Jenny Siler is twenty-eight years old. She grew up in Missoula, Montana. For much of her life she has travelled and worked her way around the world, starting as a prep-cook in the scullery of a men's soup kitchen, through working in a fish-cannery in Alaska pulling salmon roe, to being a nude sketch model at an art museum in Frankfurt. Her work, she says, has defined her and her writing.

Easy Money

JENNY SILER

ORION

An Orion paperback
First published in Great Britain by Orion in 1999
This paperback edition published in 1999 by
Orion Books Ltd,
Orion House, 5 Upper St Martin's Lane,
London WC2H 9EA

A CIP catalogue record for this book
is available from the British Library.

Typeset at The Spartan Press Ltd
Lymington, Hants

Printed and bound in Great Britain by
Clays Ltd, St Ives plc

For Jocelyn Siler
my mother,
who taught me to believe in beauty

Acknowledgments

For their invaluable help along the way, I would like to thank the following people.

Nat Sobel, my agent, for his belief in me and my writing. Rachel Klauber-Speiden, my editor, the best reader a writer could hope to have. Jack Macrae, for his kindness and patience. Martin Duffy, who let me steal his stories. My grandmother, the real Jeannette Decker, for her grace and wisdom. Christine Gallagher, Libby Lawson, Ken Stubblefield, Meredith Norton, Dave Clark, Gary Berg, and Mike McCarthy for their friendship and the sustenance of good conversation. Denis Kempe, for the much-needed calm his presence in my life provided. Mike McCarthy, for nourishing me in so many ways.

Thanks also to my father, John Siler, who, along with my mother, taught me the love of place and the wonder of words.

I owe a special debt of gratitude to Jocelyn Siler, my mother, my teacher, my friend, my guide in all things. Her unwavering faith in me made everything possible.

First there was just a dull trace of ivory in the loam, the smudged surface of a single tooth unearthed by a farmer's rust-pocked shovel. Next part of a boot emerged, its rotted canvas fragmenting, its metal eyelets crusted with mud. Then came the spidery shape of a hand, the bones resting casually across the bulbed joint of an arm. Finally, the whole knotted, snarled treasure was revealed, the half-clothed corpses slumped together like sleepers seeking warmth.

David Callum could see the bodies now, whenever he closed his eyes. He imagined their faces turned to the white heat of the sun, their jaws hanging slack, and the great commotion around them, the digging and prodding that had brought them into the light.

Callum snapped his eyes open and looked out the windows of his study, trying to shake the images. His hand lay on the sill, the knuckles knobby from years of use, the skin mottled and freckled with the brown spots of age. Fall was definitely upon them. A gust of wind swept across the tall grass, rolling through it like the muscles of a great animal might ripple beneath fur, the briefest suggestion of power. The day had been a blustery sequence of sun breaks. Now, under heavy cloud cover, the afternoon moved into premature dusk. A patch of autumn crocuses bloomed in a cluster around the roots of a pine tree, their white petals glowing like droplets of fire in the steely light.

There was, he knew, a specific phrase for such heightened luminescence, for the illusion of phosphorus on a petal. The effect had something to do with the diffusion of light, the mysterious twisting of the sun's rays that caused colors to leap at the eye. Callum waded into his memory to find the forgotten phrase. Lately, his ability to recall such things had dulled. Like the flash of crocuses in changing light, some words or events stood out in visceral reality while others receded into shadow.

He remembered a field of clover just after sunset, like thousands of bright eyes blinking through the blue dusk. It was amazing to him how these moments flashed out of nowhere. Earlier today, standing at the kitchen sink getting a glass of water, he had been wrenched back to being thirteen again, hanging from a thick strand of rope over the green surface of a pond. He felt the bristling rake of the twine against his palm, the second of weightlessness as his body reached the top of the swinging arc, the exhilaration of release, and the long fall through the air.

And he remembered the voice, just days ago the warning humming through the static of distant phone lines, carrying with it the one great, snapping, crackling, live-wire loose end of his life.

I just thought you might like to know, the voice had said. It'll get out eventually.

Who knows about this? Callum had asked.

Just the people on the recovery team and a few of us in the Agency.

The press hasn't got wind of it yet?

No, but they will. What are you going to do?

I don't know. I may need your help.

Whatever I can do.

I'll be in touch.

Then the line had gone dead and there was only the rustling of Patricia's skirt as she moved through the kitchen, the sharp whistle of the kettle she had put on coming to boil. He had set the phone back in its cradle and taken Patricia's hand.

Callum turned from the window, from the tiny white flowers, from the shadows pooling in the recesses of the yard. Across the study his golden retriever, Charlie, lifted his head from the warm patch of sunlight where he had been sleeping and opened his mouth in a wide yawn.

Though overcast, the day had been warm for November. Callum had left the front and back doors open except for the screens. Now a cold breeze blew in off the water and circulated through the old house. He heard the faint murmur of tires on the gravel driveway to the front of the house and Charlie rose and padded over, his tail wagging furiously.

'How was your nap, old man?' Callum asked, scratching the dog's broad head.

The car grew closer and stopped. Callum opened the top drawer of his desk and drew out a small computer disk. A door slammed outside and heavy footsteps sounded on the planks of the front steps. Callum crossed through the study and down the hall into the living room. The reassuring jingle of Charlie's collar followed behind him. Through the fine mesh of the screen door he made out the figure of a man with one arm hooked around a sack of groceries. A van with bold lettering reading SUQUAMISH MARKET was parked in the drive. Callum lifted the flimsy door latch and stepped out onto the porch.

'Here's the order you called in this morning.' The man smiled. 'I'm afraid we're all out of tuna, so we threw a small snapper in instead. I've got everything else, though.'

'Just like old times,' Callum answered, nodding. 'How much do I owe you?'

'Twenty-seven fifty, sir.'

Callum reached into his pocket and pulled out three ten-dollar bills. He placed the money and the disk into the man's free hand and took the groceries.

'Keep the change,' he said, smiling too.

'It's the right thing to do,' the man said. He slipped the money and the disk into his pocket.

'No one knows?'

'I haven't told a soul. As far as the Agency's concerned, I'm just up here doing a little fishing. Nothing can go wrong.'

'Thank you,' Callum said.

The man waved and bounded down the steps toward the van. The sun had slipped once again through a rift in the clouds. It sat low in the sky, bathing the man and the van and the woods beyond them in harsh orange light. Callum listened to the engine roaring to life and the grinding of wheels spinning in the loose rock of the drive. He watched the flash of the chrome bumper and the fleeting face of the happy fisherman painted above the market's logo, LIVE BAIT, COLD BEER, GROCERIES, as the van disappeared around the bend into the trees.

'C'mon, Charlie,' Callum said softly. He held the screen door open and followed his dog back into the cool shade of the house.

*

In the kitchen, Callum set the groceries down gently on the counter and stood for a while gazing out through the wide windows above the sink. Beyond the sloping green of the backyard, the flat surface of Puget Sound reflected the glint of the late-afternoon sun. Large gray geese floated and bobbed close to shore, their throaty cries skipping across the barnacled rocks of the beach. In the dense woods on the other side of the bay, slant of shadow and light shifted. Pools and eddies drifted slowly with the tide. Out at the mouth of the bay, far across the Sound, the lights of the Seattle skyline brightened against the impending darkness. To the east, beyond the city, the snowcaps and rocky faces of the Cascades towered like a theatrical backdrop.

When he finally turned from the window and began putting the groceries neatly away, the first ruddy hints of sunset had appeared in the west. Callum unwrapped the small snapper from its clean white paper and ran his fingers along its tough scales. He opened its stomach and ran a sharp knife between the fine bones and the white flesh, deftly separating the prickly skeleton from the meat.

Callum set the cleaned snapper gently in a small glass baking dish, cut paper-thin slices of orange, lime, and sweet onion, and crushed fresh cloves of garlic, stuffing them into the cavity of the fish. He rubbed the scales with olive oil, fresh pepper, and white wine, then covered the dish and put it in the refrigerator. He set a place for himself at the table on the glassed-in porch: a clean linen napkin, a silver fork and knife, a thin-stemmed wineglass.

From the porch Callum could see the dusky outlines of his wife's garden. The flashy flowers of summer were withering now; the rhododendron bushes held only the husks of blossoms, the heavy heads of browning dahlias sagged on their stems. Beyond the garden, past where the yard sloped toward the beach, black shapes of leggy waterbirds rose from the reeds and stepped offshore, fishing for their own dinner.

And he could see his own shape in the darkening windowpanes, the few remaining gray tufts of hair springing raggedly from his scalp, the creased folds of flesh beneath his chin. Callum peered down at his hands and let his eyes trace the harsh lines of veins, the brown spots of age. He closed his eyes and imagined his wife's strong legs as she walked. Although he could look back at pictures of the two of them and know for certain that she had aged along with him, it still always seemed to him that Patricia lived in a kind of magical stasis, a permanent youthfulness.

Nothing can go wrong. The words he had heard earlier rattled through his brain. He thought of the letters written to Patricia from Italy, and later the phone calls from other posts, the same panic, the same fears. There was always something that could go wrong. Always. Except for the muffled humming of the refrigerator and the occasional rustling of Charlie in the living room, the house was deathly quiet.

In the downstairs bathroom Callum found his Lycra running pants, his windbreaker, and his old Columbia sweatshirt. He stepped out of his jeans and sweater and put on his rowing clothes. He let Charlie out the back door and watched the dog nose its way through the wilted garden to the beach. As he made his way across the damp lawn, Callum heard the retriever splashing at the water's edge.

He was a man who had lived his life in deliberate

disorder. He knew the dangers of predictability and it had taken him years to adjust to the luxuries of a routine. His nightly row was one of these luxuries.

'Charlie!' he called. The dog came bounding up out of the shadows, then darted off again. Callum watched the dog's yellow haunches disappear into the dense woods. They could be out there watching, he thought, settled quietly into the loamy autumn carpet of wet leaves and pine needles. And if they were, what would they see? An old man and his dog; a fool, unarmed; a target, naked, alone, ambling carelessly across the cool grass.

Callum followed the beach to the small boathouse he had built for his scull. A single light illuminated the wooden dock. He opened the padlock and let himself in through the wide doors. He flipped on the bare overhead bulb and gently lifted the scull onto his shoulders from its rack on the wall. Stepping carefully out onto the dock, he eased the sleek boat into the water and secured it with a piece of rope.

Patricia had reprimanded him many times for rowing in the dark, but Callum had always assured her of his safety.

He had even attached two small lights to the bow and stern so he could be seen in the winter months. Callum made his way back into the boathouse for a pair of oars and flipped off the light. Charlie's collar tinkled somewhere down the beach. Across the Sound the moon had begun to rise. It hung huge and low over the bright buildings of downtown Seattle. The last lights of dusk flickered across the small bay before him. Callum placed his oars in their locks and stepped gingerly into his scull. He untied the line and pushed the small craft free of the dock.

Callum set his blades in the water and pulled. He loved

7

the fluid motion of gliding soundlessly over the bay, the power of his own movements.

Tonight, as he picked up speed and settled into a rhythm, he watched the moon shrinking as it rose. The first full moonrise he had seen had been over Italy during the war. 'The good war,' they all called it. As his legs pumped back and forth he thought about sitting in the darkened body of the plane that night, listening to the hum of the engines as they gained altitude. There were three other men with him waiting to jump, and they smoked Pall Mall cigarettes and joked nervously with each other.

It had been different later, in South America and Korea and Vietnam. The wars they fought had changed, the reasons for them, the nature of them. But that night over Italy when they opened the hatch, they all saw the huge globe of the moon shining low over the countryside; when he was thrust from the body of the plane into the cold rush of empty space, he was buoyed by a great sense of morality.

Callum was halfway down the bay now. A trickle of sweat dropped between his shoulder blades. The oars creaked in their locks and his seat hummed, sliding forward and back. The bow and stern lights glimmered over the rippled water. He thought about how easy it had been today, passing the small disk like the priests at Catholic school passing the wafer.

Callum rounded the curve of the bay and turned his scull back toward home. Clouds of his breath hovered in the stern light. He thought about Patricia, who was in New York visiting her sister, of how they would make love when she came home. He wondered if she would wear his favorite dress on the plane, the one with the tiny blue flowers and the soft silk piping around the neck. He thought of the thin line of buttons running down her back, the joy of undoing each one, of watching the crease of Patricia's spine appear from under the thin cloth. The time I have left, he thought, will be for her; nothing more to be wasted.

Callum felt the strength of the twenty-year-old he had once been in every stroke of his seventy-five-year-old body. He felt the disk slip from his fingers, the parachute opening, the patchwork of the Italian farmland rising to meet him.

In the distance Callum could see the lights of his house through the woods and the lone light at the boathouse. He sank the blades of his oars for the short sprint home, and as he pulled back he felt something tugging at his portside oar. The thick weight of fear he had felt earlier had disappeared and he eased the scull to a stop. A crab trap, he thought, as he pulled his oar in and laid it across his lap. He ran his hands down the length of the shaft, groping for the thick line he would have to untangle. He felt nothing but smooth wood.

He looked up past the stern light. Circles spread, widening, across the surface of the water. Slowly, the gleaming face of a man rose from the small waves. A gloved hand reached up past the side of the scull, and Callum felt a deep chill as his legs hit the water. For a moment he grappled with the man, pulling at the spare regulator that dangled at the diver's side. As he felt himself go under for the last time, he thought, *They have not won.*

The current sucked at his feet through the thin canvas of his shoes and he remembered his body, some sixty years earlier, slicing into the green murk of a pond. He felt the slimy rocks as his toes brushed them, the mud, soft as corn silk, the scales of a bass rasping across his skin, the force gathering in his legs as he propelled himself up into the summer afternoon. And before the dim haze of unconsciousness overtook him, he imagined the disk, a warm body of truth pulled up from the cold sea of lies, traveling even now through the darkness.

One

The first time my father died I was twelve years old. He fell down drunk in the alley behind the bar he and his best friend owned in Key West, Florida, hit his head on a drainpipe, and stopped breathing. If his Cuban cook, José, had not found him he probably would have lain there all night in the fetid puddles of rain-soaked garbage and his own vomit, fodder for the roaches and tree rats that overran the island. José cleared the bile from my father's mouth, beat his chest, and breathed into his lungs until he sputtered to life again.

Any other person might have taken this experience to heart, maybe even been transformed by such proximity to death. My father was far beyond transformation. I think he looked at death and saw the vast expanse and thought, What the hell, I might as well live it up while I can.

That night my father's best friend and business partner, Cyrus, dragged him home. The sounds of them arguing in the front yard woke me up, and I stood on the balcony of our wrecker's house in the shadows of the royal palms and listened to their hushed voices. It was a sticky summer night, and I leaned my back up against the cool wood of the house and watched the glittering backs of palmetto bugs as they scuttled across the boards at my feet.

'Have you thought about Allie?' Cyrus asked. 'Have

you thought about what she would do if you were gone?'
My mother had died eight years earlier and I realized then
how close I was to being completely alone.

'Allie's my daughter, she'll always be able to take care
of herself,' my father muttered drunkenly.

'Don't forget, Joe, you died tonight.' I could hear the
disgust in Cyrus's voice and his footsteps receding into the
humid night.

I crept to the edge of the balcony and craned my head
over the side. In the deep summer on Key West the air is
so wet that the cast of light takes on a glow, like that of a
streetlight through fog, but softer, subtler, so that what
little light there is at night from porches and streetlamps
and passing cars disperses and reflects off everything. It
was in that light that I saw my father from the balcony.

He fumbled in his pocket for his cigarettes and lighter,
pulling them out with exaggerated care, cursing as he
dropped them on the ground. I watched him hunch down
to pick them up, saw the slump in his shoulders, the
vulnerability of the bare nape of his neck as he searched.
When he finally found the pack he rose and staggered
over to a little iron bench we kept in the front yard and sat
down heavily. I heard the click of his lighter snapping
open and saw the angles of his face lit up by the bright
butane flame.

I stayed on the balcony for a long time, while the tree
rats ran back and forth overhead through the thick
canopy of banyan and poinciana trees. My father smoked
cigarette after cigarette, the red cherries flaring as he
inhaled. After several hours he heaved himself off the
bench and stumbled up the stairs to the veranda. I found
him sleeping on the couch the next morning and made
him thick Cuban coffee and toast. My father and I never

spoke about that night, though I'm sure he knew I'd seen everything.

He never did quit drinking. Even in Key West, a town full of drunks, he held his own. When I first went off to college, before I quit and became a courier, he proudly sent me a clipping from the *Key West Citizen*. He had been arrested one night. 'Police arrested a drunken bicyclist,' the article began, 'who planned to swim home on a city street which he cursed and blamed for his repeated falls.' I can see him now, belly down on the dry asphalt, his arms flailing in a desperate breaststroke as he tries to move his body through the air.

My father came from an Irish immigrant family in Brooklyn. We didn't move down to Florida until after my mother's death. Cyrus already had the bar and was looking for a partner. I was too young when she died to remember much about her, so my mother remains an odd, shadowy collection of smells and movements not quite real enough to miss. I catch glimpses of her occasionally, an odor of perfume in a crowd, the angle of hair across a stranger's face. These moments pass in and out of view like the silver fins of tarpons we used to see leaping out of the wake of Cyrus's boat.

They named me Alison Yana Kerry, but I have always been Allie. So when Cyrus called from the Keys two nights ago and I heard his low voice saying, 'Alison, I have some bad news,' I knew something was seriously wrong. Fifteen years after he first died, we will finally be burying my father.

Now I lie in bed and hope that it's cold outside and very gray. There is nothing more odious than sunshine when I am hung over. When Cyrus told me the news I didn't even wait to find out how it happened. 'Thank you for calling,'

I said. I hung up and walked down the street to the closest liquor store, bought a bottle of Wild Turkey, returned to the grimy little motel room I'd rented on the outskirts of Oakland, and just started drinking. By the time Joey called I was too far gone to say no to his offer.

Bright, hovering clouds of fog filter through the slits in the room's dirty louvered window shades. At first, because of the strange blue glow the fog has cast, I think it has snowed. Then I remember it is still early November and it rarely snows here anyway. Thank God, I think, as I lie under the cheap chenille bedspread trying to piece together the events of the last two days. From the room next door comes the muffled thump of the bed hitting the wall and the rhythmic creak of the box spring. I reach over and touch the tangle of empty sheets next to me. Often there is that awful moment for me, before I open my eyes, before I move, when I wonder where I am and who I will find sleeping open-mouthed beside me. Today I have two things going for me: I know I am somewhere outside of Seattle, Washington, and I am alone.

The noises from next door have stopped. The only sounds in the musty room are water running in the pipes and the sharp, sputtering *tick-tick* of rain on the windows. I trace my fingers down the nubbed rows of the bedspread. My head is killing me and this is all the movement I can manage. I run my tongue over my dry lips and taste last night's whiskey. The red numbers on the alarm clock glow: 10:07 A.M. I should be halfway to Florida by now. I curse myself and Joey silently for setting up this meeting tonight. Then I think about the money.

Money like this is what we all hope for. We are like gambling junkies waiting for a thousand-to-one horse to be the first to streak past the finish line. We all want the big job, the ride that lets us retire. Money like this could give me direction, or at least a nice long vacation, during which I could collect my thoughts. I don't want to do this work forever.

I throw the covers back and swing my legs over the side of the bed, grab an aspirin bottle from my purse, stumble over to the sink, and peel the paper off one of the glasses. The water from the taps is tepid and tastes faintly of rust. The cool surface of the Formica counter brushes against my naked thighs.

I flip on the overhead light in the small bathroom and step into the shower, letting the scalding-hot water run over me for several minutes. If I stop thinking about the money I'll leave now. Joey will find someone else to drive the package, and I'll make it down to Florida a day sooner, maybe in time for whatever funeral or drunken wake there is going to be.

The shower helps to dull the headache, but my body is screaming for coffee. I wrap myself in one of the cheap white motel towels and wander back into the main room, trying to remember exactly what I said to Joey, and if I agreed to run the package at all. I find my cell phone and dial, then wait for Joey to answer.

'Yup.'

'Joey, it's Allie.'

'Allie, baby. I was worried about you.'

'I bet you were,' I say sarcastically. I can't really say that Joey was ever my boyfriend. We used to sleep with each other back before I got cleaned up. I only deal with him now because he gets me really good rides.

'No, really. I'm sorry about your dad. He was a good guy. You know I always liked him.'

Joey's father and mine knew each other in Florida long

before Joey and I ever met. They ran in the same circles together in the late seventies, ferrying bales of dope up the coast from the Keys.

'I know,' I say.

'Anyway, Al, I'm sorry.'

'Is this thing still on?' I ask. I don't want to talk about my father; I'd rather hear about the money.

'Yeah. Listen, baby, it's gonna be real easy money, like I told you before. All you have to do is meet this guy tonight. You go to this bar in Bremerton, the Nightshift, around six o'clock. They got pool tables, music. He's gonna know who you are. They got a parking lot out back. You park the car and go inside, play a game or two of pool, buy yourself a cocktail. Easy, right?'

I listen to the soft clip of Joey's voice and think to myself how little he ever changes. With Joey everything is easy.

'Yeah, Joey,' I say, 'easy.'

'Okay,' he continues, the lilt of his Key West Cuban accent ringing over the lines, 'you don't talk to this guy. You don't need to know anything about him. You just fuck around in the bar for a little while like you're a nice single girl out for some fun. He'll find you with the package.'

Joey pauses for a minute. 'So that nice-girl part might not be so easy.' He chuckles. I don't laugh. 'Sorry, baby,' he goes on. 'Anyway, you wait maybe an hour, give him a little time. Then you go back out to the car and you drive away. They don't want to be fucking with money on delivery, so you get the payoff with the package.'

'All of it,' I say coldly, 'or I don't go.'

'Who you talking to right now? Baby, this is Joey. Of course you get the money.'

'Joey.' I pause for a minute and think.

'Yeah, Al.'

'This isn't what I usually do, is it? I mean, nobody in their right mind pays this much for a regular ride.'

There's a long silent pause. Finally he breaks in. 'Like I told you last night, with the package there'll be a contact number, information about where the drop is set for. Once you know you've got everything, you stop at the nearest pay phone and call me, just to let me know you've got the package. Don't call the contact until you get to where you're going. They'll let you know then where exactly you're supposed to meet. Two calls, Allie, that's it, okay?'

'Two calls,' I repeat. I'm not exactly in the habit of chatting away to my customers on the phone. I never even speak to most of them.

'Just like any other ride you take,' Joey says, in his slickest, most reassuring voice.

'I'll talk to you later.'

I lay the phone down beside me on the bed and tap a cigarette out of the pack on the night table, catching a dim glimpse of myself in the mirror on the opposite wall. A swath of light from the open bathroom door lies across the dull orange carpet at my feet. I light my cigarette and watch myself exhale, letting the smoke filter out in a slow stream. Still wet, my hair hangs at my bare shoulders in dark, uneven curls.

'Just like any other ride,' I say to myself in the mirror. I watch my lips form the words, watch each muscle in my face change as my mouth moves.

Usually it is easy money. Joey calls me, or Michael, or one of the others. Mostly I don't know what it is that I'm driving; mostly I don't want to know. I'm not supposed to ask. Sometimes it's smack, sometimes cocaine or big bales of marijuana. Sometimes, like tonight, it's other packages. I don't have a permanent address. When there's no work I stay in the Keys with Cyrus and my father, or I visit friends, or sometimes I just drive. I have been doing this for seven years now, drifting, since my second year in college.

When I was eighteen I left the Keys with a scholarship to NYU. I got a waitressing job at a bar in Alphabet City and a tiny apartment across the river in Brooklyn. That's when I first saw Joey. My friend Christine introduced him to me one night after work. She and I had been down in the basement office doing a few lines, and when we came up the stairs he was standing in the doorway talking to our boss. He didn't move for us to pass, and we had to squeeze by him to get back into the bar.

'Hey, Joey,' Christine said as we passed. 'How's it going?'

'Not bad.' I could feel Joey's eyes taking me in, checking me out. 'Who's your friend?' he asked.

'This is Allie. I thought you guys might know each other. She's from Florida, from the Keys. Aren't you from down there?'

I didn't say anything, just stared hard at Joey.

'Nice to meet you, Allie,' he said. I turned and walked toward the bar.

I was driving back then also, but nothing big like now. My father got me the rides. Christmas vacation or summer I'd get a job driving rental cars from one city to another. It was easy. I didn't even carry a gun at first. Say I was taking a Grand Am from Miami to Orlando for Hertz, I'd call up my dad and ask him if anyone needed transportation. There was always someone looking. After my second year at NYU I figured I could earn more money driving than I could making espresso with an English degree, so I quit.

I wasn't working for Joey then, just sleeping with him every once in a while. Joey doesn't hire junkies, and I was too far gone. Drivers always get a nice little bonus if they want, something to keep them awake on the road, and I took full advantage. I never shot heroin or really liked dope, but I had one of the world's greatest love affairs with cocaine.

I've been clean for over four years now, but I still get a little twinge every once in a while. I sometimes wonder if the whole ritual of cocaine is not more powerful than the drug itself. When I first quit I used to dream that I was laying out fat, fluffy rails, chopping and cutting the flaky rocks. I would wake feeling the click of the razor blade on the glass, the clink of the pipette against the mirror.

I stub my cigarette out in the ashtray by the bed. The rain has stopped and traffic whispers on the wet street outside. I reach for my purse, pull out my Walther PPK/S, pop the clip, and check that it's fresh. Something tells me Joey's wrong this time; this is not going to be easy money. I run my fingers along the sleek, cold metal of the barrel.

The Walther's not my only gun, but it's my favorite. My father gave it to me when I first started driving. It's compact enough to fit in the back of my jeans. When I shoot the Walther I can be pretty sure I won't miss. I have a Browning Hi-Power auto that I keep for dicier situations, when I need the extra power and the big magazine.

I dress quickly, slipping into my favorite pair of jeans, black boots, and a black sweater, tucking my wet hair up into my Yankees cap. Slinging my duffel over my shoulder, I make one last check around the room, then pick the Walther up, slide the fresh clip into the handle, and tuck the gun into the back of my jeans.

When I open the door and step out into the parking lot, the fog has already begun to lift. A neon sign reading EMERALD CITY MOTOR INN towers over the single-story complex. A cutout of a large green jewel revolves, blinking, over the bright letters. A maid's cart is parked at the unit two doors down from mine and the door is wide open. Though I can't remember parking it last night, my '69 Mustang is in the slot right outside my door. I throw my bags into the back seat and slide in behind the wheel. A box on the passenger side floor is filled with maps, and I pull out Washington. I want to make sure I can take a ferry over to Bremerton from Seattle. Unfolding the map, I find the blue of Puget Sound. A tiny green line marks the ferry from Seattle to Bremerton. I can feel the cold weight of the Walther against my back and I shift slightly in my seat, turn the ignition switch on, and pull out of the parking lot, leaving the Emerald City behind.

Two

The four-fifty ferry to Bremerton is crowded with the first wave of commuters going home. I leave the Mustang on the car deck and climb up through the warmth of the main cabin. A cold wind slams into me as I push the door open and step out onto the upper deck. Night is already falling. A bright amber strip of sun gleams through dark clouds on the western horizon. I lean into the wind and make my way toward the bow, where a glass enclosure houses rows of dirty white plastic chairs and heaters. A young woman sits in the corner playing a cello. Several people have gathered around her.

I take a seat just outside and pull a cigarette from my pocket. A group of small children in bright winter coats careen in circles around the deck. They all have their arms stuck out like wings, and their high-pitched screams doppler into the wind each time they pass by. I lean back in my chair and cross my legs in front of me. The sea air whips at my face.

When I was twelve my father started taking me with him on the boat while he worked. The first time I hid in Cyrus's truck and they had no choice in the matter. From then on I think my father figured I would get in more trouble if he left me at home. Later he would teach me how to use a gun and how to fight as well as any of the men we worked with, but in the beginning I just sat quietly next to him drinking Coca-Cola and watching his face and Cyrus's in the lights from the instrument panel. He always worked at night, and sooner or later I would drift off to sleep in the tiny cabin.

Everyone knew my father and Cyrus owned the bar, but their real work was one of the many mysteries that we shared. Closing my eyes and thinking about my childhood, I remember waking again and again to the hushed sounds of men's voices in the dark. We would be moored somewhere along Sugarloaf or Islamorada, and I could smell the salt water and the pine trees. I would poke my head out of the cabin and see the men's backs, hunched and slick with sweat as they worked. The boat's radio crackled softly, sometimes in English, other times in Cuban Spanish or Haitian patois.

There were other secrets, as well. On the hottest nights my father would cry out in the darkness of our house. I crept to the door of his room and listened to him fighting his dreams. 'PIC dreams,' he and Cyrus called them. I never knew what that meant, but the words became part of the private language of our strange family.

The engines slow and begin a rhythmic pulse of vibration as the ferry slips past a red channel buoy and heads into the spit toward Bremerton. I get up, walk across the deck, and peer over the railing. A flock of gulls hover and dive in currents of air just above my head, keeping perfect time with the boat. Rafts of seaweed and great chunks of cedar driftwood tumble and churn, crushed beneath the flat iron bow.

In the Keys the water was safe, inviting. Even in the depths of channels it was water you could survive in, milky with salt and sediment, warm. Here the waves are matte black and impenetrable. Stilted houses cling to stony beaches backed by cliffs. All around us are dark hills and dense forests, miles of shaggy cedars where you could lose yourself forever. Up ahead are the lights of Bremerton and the hulking shape of the huge crane at the navy yard. The crane is swathed in a billowing sleeve of white plastic and lit up from within.

Back in the enclosure, the cellist has stopped playing and is packing her instrument away in its case. I leave the rail and make my way over to the stairs. The passage to the car deck is crowded, and I edge down with all the other bodies moving toward home.

Bremerton is a navy town. As I drive off the ferry I see the sprawling lights of the shipyards and the hillsides studded with blocks of old navy housing. I follow the road from the ferry into downtown, past shuttered storefronts and a few seedy bars. Ahead of me, on the right-hand side of the street, the neon beer signs of the Nightshift gleam like beacons. My heart speeds up. Fear has never excited me. I keep my eye on the bar as I drive by and think hard about the money.

I pull around the corner and into the back parking lot of the Nightshift, edging the Mustang into a space close to the alley before cutting the engine. The back door of the bar opens and a sailor with close-cropped hair and a woman in a tight dress stumble out and walk over to a red Jeep.

The clock on the dash reads 6:09. I take a deep breath and survey the parking lot one more time. The sailor and the woman have driven away, and there are only two other cars besides mine. Both are empty. The lot backs on an alley.

The windowless brick walls from the Nightshift's neighboring stores run down either side, and the back of the building across the alley has only two small windows. Both are unlit. I take my keys out of the ignition and step out of the Mustang. Easy money.

When I swing the back door of the Nightshift open and step inside, the stale odor of liquor and old cigarettes hits me full on. I make my way up past the pool tables to the main bar.

A short, wiry woman whose gray hair is pulled back in two barrettes stands behind the wooden counter. She's pouring cheap well scotch into a tumbler. Besides the bartender, I'm the only woman in the room. Half a dozen old men sit quietly sipping drinks, their elbows propped on the counter. A small group of sailors are gathered around a table in the back playing doubles.

The woman shoves the scotch across the bar toward one of the old men and turns to me.

'What'll it be, young lady?' she asks.

My stomach is still turning from last night, but I have to drink something while I wait.

'Just give me a draft,' I say.

I sit down at one of the stools on the side of the bar facing the front door and slide a five-dollar bill onto the counter.

'Louise!' one of the customers yells.

'Yeah, yeah, I'm comin'.' The woman slides my beer across the bar and waves her free hand dismissively over her shoulder.

There's a large sign in bold lettering over the back bar that reads, IF OUR SERVICE DOESN'T MEET YOUR STANDARDS, LOWER YOUR STANDARDS. Below the sign is a faded picture of a softball team and several dusty trophies. Small bags of potato chips and pretzels hang on a rack over the cash register alongside packets of aspirin

24

and Alka-Seltzer. A hand-lettered sign on the far wall lists the Nightshift rules for pool, including a twenty-five-cent charge for each dropped cue. At the bottom of the sign, in a childish scrawl, someone has added, *No weapons*. I pull the back of my coat down.

'Hey, Louise, turn that up!' someone yells. Louise climbs onto a bar stool and fiddles with the volume on an ancient television that's hanging in the corner. The local news has just come on, and the booming voice of the announcer and the unmistakable news theme music blares through the bar.

'Good evening,' the anchorwoman starts out. 'Our top story tonight: Still no signs in the search for David Callum.'

Around me in the bar there is muted activity as several of the customers stir and look up from their drinks with mild interest. The name Callum sounds vaguely familiar to me. I focus my eyes on the television.

'Callum, once a top-ranking CIA officer, disappeared from his home on Bainbridge Island sometime last night,' the anchor continues. Her face is replaced by a picture of a quaint seaside house. 'Friends say Callum was an avid rower. He apparently took his scull out last night and never returned.'

'Now *there's* a man with no enemies,' a man with a graying beard and a baseball cap sitting a few stools down from me mumbles sarcastically.

I glance back up at the TV. A man in a yellow slicker with a badge pinned to it is being interviewed. 'The neighbors called in when they heard the Callums' retriever barking all night. They came over this morning to see what was wrong and couldn't find Mr. Callum anywhere. We checked the boathouse, and his scull's gone.'

'Does it look like the worst?' the young woman reporter asks dramatically.

'Ma'am, we're still in the process of looking for Mr. Callum. We're talking about a seventy-five-year-old man, here. Anything could have happened to him. It was a full moon last night, and the tides around here can get pretty rough.'

The images on the television break back to the studio. One of the pool players in the back has switched on the jukebox. The opening lines of Nirvana's 'Where Did You Sleep Last Night?' drown out the voices of the news anchors. I look around the bar, wondering if any of these men is my pickup. The front door opens and a middle-aged man steps inside. He's wearing standard fishing garb: brown neoprene fishing boots over his jeans and a tan canvas jacket. He surveys the room, letting his eyes linger for a split second on me, then sits down at a stool with his back to the front door and orders a bourbon. He picks the glass up from the bar and tilts the rim toward his lips. Even in this dim light I can see the clean fingers, the white half-moons of his immaculate nails, the freshly shaved hollows of his cheeks. Tilting my eyes down toward my beer, I keep the man at the edge of my field of vision. I have spent enough of my life around the sea to know his are not the battered hands and weathered face of a fisherman.

The man sets his bourbon down and stares past me toward the back door. The group at the pool table has grown boisterous. Their voices travel over the loud drone of Curt Cobain's howls.

'Nice bank,' one of them calls out.

'Lucky shot,' another voice booms.

The phony fisherman reaches his hand nervously inside

the left front of his jacket. This is the guy, but I don't see the money. I get up from my stool, shove a couple of quarters into the jukebox, then bend down over the brightly lit glass case and start flipping through selections.

One of the sailors glances at me and I straighten myself and make my way over to the pool players, weaving slightly, flashing them my most convincing drunk-girl smile. I set my beer down and lean over the green felt of their table, letting my jacket hang wide open. If it weren't for the Walther, I'd take it off. The tops of my breasts press against the deep V of my sweater.

'Mind if I get in on your game?' I look up past the bright pattern of balls and see the fisherman rise from the bar. He pushes his stool back, his hand still deep inside his jacket. Nervous amateur, I think to myself, smiling up at the sailors.

'Sure, baby,' one of them says.

Out of the corner of my eye I can still see the fisherman. He has ordered another bourbon and his eyes are locked on me. Standing up from the table, I move over to the rack of cues along the wall, lift one of the wooden sticks from its clips, and slide my hand along its smooth surface. Turning my back to the wall, I lean over the table and start racking the balls. Louise stands at the well behind the counter, mixing a drink. The aging customers stare up at the flickering colors of the television. The sailors are all watching me.

The fisherman downs his bourbon and heads toward me, his boots squeaking as he crosses the wood floor. Keeping my eyes on the triangle of balls and the blazing green felt, I take my time ordering the balls, sliding the black eight into the center of the rack. The squeak of the rubber boots grows closer and the fisherman passes right behind me between the table and the wall. The odor of his aftershave is slightly antiseptic and the knuckles of his hand graze my thigh. Something slides down inside the pocket of my jeans. I lift the rack away from the balls and set it on the light above the table, pick up my cue, sight down the smooth wood, and break.

The fisherman moves past me and disappears into a small alcove in the back corner of the bar marked REST ROOMS. I've sunk two low balls on my break and I take my time with my next shot, walking slowly around the table, surveying the setup of the game.

The fisherman has still not reappeared from the men's room when I lean down again and call my shot: seven ball in the side pocket. The back door swings open and a blast of cold air crosses my neck. I miss my easy shot on purpose, move away from the table, and pick up my beer. A gray-haired man at the bar, in stained Dickies work pants, boots, and a flannel shirt, has stood up and is looking right past me. He nods his head in the direction of the rest rooms.

Turning, I watch the newcomer as he makes his way to the men's room. He's not a large man, maybe five-nine, but his body bristles with danger, like the scorpions we used to catch under our house when I was a girl. The first time I saw one we had just moved down to the Keys, and I woke up in the middle of the night needing to pee. I made my way barefoot down the dark hallway to the bathroom and flipped on the light. The open door threw a square of light into the hallway where I had just stepped, illuminating the creature's frenzied movements. The scorpion's shiny black tail stood erect and tense; its pincers flailed wildly, and I knew it wanted to hurt me. I stamped my foot and it scuttled away, its shell clicking against the polished wood floor. Only some marvelous stroke of luck had directed my feet in the darkness. After that night the hall light was kept on and I slept with the knowledge that the scorpion was somewhere in the house, ruing its missed opportunity to strike.

I meet people like this man all the time in my business. They take a distinct pleasure in their work, in the varying degrees of pain and fear they can inflict. The man in the bathroom, with his nervous face and clean hands, would be no match for such authority.

'You're up,' one of the sailors says. The back of the scorpion man's balding head rounds the corner and disappears into the alcove. I look down at the table. My opponent has not dropped a single ball. I try for the seven again and bank it off the rail into the side pocket, then aim for the five and miss. The door to the men's room slams; the balding man comes out and crosses in front of me. His gait is solid, not cocky but strong and purposeful. It makes me think of the tomcat, Max, we had when I was growing up. He pushes his way through the door, and I can't help but tag him with the old tabby's name. Max, the scorpion man.

The man at the bar has sat down again.

'You boys keep my turn, okay? I've got to use the ladies' room.' I lay my cue down on the side of the table and head for the partition.

I turn the corner and lean my back up against the men's room door, thinking about the man at the bar and Max, who is probably waiting outside. With luck, they only knew the fisherman. Otherwise I'm as good as dead. I slide the Walther out of the back of my jeans, check the clip, and jam it back into the handle so that it engages. Easy money. I open the bathroom door and step inside.

The first thing I see are his boots. The brown rubber sticks out almost comically from under one of the stalls. The fisherman is lying on his back with his head slumped up against the base of the toilet. His eyes are wide open and a thin line of blood seeps from a jagged hole in his forehead. I squat down over him and reach into his jacket. His body is warm and bright tears well in the corners of his eyes. He's close to my father's age, maybe a few years older, with a slight paunch that his bent posture exaggerates. There's a gun in his inside pocket, a Colt government-model nine millimeter. I tuck it into my coat, reach underneath him, and slip his wallet out of the back pocket of his jeans. There's a couple hundred dollars in the leather billfold, but that's all the money he has on him.

Max and the man in Dickies are nowhere in sight when I come out of the men's room. The sailors are busy with their game. I slip out the back door unnoticed.

The only light in the parking lot comes from a bare bulb above the back door to the bar. Keeping the Walther glued to my side, I head for the powder-blue glimmer of my Mustang. I'm halfway to the car when something hits my legs. They fly out from under me. My left shoulder goes to the ground first and I bite my lip against the pain of the impact. The Walther slips from my hand and scuds out of reach.

'Give me the disk,' Max says into my ear. His breath is hot and rancid. The weight of his body presses on my chest. His thighs grip my arms, pinning them to my sides. He's not young – somewhere around sixty – but a youthful sixty. He curls around me, all muscles and angry strength, the whites of his eyes glowing.

'I don't know what you're talking about,' I lie, trying to sound calm, twisting my head back to see the outline of my Walther a few feet away. The fisherman's Colt is still in my pocket.

Max raises his gun to my face. It's a small weapon, a Beretta Jetfire, twenty-five caliber with a long silencer. Perfect for taking someone out noiselessly in a filthy little bathroom. The odor of spent powder wafts from the barrel. He jabs the tip into my cheek and leans down and puts his lips to my ear.

'Where's the disk?' His voice is intimate, as if we are lovers. His lips are dry. A shiver runs through my body. I jerk my face away from the Beretta and bring my knee up hard between his legs. Max's eyes register a split second of surprise, and for an instant his legs go slack. The gun discharges into the pavement next to my ear.

Slipping one arm free, I bring his gun hand down hard against the asphalt. The twenty-five clatters against the pavement, and I jam my knee up one more time against the soft flesh of his groin, pull my feet up to his chest, and kick myself free. Max staggers backward, his right hand probing the inside of his coat. I roll up onto my knees and bring the nine millimeter out of my pocket, aiming it at his chest, reaching for the Beretta and the Walther.

'Don't even think about it,' I say, slipping the Colt back into my pocket, edging toward him.

'Drop it! Drop the gun!' a voice calls.

I turn to see the second man on the other side of the lot, his elbows propped on the trunk of a sedan. Tucking my head into my chest, I dive for the ground, wrapping my finger around the trigger of the Walther, aiming for the bulb above the doorway. Glass shatters as the parking lot is plunged into darkness. I crouch down low and start moving backward toward the ghostly blue of my car, my eyes straining to make out the shape of the man in

31

Dickies. For a moment the only sound I can hear is the ringing in my ears from the first few shots.

I'm closing in on the Mustang and I pick up speed, firing blindly. The force of the semiautomatic tugs at my arms with each squeeze of the trigger.

'Motherfucker!' The voice of the man in the Dickies rings through the darkness.

Max is still out there somewhere and more pissed off than before. A loud blast erupts from one of the parked cars, followed by an explosion of glass from the passenger window. There's a sharp pain in my cheek and the warmth of my own blood. Someone's moving along the far wall, keeping pace with me. I fire again and crouch down behind the parked car. My clip's almost spent and I reach into my pocket to pull out a fresh one, trading it for the empty cartridge in the Walther. The parking lot is dead quiet. My cheek is throbbing and my fingers find a large sliver of glass in the soft flesh.

The man in Dickies groans softly from the far end of the lot. I take a deep breath and creep toward the direction the shot came from, pressing myself against the cold metal of the cars, keeping my head down.

It's his shoes that give Max away, the barely audible rasping of leather soles on blacktop as he shifts his feet. Sticking to the brick wall, I hook around behind him.

'Give me the gun,' I say, pressing the Beretta right up against his head. He's squatting behind the Mustang, his left hand touching the bumper for balance. 'Now!'

Smirking, he offers me the gun, balancing the trigger guard on his index finger. I could kill him if I wanted to, but that's not the way I work. Besides, I have a feeling these guys are not just ordinary crooks, and I wouldn't want to piss off the wrong people. It's clear I'm already into some pretty deep shit.

'Stand up,' I say, following his head with the barrel of the Beretta. 'I'm going to get in my car, and you're going to wait till I'm gone. Then I want you to go see about your friend over there.'

The man's uneven breathing echoes across the darkened parking lot like the scratch and rattle of a shiny exoskeleton on hardwood, like that scorpion sliding back into the shadowed corners of our old house. I sidle to the Mustang, pop the driver's door, and climb in.

Three

It wasn't until nine years after my mother's death that my father finally let go of what was left of her. By then we were living in Key West. The outlaws' outpost, Key West has been a navy port for many years, and the military has dug countless channels through the flats for their deep-hulled ships. Ironically, this labyrinth now provides refuge for local smugglers, who, unlike the Coast Guard, have the benefit of generations of experience with the flats and backcountry wilderness. Like my friends whose fathers and uncles were also in the business, I spent a large portion of my childhood learning how to navigate these waters.

Most of the sand from the dredgings was hauled up on shore to make the beaches that line the islands, but the rockier bits were simply shoved aside into piles that still stick up out of the shallows. Halfway out toward Woman Key, two of these piles form a kind of deep, protected lagoon.

When I was a teenager we would go out to the lagoon on unbearably hot summer afternoons, drink beer, and swim in the cool depths. There was a small wooden dory sunk at the bottom and a giant grouper that lived in its hull. If you jumped into the water at night and waved your arms, you could see the dull lights of the tiny bioluminescent creatures that swarmed there. An anomalous hole in an otherwise shallow stretch of water, the lagoon was not a particularly picturesque place.

It was into this hole that my father had decided to sink my mother. Perhaps he wanted to leave her someplace where the current was less likely to grab her; perhaps he wanted to be able to share a beer with her on a hot day. Whatever his reason, he asked Cyrus to drop the anchor there one afternoon. We had packed a lunch of *media noche* sandwiches and conch salad from the Cuban bakery down the street from our house. I was thirteen at the time and my father had put a Guanabana shake, alongside his and Cyrus's Red Stripe beer, in the cooler for me.

After we had eaten, he took the urn and bashed it across the side of the boat. He must have been a little tipsy by then, for he didn't quite break the clay on the first try. He brought it up over his head again and slammed it down hard against the hull. The urn cracked like the shell of an egg and we all watched as shreds of newsprint fluttered down over the calm surface of the water.

For years my father was convinced that the crematorium in New York had duped him. I don't know what he thought their motivation might have been for keeping the ashes. Maybe he envisioned a conspiracy involving dead loved ones and garden fertilizer, or the secret sale of body parts to some remote corner of Asia. If anything, I believe the missing ashes proved more of a reason for liking the place, as if the deep water there was some kind of witness to my father's having been cheated. It was not until I was sixteen that we would know my mother had been lying there after all.

I had gone to the lagoon with my best friend, Meredith Norton. It was a perfect April day and we were playing

36

hooky from high school. Meredith's parents were out of town and we took their cabin cruiser from the marina. We anchored the boat and stripped down to our bathing suits. The weather had been calm for weeks and the water in the lagoon was gin clear. We sat with our feet hanging over the side of the boat and watched the wavering shape of the sunken dory below. We each took turns diving down to the bottom of the lagoon and bringing something back to prove we had made it all the way. My first trip down I grabbed a Red Stripe bottle, probably a relic from one of my father's trips. Meredith dove next and came up holding a shard of pottery. She threw it next to me on deck, and I recognized the rounded surface of my mother's urn. I slipped into the water for my next dive.

I adjusted the seal on my mask and headed straight for the spot where Meredith had been. The water was still clouded where her hands had touched bottom, but I could make out more pieces of the urn. I held my breath and moved the shards aside, waving away a thick layer of algae. The green film broke apart and floated free and I saw a small plastic bag filled with gray powder. When I picked the bag up, the plastic broke apart gently in my hands. The powder sifted through my fingers, heavy and sharp with small bits of teeth and bone. My lungs were beginning to give out and I waved the plastic a few times, trying to free the pieces of my mother still trapped inside. When I surfaced, gasping for breath, I could still feel the silt of her body on the cool skin of my hands.

When I got home that night I told my father about the ashes. He called Cyrus, and they both had a good laugh over the phone. I still don't know how the three of us missed her that day, how we could have failed to see the plastic bag containing what remained of her body slip like a yolk from the cracked shell of the urn. Maybe, in one last urge to keep her from going, my father used sleight-of-hand to conjure up his own deception.

The phony fisherman had used sleight-of-hand, too, sliding the disk unseen into my jeans. It's nearly ten o'clock and I've been driving since I pulled out of the Nightshift's parking lot, trying to put some distance between me and what just happened. Somewhere along the highway outside of Tacoma, my stomach heaving and turning with panic, I pulled over to the shoulder and vomited into the bushes. My body emptied itself completely, and then I got back in the Mustang and headed toward Interstate 90.

It has been over an hour since I skirted the brilliant towers of Seattle and started the long climb into the Cascades. The light rain that followed me east is turning to snow, and wet flakes collect on my windshield wipers. I watch the dividing lines on the asphalt, praying this front has almost snowed itself out. The scene at the Nightshift plays over and over in my mind, as I struggle to make sense of my jumbled thoughts.

I can't shake the image of the fisherman and all the little details that gave him away: the clean fingernails, the unscuffed surface of his boots, the close shave. The other two men were professionals, but the fisherman had all the markings of a federal agent. The feds I've dealt with before have all been amateur James Bonds.

The grade of the highway has grown steeper. Shifting the Mustang into a lower gear, I press my foot down on the accelerator. I'm almost at the top of Snoqualmie Pass. The motionless shapes of the ski lifts and cables are barely visible on the mountainside to my right. The needle on my gas gauge has edged down toward empty, and I ease over to the left-hand side of the road. Up ahead, a brightly lit Arco sign and a few buildings gleam through the light curtain of falling snow. A green highway sign, reading HYAK NEXT EXIT ¼ MILE – FOOD – PHONE – GAS, glides by my window.

Hyak consists only of a clump of cheap Bavarian-style buildings that house the gas station, a little store, and an all-night diner. I roll into the parking lot at the back of the buildings and bring the Mustang to a stop out of sight of the highway. Turning the ignition off, I lean back in my seat and stretch. I need coffee and gas, but I need to clean up a little before going inside. The skin on my cheek has tightened under the smear of dried blood.

The guns I picked up back at the Nightshift are lying on the passenger seat. I switch on the overhead light. Max's forty-five is a Heckler and Koch, a P9S with open combat sights. I test the weight of it in my palm. It's a mean take-down gun, not feisty and discreet like the Beretta but heavy and powerful, designed to do serious damage. I'll have to stop first thing in Montana and pick up some clips for it and the twenty-five.

Beneath the words MADE IN GERMANY someone has etched the letters R.B.H. into the metal. I stow it and the Colt and the Beretta under the seat.

The only other cars in the parking lot are a ski-rack-laden minivan and a Washington State patrol car. I'm almost positive the cops aren't looking for me. It's a pretty sure bet that whoever killed the fisherman won't be calling the local authorities for help. They have other ways of finding a person.

I flip the mirror on the back of the sun visor open. My face looks awful. My lower lip is split, chunks of black asphalt are lodged in my chin from the fall in the parking lot, and the gash on my cheek could probably use stitches. I pick a few shards of glass from my cheek and flake off some of the dried blood with my fingernail. Finding my first-aid kit, I pull out tweezers and moist disinfectant pads and set to work in the dim light. Inside I'll be able to wash my face properly. I untangle my matted hair, brushing it down over most of my face, and check myself in the mirror one last time.

The air outside the car is cold and thick with the smells of ozone and fresh snow and pine. The brown cedar buildings of Hyak are edged in a sugary cloak of white, their eaves sparkling in the harsh light of the tall streetlamps that dot the parking lot. The smoke of my breath dissipates into the whirl of snow.

I trudge across the parking lot and step through the door of the convenience store. A stout man in his fifties wearing a quilted flannel shirt sits behind the counter reading a magazine with a large buck on the cover. He looks up and nods when I come in.

'The snow's really coming down out there,' I say, rubbing my hands together and stamping my boots on the mat in front of the door.

'Yup.' He nods again and turns his eyes back to the magazine.

'Mind if I use your rest room?' I ask.

'Through the café,' he mumbles, nodding his head toward a door in the wall behind me.

The small café is brightly lit and crammed with postcard racks and other souvenir paraphernalia. T-shirts reading I SKIED SNOQUALMIE and plush stuffed bears on skis with HYAK imprinted on their chests adorn the walls. A bank of booths runs along the front of the café by the windows, and a row of stools is fixed in place along the

Formica counter. A family sits crammed into one of the booths, eating burgers and fries. The state trooper sits at the counter with his back to me and his hands cupped around a coffee mug. The air is heavy with old grease.

I make my way toward the rest room sign at the back of the room, passing the minivan family on the way. The parents, both in their late thirties, are wearing ski sweaters in ungodly shades of neon. The mother's blond hair has been teased into a high pile of curls and her mouth sports a bright slash of red lipstick. The two pudgy children are silent as I pass the booth, and the daughter looks up at my battered face, a piece of half-chewed fry lurking in her mouth.

'Stop staring!' The mother commands.

Of all the shit I have to deal with when I'm working – bungled connections, bad packages, cops – the most difficult thing for me is the American family. Once you leave the coasts and enter the belly of the country, the great blind central states with their barn-sized churches and bland food, it is difficult to escape the ubiquitous maw of their distressing normality. I'm not quite sure why I find these families so unnerving. Perhaps it's simply that I never grew up around such wholesomeness. My father and I never took trips to Disney World. He and Cyrus and I never sat around a plastic table at a Howard Johnson's. I have always been part of the underworld.

Seeing these little tribes now, with their Volvos and their Plymouth Voyagers, I can't help but wonder at the secrets of their lives. Are they happy? Do the men go home at night and lie on top of their quiet wives and not think for a moment of what else is out there? Whenever doubts arise about my profession, I picture myself in a spacious suburban kitchen pulling tuna casserole out of a clean oven, going to a hateful job, letting a man I don't desire into my body, and I know I have made the right choice. I have learned to glide anonymously among them, invisible.

Locking the door to the women's room behind me, I survey my face under the fluorescent lights. By tomorrow I'll have some bad bruises. I pull the fisherman's wallet out of my coat pocket and start laying the contents out on the counter by the sink. There's a reminder card for a dentist's office in Falls Church, Virginia. Someone has scrawled the words *Thursday, December 5th, 10:00 a.m. cleaning* on the back of the card. He's a fed, all right. The front of the card is emblazoned with a smiling mouth and two rows of shiny teeth.

The sheaf of bills is mostly twenties and fives. Obviously Max wasn't interested in petty theft. A folded piece of paper is tucked in one of the corners. There are handwritten directions to the Nightshift on it and a brief description of me, but no instructions for a drop. Whatever credit cards and identification the wallet may have held have been removed, either by the fisherman or by the man who killed him.

Crammed deep inside one of the leather pockets of the wallet, folded in quarters, is a playing card. The back of the card is decorated with an elaborately designed depiction of a bird. Its wings are stretched out to reveal brilliant feathers, each with a single eye at the top of the shaft. The bird isn't a peacock; it looks more like a mythical creature. Flames spring from its feet as it lifts off into the air. A cross of creases cuts through the picture from constant folding and unfolding. The front of the card is the Ace of Spades. In the white space in the upper righthand corner, someone has drawn a small crude picture of a disembodied arm holding a bloody sword.

There's nothing else of any interest in the wallet: a receipt from a gas station, a frequent coffee drinker's card from Starbucks with only one punch to go toward a freebie, a stick of gum. I take the disk from my back pocket and unwrap it and hold it up in the light. It looks like a smaller version of the CDs I play in my car. Someone killed the fisherman for this disk. They would have killed me, too. I should call Joey and tell him everything went wrong. Here is my bargaining chip. If I give up the disk now, I give up the money and, most likely, my life.

I turn the taps on and let them run until the hot water comes out steaming, then wet my palms and squeeze a pearl of pink soap from the dispenser. After cleaning the blood and grime from my face, I dry myself, put the disk back in my pocket, and return the receipts, cards, and papers to the wallet.

When I make my way back through the café, the trooper has gone and the minivan family is just finishing their meal. The man in the convenience store is still engrossed in his hunting magazine.

'I need to fill up my tank.' I slap two twenty-dollar bills down on the counter in front of him and head out into the parking lot and unlock the Mustang. When I'm done at the pumps I step back inside and grab a large cup of coffee, two packs of cigarettes, and my change.

I will call Joey later, I think, as I ease the Mustang up the grade of the entrance ramp to the interstate. I pull a cigarette from one of the fresh packs and press it into my lips. Keeping one hand on the wheel, I flip open my Zippo and watch the end of my cigarette bloom into a fiery coal.

I think about the handful of people around the country I know I can trust. In the darkness before me, the cold topography of the earth fans and rolls like a surging sea. Mountains spring up and old mining towns appear in the creases of valleys. The flat spine of the highway winds through the snowy desert of eastern Washington and up into Idaho. Two more passes loom between me and sleep. By dawn I'll have crossed into Montana. If my father were still alive, I'd call him and ask him where to go from here.

Four

There is a certain strange sense of illusion to driving a state like Montana, where towns have names like Paradise, Wisdom, and Opportunity. You know in your heart these were promises thought up to entice homesteaders or miners to this barren stretch of land. But another, deeper part of you believes the lie. You begin to wonder if the retreat of the great inland sea really left mussel shells in the county so named. You can imagine fields of kelp where the wind now stirs wheat. Low clouds glide above you like pods of prehistoric whales.

It is after six o'clock when I nose the Mustang off the interstate and down into Missoula. In the early light, the three stars of Orion's belt hang on their tilted axis, about to disappear over the black mountains. The paper mill on the far side of the valley is working overtime, churning plumes of smoke and steam from its industrial turrets.

The familiar lights of the Thunderbird Motel spew a purple haze across the railbeds at the mouth of Hellgate Canyon. The neon wings of the great bird stretch out over the ratty two-story complex. When I'm driving like this, the car is my cocoon. The soft green light from the dash panel comforts me, and the black rubber of the tires insulates me from the road.

Drowsy, I crack the window as the car climbs up through Rattlesnake Canyon, past houses with neat picket fences. There's a pungent odor of woodsmoke in the cold air, and except for a few windows that are lit up like bright slices of a ripe orange, the neighborhood is dark.

As the canyon grows narrower and edges up into the mountains, the houses fade away. The road bends into a long series of curves, and the limbs of the ponderosa pines hang down low, forming a twisting tunnel through the woods. I flick my headlights to bright. Up ahead, the black asphalt peters out to gravel and the road steepens. Easing up on the gas, I shift down into second gear for the last mile of the trip. The Mustang labors over rocks and scree, tires spinning. I peer through the cave of ponderosas, waiting for the break in the dense trees, for the sudden clearing and the bright beams of my headlights thrown up against the rough walls of Mark's cabin.

I met Mark when I was still driving rental cars. I stuck mostly to the east side of the country then and he couriered out west. Anything that had to go farther than Kansas City, I usually passed on to Mark. We would meet at some motel reminiscent of the one in *Psycho*, the Dew Drop Inn or the Shady Grove, and exchange packages.

Then, about three years ago, a drop he had outside of Reno turned bad. It wasn't Mark's fault; his connection had screwed a higher-up. But Mark was caught in the crossfire and took a bullet in his knee. He hasn't worked as a driver since.

The trees open into the clearing surrounding the cabin. I wheel the Mustang around back, next to Mark's beat-up Land Cruiser, and cut the engine. Perched just below the ridge where mountains converge from east and west into one jagged range, Mark's place is the last house up the canyon. The dirt road ends, and beyond there is nothing but wilderness. I step out of the car and let the silence overwhelm me. The first gray light of dawn appears over the eastern mountains and the last of the stars fades farther west.

I bend over the back seat of the Mustang, grab my duffel bag, and lock the car. The grass in the clearing is dusted with a coat of white frost, and my feet leave empty footprints as I make my way around to the front of the cabin. I find the familiar flowerpot by the front door and lift it up, revealing the shape of the key hidden underneath. Whenever I visit, I marvel at this small act of faith, the imprint left by the key signaling the luxury of trust.

Slipping the key into the lock, I step inside the dark cabin, turning the bolt behind me, hearing the heavy click of metal sliding into metal. I kick my boots free, let my duffel fall from my shoulder, and peel off my coat and jeans. The living room curtains are open, and the half-light reveals the closed door to Mark's bedroom. The hulking shape of his computer is shoved up against the far wall. There's a horse blanket flung across the back of the couch. I wrap myself in the warm wool, lay the Walther down on the floor beside me, and fall asleep.

I keep a picture of my father tucked behind the false back in the glove compartment of the Mustang. He would have been sixteen or seventeen when it was taken. Standing outside St. Mary's convent school in Brooklyn, he's wearing a suit he must have inherited from an older brother. The time of year is clearly late spring, because the branches of a horse chestnut are in full bloom above his head. The white cones of the flowers stand straight up out of the foliage, making the tree branches look like giant

47

blazing candelabra. My father's curly brown hair is cut short and slicked back against his head.

He's looking straight into the camera, his round cheeks almost completely consumed by the wide smile spread across his face. The words *Sister Magdalene's Junior Boys dance class, graduation* are scrawled on the back of the photo in my grandmother's faded handwriting. The reason for my father's smile is easy to understand: after weeks of dancing with the other boys from his Catholic school, after leading Jim Leary or sweaty Charlie Girvin in waltzes and box steps around the basketball court, today he will finally be able to dance with a girl.

Of course this day in Brooklyn is long before my mother or I entered his life, long before the war. I think back now past my own birth and try to imagine my father dancing under the watchful eyes of the nuns, his hand perched lightly on the peach folds of his partner's dress. I try to imagine his face as it is now consumed by such a smile, the day unfolding, pregnant with possibility.

When I was a little girl, my father would pump nickels into the jukebox in the bar and I would step up onto his toes. My tan feet would cover the tops of his boots. He would bend way down over me and rest his hand on the top of my back. I would cling hard to his waist, gripping his shirt in my tiny fists as we spun in movements of three across the floor.

Today, as I drift out of sleep in the cabin, I am gripping the horse blanket. In the strange haze of half waking, I feel the gentle weight of my father's hand on my back, the dizzying whirl of the waltz. I open my eyes and stare at the brown back of Mark's couch. The TV throws flickering shadows up through the wintery late-afternoon light. It must be on without sound. My first thought before I turn and move completely out of sleep is that I forgot to ask Cyrus how it happened. I have no clear picture of the way my father entered death.

Raising myself up, I swing my legs off the couch with the blanket still wrapped around me. On the television three couples are arranged on a stage facing an audience. The host of the show, a large man in a tentlike suit, is galloping through the studio fielding questions. Mark is sitting at his computer with his back to me. He is shirtless, and the large black spider he has tattooed on his left shoulder blade jumps as his hands move furiously between the keyboard and the mouse. A pair of earphones is clamped over his shaved head. A tinny whine filters out through the headphones.

He is singing along silently to the music, and the delicate veins and muscles in his brown neck work with his jaw. Half Gros Ventre, Mark was brought up by his mother on the Fort Belknap reservation way up in the northern edge of the state. After he decided to quit driving, he came back here to live. Now he does freelance work for big computer firms, testing new games for bugs and writing code.

'*Pow, pow, pow.*' He makes soft shooting noises. His hands speed up, then come down hard three times on the keys. '*Pow, pow.*' He leans back, peels the earphones from his head, and laughs triumphantly. He swings around in his chair and sees me staring at him. I throw him a sleepy smile.

'Allie,' he yells, hurling himself toward me. He pounces on me and wrestles me to the ground. 'Man, I freaked out when I saw you here this morning. You gotta quit sneaking up on people like that.'

I look up into Mark's face. He's shorter than I am but

twice as strong. He's got me pinned to the ground and he's sitting over me with his feet tucked up under him.

'God,' he says, his smile fading, 'you look awful.'

'Gee, thanks.'

'You okay?'

I shrug. 'It looks worse than it is. I'll be fine.'

Mark straightens up and extends his hand, helping me to my feet. 'You working?' he asks.

'I had a pickup outside of Seattle.'

'I take it it wasn't a grand success.'

'To put it mildly, no.'

'When are you gonna learn, sis?'

'About the same time you do,' I say, grinning.

'Seriously, I worry about you, Al.'

'Don't.'

Mark shakes his head. We've talked about this before and he knows when to give up. 'You hungry?'

'Starving.' I reach across the floor and grab my jeans and wriggle into them. The Walther is still lying where I left it, and I pick it up and put it on the coffee table.

'I've got some good antelope steaks.' Mark hobbles toward the kitchen, favoring his good leg. 'Why don't I fix you something to eat and you can tell me the whole ugly story.'

I follow along to the kitchen, slipping the disk out of my back pocket and setting it down on the table. Mark grabs a carton of eggs from the refrigerator and lights the gas burner under a heavy iron skillet. He pours me a cup of coffee and unwraps two thick steaks from their white butcher paper.

'My cousin got this down by Dillon,' he explains, motioning to the meat.

I take a sip of the coffee and nod. My stomach is

growling at the thought of food. I can't remember the last time I've eaten.

'How's work?' I ask, watching Mark's hands as he cracks eggs into the hot pan.

'Same old same old. I've got some great new stuff for the computer, though.' Mark flips the eggs and pushes them to the side of the pan, making room for the meat. 'I did this job for Microworks and they gave me a test model of their new camera. Amazing. I can hook one up and talk face-to-face with anyone. You should see the shit that's out there, though. I'm talking weird. Chicks doing insane stuff with their animals, insane. Fantasyland, man.' Mark talks rapidly, his voice shattering the quiet of the cabin like gunfire.

Pulling a plate from the cupboard above the sink, he flips the eggs onto it. He slices two thick chunks of bread from a brown loaf, slathers them with butter, and slides the plate in front of me. 'Steak'll be ready in a second.' The disk is lying on the table by my hands and Mark's eyes graze greedily over it.

'This what you're working?'

I nod.

'What else are you carrying?'

'That's it,' I say.

Mark fingers the disk, his eyes widening. 'Seems like they could have just dropped it in the mail.'

'Seems like it, but they didn't.' The yolks of the eggs are soft and runny, and I dip chunks of the bread into them. 'Listen, I don't want to drag you into this, but I need to find out what's on here.'

Mark watches me eat, silent. The fresh meat sizzles and pops in the skillet. 'Events have taken a wrong turn?' he asks, finally.

'You could say that. I almost got killed back at the pickup.' I stop eating, lean back in my chair, and give Mark a long look. 'I don't know what this is about, but it's pretty serious. You just say the word and I'm gone.'

'You know, sis, we've been through a lot, but I just don't want you here. Why don't you go out and get yourself killed?' Mark rolls his eyes to exaggerate his sarcasm. 'You stupid or what? You're not going anywhere.'

'Thanks.'

'Who're you running this for?' Mark asks.

I hesitate a moment. Mark has always hated Joey. 'Joey got me the ride, but I think this is even over his head. These guys in Seattle had professional written all over them. They weren't mob, though. Maybe contract hires. You know, freelance.' Mark lifts the skillet from the stove and passes the steak to my plate. His long brown eyebrows are knit together in a look of deep concentration.

Between bites of steak I tell him the story of the Nightshift and the dead fisherman.

'It could be some kind of corporate thing,' he says, when I've finally finished. 'The software business can be cutthroat.' He has refilled our coffee cups several times and the afternoon has moved into evening, taking the last of the day's light with it. Our faces reflect in the blind kitchen windows.

'I'm telling you, Mark. This guy who slipped me the disk was a fed. He gets his teeth cleaned in Falls Church, for God's sake. Why would the feds be messing in a private concern?'

'Only one way to find out,' Mark says. He stands up from the table, grabs the disk, and crosses from the

52

kitchen into the shadows of the living room. I follow him with my coffee. He pulls up an extra chair next to his at the desk and motions for me to sit down. The computer's screen saver is on, and a tiny, pixilated spider crosses the monitor. It stops at the center of the screen and spins a fine web, working its way steadily outward. Mark goes to the stereo to put some music on, and I watch the plump, leggy body crisscrossing the screen, throwing out its computerized silk.

'Have you told Joey about the problem with the pickup?' Mark comes over and sits down next to me.

'No. I haven't told anybody. Are you sure you want me to stay?'

'How many times do I have to tell you? Relax, little sister, no one's gonna find us out here.'

Mark slips the small CD into the mouth of the computer and the drive clicks to life. The spider lingers for a split second more on one of the outer strands of the web, its legs trembling with imagined effort. In a flash of color, the monitor springs to life. The muscles and the copper skin of Mark's chest gleam in the light of the screen, and the tendons in his wrists scramble to keep up with his fingers on the keyboard. I know nothing about this secret world of his. I sit back quietly and let him work.

The stereo has kicked in and the cabin is alive with the screaming of guitars and drums. Names and colors dance across the monitor. I get up and find my cigarettes and Mark's pipe. I have some leftover pot from a ride last week, and I stuff a big green bud into the bowl.

Mark's fingers stop suddenly and hover in midair. 'It's a game,' he says excitedly, turning away from the computer.

The word SPYMASTER glows in huge stylized print on the screen. Ominous music blares from the computer's speakers. An American and a Soviet flag wave above the letters. Mark moves the keyboard aside and replaces it with a game panel. 'Wanna play?'

'You know I'm no good.'

'C'mon, Al. It's not as hard as it looks. It's more a matter of remembering all the tricks than anything else.'

I cross the room and take my seat next to him and hand him the pipe and a lighter. 'Leftovers from my last delivery. I thought you might enjoy them.'

'Perfect!' Mark beams. He flicks the lighter on and takes three or four deep pulls, exhaling slowly each time. 'Okay,' he says. He rubs his palms against each other. 'Let's play. I'm assuming in this game we'll have some James Bond-type weapon like a Walther.'

'Any idea how old this is?' I ask.

'The copyright said 1987.'

An unwholesome figure appears on the screen. He's dressed in a computerized version of a rumpled suit, and a cigarette dangles from his lip. A short bio flashes below him:

KGB head General Nikolai Gregorovich, one of the most villainous figures in the war for democracy. Your mission – to defeat him in the spying game.

'This can't be real,' I groan.

'I don't think this baby ever saw production. At least I've never heard of it before.' Mark bounces gleefully in his chair. 'Look, there's more.'

The shady Gregorovich has been replaced by a crisp-suited figure with (sure enough) a shiny Walther in his right hand. The text at the bottom of the screen explains:

You are David Callum with the American Central Intelligence Agency –

'This guy, this Callum guy,' I say, not bothering to read the rest of the bio, 'he really was CIA. He was on the news last night in Bremerton.'

Mark's not listening to me. The introductions are over and the game has started. In the foreground of the screen is the short nose of the Walther. Mark spins his ball and the Walther moves through corridors and around corners. Some of the pathways are dead ends, and Mark has to turn Callum around and head back in the direction he came from; others have hidden doorways or life-extending charms. Apparently we are penetrating deep inside the Kremlin.

I stay with Mark for over an hour, watching his supply of lives shrinking, his repeated deaths at the hands of stiff Soviet soldiers. Every time Mark restarts the game he's a little wiser to the intricacies and secrets of the maze and manages to go farther into the game before dying.

'You'll be at this for hours, won't you?'

Mark is about to start for the fourth time. I leave the computer and start packing him another bowl.

'I think those long winters up in Havre did something to your brain,' I say, joking.

'This is fucked up.' Mark is suddenly serious. He joins me on the couch, and I pass him the pipe.

'One guy's dead and someone's looking to kill you, and all we have is a shitty game.' Mark pauses for a moment and puts the pipe to his lips. He sinks back into the couch

55

cushions and lets the smoke drift out of his mouth. 'The graphics on that thing are ancient. Besides, the Cold War's been over for a long time. Maybe your fisherman gave you the wrong disk.'

'I should call Joey and find out what's going on. I just want to get rid of this thing and get my money.' I pull my cell phone out of my bag and dial Joey's Miami number. Mark takes another pull on the pipe and leans forward, setting the pipe down gently on the table. His shoulder catches a shaft of light from the kitchen and his tattoo is illuminated, the bulbous abdomen, the eight long crooked legs, the ink line of silk from the spinneret that drops down over Mark's collarbone and connects with the web etched on his chest.

No one is answering at Joey's. I'll call back later. The lack of sleep from the last few days is catching up with me. I pad into the bathroom and slip out of my clothes. A long mirror hangs on the inside of the door, reflecting the yellow shapes of bruises forming on my skin. They are like small continents of pain drifting across my body.

I lean down and trace the old scar on the top of my calf, caressing the raised half-moon shape with the tips of my fingers. The night in Miami when Joey pushed me through the glass door of his condominium on South Beach, I was too high to feel any pain. We rode in his car to the emergency room at Mercy Hospital, with towels shoved under my leg to keep me from bleeding on the seats. Somewhere on the MacArthur Causeway I opened my eyes and saw the thick smear of blood and heard Joey saying over and over how sorry he was.

Joey had a little red MG convertible back then, and the top was down as we sped across the bay. I stuck my head outside the shelter of the windshield and let the warm air stream over my face. The force of our motion pulled at my lips, pressed in on my cheeks. The Miami skyline loomed before us, the bridges gilded with neon, the tiny bright windows in the cars of the Metro trains snaking through the city, the royal palms along the bay bending and rustling in the breeze. When I ducked my head back behind the windshield, Joey had one hand on the wheel and one hand stretched out toward me. He was holding a small glass coke vial with a silver lid like it was an offering of peace or an act of contrition.

I step into the steamy warmth of the shower and pull the curtain closed. Even now I forgive Joey for all his excess, his wild violence. We live lives of violence that we still think are normal. The water hits my face, and the raw cut on my cheek stings and throbs. Someday, I think, I will touch the smooth tissue of a scar there and remember this distant pain, some fragment of my life's events breaking through the skin of time. I read once that the body doesn't get rid of glass. Our cells grow around it and hold it, just as a heart might hold the three-step of a waltz.

Five

'Allie, wake up!' Mark's voice jolts me out of sleep. He's standing over the couch shaking me. I rub my eyes and struggle to sit up. My hair is still damp from the shower, and the cool length of it brushes my neck. The cabin is completely dark except for the glow of the computer. I focus on the flashing monitor.

'I made it!' Mark yells, tugging me up from the couch. 'I beat the General!'

I stumble over to the desk and sit down. 'What's it doing?'

'I don't know. After you fell asleep I decided to try the game again. You know how I hate to lose. Anyway, I made it to the fifth floor of the Kremlin and there was Gregorovich. I must have shot him because that's when the whole program went nuts. It started doing this.'

'Can you slow it down?'

'I can try.'

Mark unplugs the joystick panel, hooks up the keyboard, and starts tapping away. Still half asleep, I pad into the kitchen to start a pot of coffee.

'Holy shit! Allie, get in here! You've got to see this.' Mark's voice echoes through the cabin. In a second I'm beside him at the computer. The screen has stopped flashing.

'It's some kind of topographical map,' I whisper,

putting my hand up to the monitor, tracing the concentric rings that suggest mountains or hills. There are no place names on the map, only numbers that must be altitudes.

'It's fucking Vietnam, Al,' Mark says softly. He's close to me and I can feel his breath on my cheek as he says the words. I stare at the uneven border and try to remember the shape of the country from high school history classes.

'Look.' Mark points to a spot where half a dozen small rivers flow in from the line of the western border and converge into two thick threads. 'This is the Mekong Delta' – his fingers move north – 'and right about here would have been Saigon.' The curving shape of the country floats like an elongated embryo on the deep blue background of the monitor.

Mark pecks at the keyboard and the map disappears. *December 18, 1969* appears in the upper right-hand corner of the screen, followed by some kind of official letter. At the bottom of the text is a round seal with a picture of a bird set into it. Just above the seal are the looping scrawls of two signatures.

'What the hell?' Mark draws his breath in and lets out a slow whistle. He peers at the screen and leans back in his chair. I scan through the letter quickly, making out the words 'necessary force,' 'pacification,' 'highly classified.'

'Okay.' Mark looks over at me. His face is creased with concentration. 'You know how a fax machine sends images? This is the same kind of thing.' He explains. 'You feed an image into the computer – a photograph, say, or a document like this – and the computer copies the image into its database. Someone's done this here. So basically what we're looking at is a picture of a document written in nineteen sixty-nine.'

'This seal looks familiar,' I say, pointing to the small stamp of the bird.

Mark has turned back to the monitor, and his lips are moving as he reads. 'Operations will begin at Chau Doc at 0300 hours,' the text begins. 'You may use any and all necessary force and each kill is to be confirmed immediately. Any outcome other than total pacification will be considered a failure. This mission is highly classified and is to be treated as such at all times. You will speak to no one before you leave or after you return of what you have seen. I repeat, under no circumstances are any of the preceding command or comments to be discussed with anyone . . .'

My eyes rest on the names at the bottom of the document. The top signature is broad and easy to decipher. I read over the large sloping *D* of the first name, followed by the open *C* and two looping *l*'s of the last.

'David Callum.' I touch the tip of my finger to the screen and look up at Mark.

'And this one?' Mark asks, pointing to the sloping scrawl beneath Callum's signature.

I shake my head. 'The first name looks like *J* something.'

'I think that's an *R* that starts the last name, but I can't be sure.'

Mark stands up and limps across the room to a large bookshelf. His long brown fingers find the spine of a thick oversized atlas, and he pulls it off the shelf. He walks back toward me, flipping pages as he goes.

'Chau Doc,' he says, laying the volume flat on the desk, its pages open to a map of Vietnam. His finger follows the blue of the Bassac River inland to the thick line of the Cambodian border and stops.

'Any idea what a Hmong is?' I ask.

'I think they're some kind of Laotians. There's a whole group of them that live down the Bitterroot Valley south of here. They're farmers, mostly. I guess they came over with the wave of boat people checking out of Indochina after the Communists took over. They sell vegetables at the local farmer's market. My father used to run some English classes for them at the Vo-Tech in town.'

A new map replaces Callum's document. Two thick rivers cut diagonally across the screen, branching apart and rejoining as they go. In the very center of the screen, where the southernmost river crosses out of Vietnam, Chau Doc is marked by a red circle. Just inside the Cambodian border, northwest by Chau Doc, is a thick red X.

'C'mon, baby, show me something I don't already know.' Mark is talking to himself as he works. Once again the monitor flickers and the image on the screen changes. What appears to be an aerial photograph of a compound flashes before us. The words U.S. ARMY CORPS OF ENGINEERS are typed in neat letters in the bottom margin of the picture. Someone has stamped CLASSIFIED in red ink across the page.

The grainy black-and-white photograph has been further distorted by the computer, but the flat surface of an airfield and the shadowed bodies of two large planes on the tarmac are easily identifiable. Rectangular roofs of several large buildings make up the bulk of the compound. Smaller structures which seem to be some kind of guard towers dot the perimeter fence line. The tufted heads of palm trees appear here and there.

'Didn't the CIA have a kind of private airline going in Vietnam?' I ask, trying to remember what little I know about the war. Most likely, this picture was taken before either of us was born. One of my earliest childhood memories is of watching the final pullout from the American embassy in Saigon on our little black-and-white television. I vaguely remember that we were sitting in the living room of our apartment in Brooklyn and my mother was crying. This was right before she died, and it may be the only real recollection I have of her. I can still see the small head darting out the window of the embassy for the flag, the line of people clambering up to helicopters on the roof.

I scan the picture for any more information it may have to offer. Everything and everyone must be tucked away under the tin roofs. Except for a few jeeps and several piles of sandbags, the compound looks deserted.

The atlas is still open on the desk to the map of Vietnam. I scan the names of towns along the Mekong: My Tho and Can Tho. My eyes move up along the coastline past Cam Ranh, Da Nang, and Hue to Hanoi and Haiphong in the north.

In the America of my childhood, Da Nang was where Magnum P.I. and his partner T.C. had fought the Communists, a scene of frequent flashback episodes for the popular television series. Billy Joel's sorrowful *Goodbye to Saigon* was a favorite slow-dance song at grade school parties. In history classes the war we lost was squeezed in at the end of the year between the class picnic and Watergate. The only thing I remember now from those lessons was that the NVA had surprised us during some kind of holiday called Tet. Of course there were the stories of people whose lives had been changed by what they had seen. My third-grade teacher used to let the boys in the class rub her nylon stockings during story time. It was a well-known rumor that her husband still saw the enemy creeping through their house at night. Our town must have pitied her, for her unseemly desire for physical affection was never challenged.

In movie theaters we watched a fresh-faced Charlie Sheen trudging through the jungle in *Platoon*, and as teenagers we smoked dope and watched videos of Sheen's father in *Apocalypse Now*. My father rarely spoke about the war. There were the dreams, of course, and the photographs, my father garlanded by the strap of his M-16, Cyrus beside him, his eyes bright white against the rich brown of his skin. These were the rumors of failure, the whispers of war that surrounded my childhood.

'Anything else on there?' I ask Mark. There's nothing more of interest in the photograph.

Mark types another command into the computer, and a list of names is thrown up on the monitor. I scan the list: Jason Adams, Darnell Walker, Henry Morrison. There are twenty-four names in all, and each is followed by the letters *MIA*.

'Americans,' Mark comments. He tries another command and the screen goes blank. 'I think that's it. I still don't understand the big deal here. We've got a supply base, a list of missing men, an order from Callum and some J.R. for the deployment of a Hmong unit, and some crummy maps.'

'Can you go back to the aerial photo?'

'Sure.'

Mark rolls back through the names to the photo of the airbase. Nothing.

'You think you could print these out for me?' I ask. 'There's no way I'll ever be able to get through the game.'

I get up from the desk and light a cigarette. Mark must

have stoked the woodstove in the corner of the cabin while I was sleeping; the room is hot and stuffy. Leaving Mark at the monitor, I step out onto the small porch. The air outside is crisp, and the moisture in my nose and lungs freezes. I take a long drag on my cigarette and watch the smoke snaking up into the darkness.

Somewhere in the canyon below us a car engine labors to turn over. The hollow sound of the motor engaging is followed by echoes of the car accelerating down toward town. In the woods at the edge of the clearing something rustles the branches of the ponderosa trees. The trees break open, and in the moonlight I catch a glimpse of a dark figure floating down toward the cabin. It's an owl. The square outline of the bird's head cuts a sharp silhouette; the claws stretch open at the ends of the thick, powerful legs. The owl dives, circles the roof, and moves on into the night.

The screen door slams shut behind me. 'You okay, Al?' I hear Mark's voice and turn to face him.

'My father's dead. Cyrus called me from the Keys two days ago.'

'I'm sorry, Al.'

'I shouldn't even be here. If it weren't for the bullshit with this disk, I'd be halfway home by now.'

Mark doesn't say anything. He lifts my cigarette from between my fingers and takes a drag off it. The moon is just setting over the far edge of the canyon, gilding the sharp line of Mark's jaw with cold light.

'Was your father in Vietnam?' I ask.

'Army helicopter pilot.'

'Mine was in the special forces. Though I don't know exactly what that means. He ran something called a PRU for a while, some kind of South Vietnamese army unit. He

65

and Cyrus never really talked about it while I was around.'

Mark rubs his hands together, trying to warm them. From inside the cabin comes the steady drone of the printer.

'Hey, Al, you said something about seeing David Callum on the news. What was it about?'

'Oh, some kind of boating accident, he'd been missing overnight. He and his wife have a house on some island outside of Seattle.'

'And where was your pickup?'

'Bremerton, across the sound from Seattle.'

'What do you think the chances are that Callum would disappear "accidentally" the night before you get this disk that's got his name all over it at a pickup an hour's drive from where he lives?'

I peer through the diminishing moonlight toward the woods. 'It doesn't make sense. Do you think someone would kill him over a picture and a couple of maps? The Vietnam War's been over for twenty-some years now. No one could possibly have anything to lose from something that happened so long ago. Besides, I told you I thought the guy that died in Bremerton was a fed. If the feds already have the disk, why kill for it, and why give it to me?'

Mark hands my cigarette back, and I take one last drag and flick the butt off into the frosty clearing.

'It's freezing out here.' I turn toward the door of the cabin and start inside.

'Allie.'

'Yeah.'

'I really am sorry about your dad.'

'I know, Mark. Me too.'

66

Mark steps inside the cabin behind me and closes the door. I look over at the television. The green numbers on the VCR say 2:30, but with the way I've been sleeping it could be any time of the day or night and I wouldn't know the difference. I rub my eyes and try to remember the passage of events since Joey's first phone call, the night I talked to Cyrus. It's four-thirty in the morning on the East Coast. Cyrus will be waking up in a couple of hours, and Joey will probably just be getting ready to sleep. I should call them both, Joey to find out what's going on, Cyrus to tell him I won't make it to the funeral.

Mark limps over to the television and switches it on, muting the volume. He heads into the kitchen and starts the pot of coffee I left unfinished. My cell phone is lying on top of my duffel bag, and I call Joey in Miami.

The phone rings four times and a sleepy woman's voice answers. 'Hello?'

'Let me talk to Joey.'

The woman's muted laugh mingles with the rustling of bedsheets. 'Joey, honey, it's for you.'

'Who the fuck is it?'

'She didn't say.'

Joey sighs, exasperated. There's more rustling as he picks the phone up.

'*Hola.*'

'Ever the charmer, aren't you,' I say. 'I guess there's always some woman hard up enough to sleep with you.'

'Careful, baby. You sure stayed for a long time. Wha' do you want?'

'What do you mean "what do you want?" This is a mess you've got me into here. People are getting killed over this pickup, and I'm not sure I won't be next.'

'Where are you? Are you at Mark's?'

67

'I'm not telling you.' Mark has come back into the living room, and he hands me a hot mug of coffee. He shoots a look of hatred into the telephone. The first time I came to a drop all bruised, Mark wanted to go kill Joey. It took me hours to talk him down. 'Listen,' I say, my voice controlled, 'I don't give a shit who gets this disk but I want my money. Who the hell hired this pickup anyway?'

'Sorry, baby. You know the rules. No can tell.'

'Do you want me to sit here with my head up my ass or are you going to tell me where to go?'

'Jesus Christ, calm down, Al. We know all about the little glitch back in Bremerton.'

'Little glitch? Joey, a man's dead!'

'Baby, you need to relax about this whole thing, okay? You've got this ride 'cause I know you're the best there is. I want you to get some sleep tonight and then head on to Texas. The drop is set for Houston. Call me again when you get there. It's still just a simple ride, Al. You've done this a million times. Now get some sleep.'

There's a faint click as Joey hangs up and then the line goes dead. I keep the phone at my ear for a moment and listen to the quiet hum of the disconnection. Who are 'we,' I wonder, and how do they know what happened?

I put the phone down and think about the flat surface of Joey's open palm, the sting of skin on skin. The first time it happened we were in Key West. I was between rental car rides, and Joey had driven down from New York to meet me. My father was off on the boat with Cyrus, and we sat in the back garden under the bougainvilleas. I had spent the day at the beach at Fort Taylor, and my skin was still hot from the sun and salt water.

There had been a manatee close in to shore and my legs brushed it while I swam. As I sat there with Joey, feeling

68

the cool pattern of the wrought-iron garden chairs pressing into my thighs, I thought about the smooth intimacy of the sea creature, the foreignness of its body and skin.

There was a night-blooming cactus at the edge of the garden, and the huge, furry blossom pods had opened into brilliant white flowers. We were half drunk, and we looked up through the woody bougainvilleas and saw flashes of lightning to the east. A curtain of rain swept across the island.

We stumbled inside and I leaned my back up against the wall of the kitchen, feeling two points of dull pain where my sunburned shoulder blades connected with the wood. I closed my eyes and drew him close to me, pulling my linen dress up over my thighs, undoing each of my buttons from its hole. I looked up through the windows at the violent rain, felt my tongue slip over the sharp edges of his teeth, felt my mouth form the words against his mouth. 'Hit me.' I heard the seduction and the betrayal of myself in each clear syllable, the whispered hush of the *H*, the calm moan of the *M* striking the back of his throat like a perfect invitation.

Mark has sat down at the couch and is hunched intently over the coffee table, cleaning his pipe. *Tick, tick, tick.* The brass mouthpiece clinks against the heavy glass ashtray.

I pick the phone up again and dial Cyrus's number. The static-filled voice of his answering machine blares onto the line. He's probably still asleep.

'Cyrus, it's Al. I'm just calling to let you know I'm still on my way. I'm at Mark's and I've got some business to take care of, but I should be in the Keys in a few days if you can hang on with the arrangements till then.' I pause for a moment, suddenly struck by the absurdity of the word. I'm talking about my father, about disposing of his body. 'I'll call you later.'

'I can't believe you're still working for Joey,' Mark growls from the couch.

I move across the room and throw myself down next to him. On the television a large jet hangs in the cloud-studded sky. The words AMERICAN AIRLINES, SOMETHING SPECIAL IN THE AIR flash across the bottom of the screen.

'A girl's got to make a living,' I say absentmindedly. Mark and I have had this discussion many times. 'I just keep thinking about the money.'

'He's a jerk.'

I don't reply. I fix my eyes on the two overlapping A's on the tail of the plane. The CIA had an airline in Vietnam, and it sure as hell wasn't called CIAir.

'Mark.'

'Yes?'

'Air America,' I say quietly. I get up from the couch and head across the room to the desk where the grainy photograph of the airstrip glows in the dim light. 'The CIA's airline in Vietnam; it was called Air America.'

'I don't like this anymore, Al. Why don't you just take the disk to Langley or wherever those spooks hang out. Those guys don't appreciate people like us messing in their business. Screw the money and screw Joey. Look at me. I'm a goddamn cripple. You want to end up like me – or, worse, like the guy in the bar back in Bremerton?'

Mark heaves himself from the couch and limps toward me. He pops the disk from the mouth of the drive and grabs the sheets of paper from the printer tray. 'Or just get rid of the damn thing.' He holds the disk over the wastebasket by his desk and lets it drop from his hand. It lands with a sharp smack. 'See how easy it is? Now just get in your car and drive away.' He wraps his fist around the sheets of paper, crumpling them one by one, dropping them on top of the disk. 'There'll be other jobs.'

I open my mouth to tell Mark I can take care of myself when the phone rings, cutting me off. Mark pushes off his good leg and limps over to the phone. I can see that his knee is hurting him tonight, and it's hard for me to watch him move.

'Hello?' Mark slips the phone into the cradle between his neck and his shoulder and shoots me a stern look. Our discussion is far from over. I slump back to the couch, trying not to eavesdrop.

Mark is quiet for a moment, listening, and then I hear his exasperated voice. 'Yes, I'll be right down. . . . I'm sorry he put you to any trouble. . . . No, just keep him there till I get down. . . . Thank you.'

Mark puts the phone down. 'You want to go for a ride?'

'Sure, what's up?'

'My father. I'll explain on the way into town. Maybe we'd better take your car. I'll probably end up having to drive his truck home.'

I leave the disk and the papers in the wastebasket where Mark discarded them, thinking we'll argue about it later, knowing I'll win. Easy money.

Six

We have ridden down the canyon in silence, past the autumn night gardens of shriveled lilies, the dormant houses with their sleeping children and parents tucked in bed. We pass under the interstate, and I take a right into town. The streetlamps illuminate the interior of the car and I look over at Mark. He's leaning with his forehead pressed against the cool surface of the side window. He's wearing a watch cap over his bald head, and I can see the naked nape of his neck between the knit fabric of the hat and the collar of his canvas coat. His breath condenses in opaque clouds on the glass as he speaks.

'Lately my dad's taken to the "old ways," as he calls it, some kind of bullshit white thing about the Indians having been right all along, us knowing by instinct about nature. Shit, every Indian I know besides my mom is holed up with a quart of Thunderbird.'

I watch the curve of the asphalt as I listen to Mark's voice. I can hear his Gros Ventre accent breaking through, the plain speech of the far northern railroad towns.

'It's been getting worse since my mom left him, this Indian kick.'

I have met Mark's father, Keith, once before. Though he's a math professor, he could easily pass for a homeless person. He lives in a squalid trailer down by the riverfront, near where the old paper mill used to have its tepee burners. When I was here a couple of years ago I went with Mark to bail him out of jail. He had gotten drunk and pissed all over himself in the Stockman's bar. Mark and I drove him home and rolled him into his mildewed bed. I remember the whole time I kept thinking, Rats, there must be rats in this place.

'The last couple seasons he's been doing this ritual hunting thing, thinks he can erase his East Coast math PhD by going out and killing a couple of bucks with a bow and arrow and eating their hearts, or something like that. Anyway, last year I told him to go down by Polaris, past Wisdom in the Beaverhead National Forest. They've got a lot of mule deer there; that's where my cousin and I go.'

Mark's voice has grown muted. 'So last winter he goes down there. There's a big blizzard coming but he's thinking it's like another walk in the park back home in Connecticut. He's out there with the goddamn perfect stars in his goddamn world where abstract algebra and Native American philosophy are still relevant. He's sitting in his '71 GMC truck one night doing the WASP rain dance or whatever he does out there when a call comes through over the CB; some tourist from California is missing.

'So of course my father goes to the rancher's house and volunteers to find this shmuck. By the time they get to this guy, he's frozen solid, wearing nothing but a sweatshirt. It's my dad and three other hunters who've joined up for the search who find him. By the time the airlift chopper gets there from Butte, my dad's lost feeling in his feet.'

I take my eyes off the road for a second. Mark turns from the window to face me. His eyes are blacker than I've ever seen them.

'They cut his toes off, Al, said he was frostbitten so bad they couldn't do anything else but take the part of his flesh that was useless. Anyway, since then it's just been downhill all the way with his drinking.'

I stare at Mark and think of my own father's flesh, all useless now, all taken. I turn my face away from Mark's and back to the road. There is nothing for me to say.

By the time we park the car in front of the Oxford it's nearly four in the morning. The air is white with snow. We push our way through the grimy glass doors and into the glare of the fluorescent lighting and I know, as I always know entering places like this, that I am home. The Ox is the scene of all late-night drunken activity in Missoula. I've been here many times with Mark in the early hours of the morning to have fried brains and eggs with gravy-smothered hash browns. The saloon houses a bar, twenty-four-hour café, strip club, and all-night poker and keno games. It's a self-contained paradise.

The bar, by law, is closed for the night and a heavy wire cage has been locked down over the liquor. The wall above the shelves of bottles is lined with glass cases featuring an impressive array of firearms. There are no handguns, only rifles and shotguns, each piece marked by a handwritten identifying placard. It's a strange mix of weaponry: a World War II British army rifle hangs next to a novice hunter's Remington .22.

I follow Mark back across the scuffed linoleum tiles toward the café. The bar and café and keno game are all housed in the cavernous front room of the saloon. The keno caller, a heavy woman, sits on a high stool in a Formica booth. Under the layers of makeup and folded skin she could easily be thirty or sixty years old; it's impossible to determine which. Her bleached and lacquered hair shines like a halo under the torturously bright lights. Her firehouse-red nails have been filed to points, and her two pudgy hands are constantly in motion. Her left hand holds a smoldering cigarette, deftly passing it between her lips and the side of the ashtray.

We pass between the fake wood tables and swiveling vinyl stools of the café. Two mangy dogs eye us from the corner. Another licks the greasy floor. I follow Mark as he moves down the back hallway and into the poker room.

Two games are going on in the smoky darkness, each table encapsulated in a circle of light. Standing in the doorway, I let my eyes adjust.

The players at the far table lean back in their chairs, tossing their hands down on the felt, and I catch a glimpse of Mark as he moves past them toward the back of the room. One of the players, an Indian with a long ponytail sticking out from under a John Deere cap, is raking a mountain of chips toward his side of the table.

'Hey, professor,' he calls out over his shoulder as Mark passes, 'your boy's here.'

I squint my eyes and make out a dim shape slumped over a dark corner table. Mark turns and limps out of the light toward the figure of his father.

By the time I reach the two of them, Mark has managed to shake his father awake. I lean down over the table and smell the odor of stale urine. My stomach turns.

'It's Allie. Remember me?'

He looks to Mark, his head bobbing like a doll's, his face blank.

'Stand up,' Mark orders.

Keith presses his hands against the flat surface of the table and pushes himself several inches out of his chair.

His fingernails go white from the pressure, contrasting sharply with the accumulated filth under the scraggly tips. He's breathing hard, and his sweat and breath reek of alcohol. Unable to lift himself, he slumps back in the chair, exhausted.

Mark rolls his eyes. 'Al, would you wait here with him while I go settle his tab? I can't believe this shit.' He turns to his father and raises his voice as if he's talking to a foreigner or a child. 'Dad, I want you to wait here with Allie. Are you going to be sick?'

'No,' Keith answers.

'You sure?'

'I'll make sure he's okay,' I say. None of the players seem to be bothered by our intrusion. Both games continue in hushed tones.

I turn back to Keith. His face is down on the table and he's flailing his hands wildly about his head. I put my hand on his back and feel his body heaving. He opens his mouth and a small trickle of vomit dribbles out onto the table.

'Keith,' I say gently, 'you've got to sit up, okay?' I put my hand under his chin and lift his loose head up off the table. He's wearing a threadbare corduroy sports jacket. A crusty handkerchief is tucked into the breast pocket. He looks like a bad parody of a university professor, as if someone dressed him for the part years ago and forgot to change his clothes. I pull the filthy square of fabric out and wipe his face.

'Hey, professor,' one of the men at the back table yells out, glancing in our direction, 'looks like you got yourself a girlfriend.'

'Shove it up your ass,' Mark's father responds with a slurred insult.

'C'mon, Keith,' I plead quietly, 'let's just try to get through this, okay?'

'Goddamned gook,' Keith mutters under his breath, paying no attention to me. The man at the table turns in our direction again, and I see the Asian features of his face. He's wearing a red, white, and blue T-shirt with the words MORGAN COUNTY PICKLE FESTIVAL 100TH ANNIVERSARY emblazoned across his chest.

'Keith, shut up,' I say through clenched teeth.

'Hmong poppy farmer,' Keith whispers to me, as if this information explains his former slur.

'All right, Keith, time to go.' I hook my arm under Mark's father's left shoulder. 'You've got to stand up. Mark's waiting for us outside.'

I brace my legs and pull on the dead weight of Keith's body. 'You're gonna have to help me out here, okay?'

Keith looks up at me and nods. His weight gives way as he raises himself slowly out of the chair. The Hmong has turned back to his game and is trying to ignore us. Keith grunts and pitches his body forward, steadying himself on his toeless feet. We stagger together toward the bright doorway, skirting the two pools of light as we go, sticking to the shadows.

'Jesus, Pop.' Mark meets us in the hallway, and I pass Keith off to him. 'I'm gonna take him home. I'll meet you up at the cabin. I may be awhile.'

'Mark, I'm thinking about leaving soon. Joey's expecting me to be on the road by morning.'

'We'll talk when I get back to the cabin, okay? Don't leave without saying goodbye.' Mark steadies the two of them on his one good leg.

'You need some help?' I ask.

'Thanks, I got it.'

As they turn toward the door, they both flash me the same wide grin and I see clearly that they are father and son. They clutch each other like two freed hostages, and I follow as they stumble past the locked bar and out into the night.

The snow is falling steadily now. From across the street, the windows of the Oxford shine like bright eyes. The Mustang's heater is blowing full blast and the wipers scrape rhythmically across the wet glass of the windshield. I crack my side window, light a cigarette, and peer down the empty street, trying to collect myself. I'll have to leave in the morning. I've spent too much time here already, time enough for whoever's out there looking to pin me down.

Two blocks away a man turns out of an alley and heads toward me. I reach down under the seat for the Walther and lay it across my thighs, remembering the man in Dickies at the Nightshift, his clothes perfectly worn, the smeared stain of axle grease on his jacket, no clean hands to give him away. The man draws closer and I flick my cigarette out the window, watching his long strides, the imprints of his boots on the snow-dusted pavement.

'You keep moving, Al,' my father told me. 'As long as you don't stay in one place they'll never catch up to you.'

I click the Walther's safety off and curl my finger around the trigger. The man's soles squeak plaintively in the dry cold and his breath floats before him in heavy clouds. It could be him or anyone. It could be one of the poker players, the man who sold me gas in Hyak, the keno caller with her bright nails, and I wouldn't know until they came for me.

Ten feet in front of me the man hesitates for a moment, shifting his feet, tightening the sheepskin collar of his coat around his neck. He reaches into his pocket and my heart skips a beat. I feel the weight of the Walther and anticipate the split second it will take to raise the gun up over the dash and shoot. The man fumbles in his pocket and pulls out a Zippo lighter and a pack of Lucky Strikes. He lights his cigarette and turns away from me and into the street. I lean back in the seat and exhale slowly.

One of the poker games must have ended. The saloon door swings open and the Indian in the John Deere hat comes careening out. The door swings closed and then opens again and the Hmong comes out. He calls to the Indian, and the two men exchange friendly goodbyes. Through the closed windows of the Mustang I hear the Hmong call, 'Next time.'

The Indian smiles broadly and turns and waves over his shoulder. The Hmong crosses to my side of the street and heads toward a shiny red Chevy pickup that's parked a couple of spaces in front of me under the circular glare of a streetlamp. He looks to be in his late forties or early fifties, with a slight paunch around his middle. His boots sending a glittering torrent of powder into the bright air, he trudges through the snow to the driver's side of the truck and pulls his keys out of his coat. He unlocks the door of the Chevy and climbs inside. The engine turns over with a cold cough, and exhaust pours from the tailpipe as the Chevy warms up. The Hmong has turned the cab light on, and the silhouette of his head shows through the back window. He leans down and his shoulders move as he fiddles with the radio, then opens the door again, climbs out with an ice scraper in his right hand, and walks around to the front of the truck.

I lean back in my seat and watch his body working, watch his arms bearing down on the thick layer of frost that covers the windshield. And it is then that I see it. Trophy hats, I've always called them. My father and Cyrus never wear theirs, but I've seen them tucked away in the backs of closets or on the heads of one-legged vets rattling spare-change cups on street corners. You can buy them at any Army Navy store. 145TH CAVALRY, DA NANG, they read, or 85TH AIRBORNE. I don't usually pay attention to the words, but the Hmong's is different and I notice it right away. Stitched into the fabric of his hat in thick block lettering are the words PRU-IV CORPS. And next to the words, in the upper right and left-hand corners of the cap, are two small patches; one is a hand holding a sword, the other a many-feathered bird.

The first job I ever ran for Joey was out of Galveston, Texas. I parked my car as I'd been told out at the state park early on a Monday morning and went for a long stroll along the beach. I came back to the Mustang about an hour later and got in and drove away.

'What'll I be carrying?' I had asked Joey the morning before, in the pale blue living room of his condo in Miami.

'When you're working for me, Al, you don't ask shit like that.' He reached into the back pocket of his linen pants and pulled out a roll of hundred-dollar bills bound by a gold clip engraved with the letters JP. 'If I tell you Kansas City, you drive to Kansas City, that's it. You don't open the trunk and go snooping around. You don't talk to the drop guys. You're a courier, Al, and I'm gonna pay you good money for every ride, not the nickel-and-dime shit you were making before. But don't ask questions. I tell you the pickup and drop spot, and that's all you need to know.'

I watched Joey's hands slide the money out of the clip and peel off five crisp bills. He laid them down on the glass coffee table in front of me and lit a cigarette. 'Gas money,' he said, nodding his head toward the table. 'You get the rest when you deliver.'

I stood up and stuffed the bills into the pocket of my shorts. It was late March, and the sliding doors to the balcony were open to let in the stiff Atlantic breeze. I stared past Joey to the rows of white-capped waves stretching to the horizon.

'You still got that Walther your dad gave you?' he asked, flexing the muscle in his jaw.

'Yeah, I have it.' I blinked my eyes to keep them from watering in the cool wind.

'Good.'

The red Chevy rolls forward as the Hmong pops it into gear. I follow it out into the street, thinking about all the unanswered questions of the last few years, the silent exchanges of money for goods. That morning outside Galveston a flock of pelicans lifted off the beach and fanned out over the pale waters of the Gulf at the sound of my engine cranking to life. Across the roadway the birds' shadows skated over the sand and the rippling water. I thought about the cached nourishment in the pouches of their powerful necks, the extra weight in the trunk of the Mustang, the five new bills falling against the glass.

Training my eyes on the dim tracks the Chevy has made in the new snow, I ease the Mustang into gear. Ahead in the distance the taillights glow like two red coals. It's just after five. Part of me screams to turn the wheel and head back to the cabin, just keep thinking about the money.

They are out there, Max and the others I have yet to see. They are out there looking for me. I follow the Chevy's trail down the blind street, past the darkened shops, and through the veil of falling snow. My father drank to erase from his conscience a war he fought without knowing why. If they are going to hurt me, I will know their reasons. The truck's brake lights flare as it takes a corner. If I hurry I can make it up the Bitterroot and back before Mark gets home from Keith's. I cross the Higgins Street Bridge behind the Hmong. Below us the black waters of the Clark Fork River flow from the mouth of Hellgate Canyon and past the old railbeds. It is too late for me to turn back.

I sit in the Mustang on the shoulder of the road across from the Coyote Truck Stop with my eyes fixed on the red Chevy. The Hmong is visible through the glass doors of the truck stop's convenience store. He's talking with the woman at the counter as he pays for the gas he's just pumped. From the way the truck weaved along the four-lane road up from Missoula, I could see he's dead tired or still sobering up or both.

Three hulking logging trucks and a couple of horse trailers sit in the parking lot. The sun is still far from rising, but a pale dawn is beginning to creep into the overcast sky.

'Goddamn it, stop talking and get in the truck.' I take the last cigarette out of my pack, crumpling the empty paper in my fist, tossing it on the floor. A semi shudders by, kicking up loose gravel, spraying my windshield. Striking a match, I watch the reflection of the flame in the window.

Across the highway the door of the Coyote swings open

and the Hmong comes ambling out into the cold. In the lights of the pumps I get my first good look at him from the neck down. He's wearing worn Levi's and cowboy boots. How long has he been here? I wonder. It's been twenty-some years since the fall of the Saigon embassy, long enough to have children that can't speak his native language, to know the woman inside like an old friend, maybe long enough to begin to forget the smells of wet earth in the jungle and palm leaves burning after war, to forget the sounds a lover makes in the deepest recesses of the night.

I close my eyes and try to conjure up the garden at my father's house, the intricate layers of the cactus flowers, the sickly sweet odor of the carpet of crushed frangipani leaves, the multiple rustlings of lizards and black beetles and palmetto bugs. Already I sense the alterations in my memories, the petals of a flower deceptively more brilliant, the stirrings of the creatures less menacing, the creases in my father's skin smoothed away.

From the parking lot of the Coyote come the sounds of a door slamming and an engine revving to life. I snap my eyes back open and peer across the highway. The Chevy wheels around and hesitates for a moment before heading back out into the dawn. There are two roads that converge at Lolo. One heads up past the hot springs through the Clearwater National Forest and then down into Idaho. The one the Hmong follows runs straight down the spine of the Bitterroot Valley.

I shadow the Chevy along the flat two-lane road. Light seeps over the rolling hills. To the west are the low trickle of the Bitterroot River and jagged, saw-toothed peaks. Somewhere up in those mountains, Mark once told me, missionaries built a huge cross and named the old Nez

84

Perce land after a Catholic saint. We were strangers here once, clumsy in our new boots as the Hmong must have been, as the boys limping through Southeast Asia in their heavy fatigues.

We pass the lights of Florence; the Happy Farmer Inn, which advertises 'fresh-baked pies;' the O.K. Corral bar and casino; the Hayes Brothers feed and farm supply store. I know from Mark that this valley is now home to an odd mixture of people: ex-hippies from California looking for a quiet place to grow dope, Mormon fundamentalists, old farm and ranch families, and the occasional militia type. The Chevy seems to be driving a little straighter now, and I fall back a few hundred feet. About a mile out of Florence a flock of blackbirds sprays from a fence line across the orange sky.

Just before Stevensville the Chevy slows suddenly and turns across the river and through a stand of bare cotton-woods to the east. The truck crosses a narrow bridge and disappears for a moment down a hollow behind some tall grass. The sun comes completely up over the ridge line as I cross the Bitterroot River and the water glints like the edge of a knife in the full light. I squint my eyes and feel the curve of the road as I swing around sharply and follow the Hmong down into the hollow and then up over a ridge.

The creased valley floor spreads out before me in cool shades of blue and gold and white. For a moment I am overwhelmed, and I lose sight even of the Hmong's truck. Then the glare of the sunlight catches the Chevy in the dim snow. The truck rolls along past two large barns and pulls up in front of a small ranch-style home. Two other vehicles are parked near the house: a battered green Ford sedan and a commercial truck with an enclosed back. I pull the Mustang off to the shoulder, open my glove compartment, take a pair of binoculars, and step out of the car. I adjust my eyes to the binoculars and scan the white landscape, focusing on the vehicles and the house.

The valley is so quiet that even this far away I hear the pop of the Chevy's door opening as the sound ricochets through the cold morning air. The Hmong gets out and walks with slow, deliberate steps toward the house. He swings the front door open and disappears inside. The windows of the house remain dark for a moment; then a light switches on in one of the rooms.

I trace the line of the road to the house with the binoculars, past two larger, windowless structures, remembering Keith's drunken words at the Oxford. Of course they're farmers. They were farmers in Laos, too. Up from the barns, where the junction from the Hmong's road meets the road I'm on, is a tall wooden gate. I fiddle with the binoculars, focusing them on the inscription on the arched wooden gateway. There are no words branded into this gate, only the shape of a large bird with its wings stretched out over the width of the road like an alate protector.

The leather of my boots has stiffened in the cold and my feet are beginning to go numb. I slide into the passenger seat and rummage through the glove compartment, finding the fisherman's wallet and the creased playing card. I slide the card out, unfold it, and hold it up to the light, then trace the ornate wings with my fingers, the sharp beak, the curling fan of the tail, the eyes peering out from the feathers.

The snow is beginning to let up, and the filtered light of morning pours across the valley. I put the card down and raise my binoculars again and zoom in on the house one more time. I fiddle with the focus, sharpening the image of the commercial truck, squinting to read the license plate. Slowly the jagged line between green and white distinguishes itself and I make out the crooked outline of the Rocky Mountains, the distinct pattern of Colorado plates.

Morgan County, Colorado, a place of bad weather, tornadoes, and destructive sprays of hail, a dry square of land dotted with oil pumps and scrub grass and the occasional beet or onion or cucumber field. I know this place and the bleak desolation of it; I have been there many times. My father's navy friend, Darwin, lives just to the west of Morgan County, in a trailer near the banks of the Platte River. Darwin, with her little packets of brown powder, of stillness and sleep, that help her forget the war.

Seven

I've felt it the whole way down the Bitterroot, the awful kernel of fear, the certain knowledge that something is wrong. It is not simply the matching birds, I think, as I fishtail around logging trucks and early commuters on their way into Missoula.

I turn up the canyon toward Mark's and cross Rattlesnake Creek. The hairs on the back of my neck bristle. In the deep new snow of Mark's driveway, under the limbs of the ponderosa trees, are three sets of tire tracks. Maybe he's come down to look for me or gone to the store for a pack of cigarettes and come back. I stop the Mustang halfway up to the cabin and get out. Two of the tracks were made by the same car coming and going; the other set is unique.

I get back into the Mustang and edge quietly up the last few yards to the clearing. The weight of the Walther rests against the small of my back. As I nose out through the last layers of the ponderosa branches, I take one hand off the wheel and bring the Walther up to the front of my body.

Sometime during the summer between my sophomore and junior years in high school it became wildly clear to my father that I could not be persuaded to stay out of his business. The trips I took with him had become more and more frequent, and instead of sleeping in the hold or reading comic books I had begun to share in his and Cyrus's work. I would clamber out when we reached the Keys and start offloading the boat with the others. In the Keys smuggling has always been a kind of family business, like farming in the Midwest. I knew several boys my age who helped their fathers or uncles on runs. None of my friends had paper routes or summer jobs busing tables. We learned early where the real money was to be made.

It was during that summer that my father gave up on protecting me and consciously began to teach me how to survive. Of course by then I'd been watching him for years. I would note the curve of his arm or the shape of his fist when he threw a punch at the boxing bag that hung on the dock behind the bar. From slight hesitations of speech I had learned who could be trusted, how to spot one of the rare local cops who wasn't in on the game. There was an old pineapple plantation that had been turned into a shooting range up on Summerland Key, and we drove up there almost every afternoon that summer and pumped rounds into the paper targets. We would stop at Big Coppitt afterward and sit on the deck of the Tiki bar, my father taking long pulls off a bottle of Red Stripe and me with a mango shake or a bowl of sweet shaved ice.

The first time I fired his old Colt revolver he stood behind me, wrapping his arms around my shoulders and clenching his big Irish hands over mine. There was a hot breeze coming off the Gulf that carried the stench of the rotting sargasso weeds that always washed ashore during summer. I steadied myself on the sharp coral beneath my feet and sighted out over the chalky ground between me and the target.

'This is the easy part, Al,' he said into my ear. His

90

calluses rasped against the smooth skin of my knuckles. 'Just pull nice and slow. If you ever really have to use this thing, it won't be your aim that will screw you, but your nerve.'

I waited for him to stop talking and drew in a deep breath and squeezed the stiff trigger. The Colt fired, and the force of the kick threw my whole body back against the weight of my father. My shoulders pressed into his chest and the small of my back curved against the soft pillow of his stomach.

'Good girl,' he said, cradling my rigid body in his own. I lowered the gun and we both looked up at the empty gash in the target.

The ponderosa branches are heavy with the weight of the new snow, and they brush against the Mustang's windshield as the clearing comes into view. I have a death grip on the Walther and I loosen my knuckles a bit, thinking about the shooting lessons at Summerland, trying to steady my nerves. The first thing I see is the mud-spattered body of Keith's GMC parked in front of the cabin. The older, single set of tire tracks leads to its wheels. The other tracks stop partway across the clearing and then make a wide loop back down the drive.

I trace the curve with my eyes and shut off the engine of the Mustang. I take the keys out of the ignition, slip them into my pocket, and make my way through the snow, trying to quell the tide of panic that's rising in my chest. The door to Mark's cabin is wide open.

'Mark!' I yell. My voice echoes up through the woods. Tightening the muscles in my arms, I raise the Walther up in front of my chest, slow my pace, and edge sideways toward the gaping door. Two sets of footprints muddle the snow where the car's doors would have been and lead up the wood stairs past the flowerpot.

Peering into the dark interior of the cabin, I ease myself forward. I can just make out Mark's desk against the far wall, the spider on the screen saver working her web. The wood shudders beneath the weight of my boots as I take the four front steps. Off in the trees a crow lets out one sharp *caw*. Whoever it was, Mark would have heard them coming through the still morning, the engine laboring uphill, the rustle in the alley of trees. He would have had plenty of time to leave.

'Mark!' I call out again. The wind has blown clean snow over the threshold of the cabin. Glistening flakes lie scattered over Mark's braided rug. I stretch my arms and the Walther through the door and lunge into the cabin behind them, sweeping the barrel of the gun around the front room.

The cabin is unusually quiet and, except for the thin dusting of snow, as neat as when we left it to go retrieve Keith. It's freezing, but my face is hot and I'm shocked at the force of my own breath. The hinges on the half-closed bedroom door creak in a faint wind. I raise the heel of my boot and give the door a violent kick. It slams as it hits the wall behind it.

The heavy iron-tinged scent of blood hits me before I even enter the room. Instinctively, I take a step back into the hallway.

'Please, God,' I'm whispering to myself, 'don't let it be Mark.' But I know he is dead.

From the hallway I can see Mark's bed. The pillows have been cut open and the down comforter has been rent in two. Fine white goose feathers coat the wood floor. A thick smear of blood runs at chest level along the pine boards of the far wall.

My arms go slack and I let the Walther fall to my side, taking one step forward and then another. The brown soles of Mark's bare feet protrude from beyond the bed. My feet stir the light goose down and it clings to my wet boots as I move across the carpet of wet feathers toward his body.

Mark's eyes are wide open and his face is tilted slightly so that his left cheek is pressed into the floor. I rest the Walther on the floor, lean down, and touch the soft hollow at the base of his head. He is shirtless, and the tattooed spider's spinneret drops down and ends at a bloody hole in his back. Whatever bullet they used passed right through the delicate tissues of his chest, through the solid breastbone and the strong red muscles of his heart. Mark's right hand is twisted under his body. The fingers of his left hand are splayed open in strange angles against the rough boards of the floor, and a thin line of blood drips from his thumb. The bottoms of his Levi's are still wet from walking through the snow. I run my hands down over his calves and feel the moisture in the cloth; my fingers brush over the sharp bones in his ankles.

I steady myself into a crouch, hook my hands around Mark's side, and roll him over onto his back. Only then do I see what they've done to him. The bridge of his nose is split crookedly in the center where somebody smashed the cartilage to one side. On the side of each of his arms, in the rich brown skin of his biceps, are five red smudges of broken blood vessels, welling bruises in the pattern of fingers where someone held him firmly from behind.

Standing, I lift a torn half of the comforter from the bed and spread it over Mark's body. Whoever did this took pleasure in their work. I can see Max's pale face, smell his sour breath in the cold room. I pick up the Walther and make my way down the hall to the front of the cabin.

Soon someone will come: Max, looking for me; a neighbor who heard the distant gunshot; the police. Mechanically, I retrieve what things of mine I can and stuff them back into the duffel bag. The spider on the computer's monitor toils away, oblivious to what's just happened.

Of course they have the disk, I think. Mark might have heard them coming, might have hidden it, but they wouldn't have left without it. They must have beaten it out of him. They must have known that eventually he'd give in to the pain, that eventually anybody will. And then, when they had what they wanted, they must have shot him.

'See how easy it is,' Mark had said, as he let the disk and the papers fall from his hands. I put the duffel bag down and cross the room. There's a fresh heap of garbage in the wastebasket. I pick through crumpled papers and old candy wrappers. The ashy dust from cigarette butts coats my hands. And there, like a fresh miracle beneath the filthy layers of trash, is the perfect round shape of the disk and the balled-up paper.

I grab my duffel bag, stuff the papers and the disk inside, and head for the front door, not knowing where I'm going, only knowing I must leave. Blown snow is piling up inside the doorway. The tracks I made on the rug earlier are almost gone. Stepping into the glare of winter daylight, I don't feel the deep chill of the mountain air. Concerned only with survival, my mind has gone beyond its own scope of reason or pain. I count the hours I've been here, slightly over twenty-four. They are fast, fast enough to have found me between one sunrise and the next. Only they found Mark instead.

I turn back to the wall of the cabin, cursing myself, running over the short list of people who might have known I'd stop here. My mind keeps racing back to Joey. My right hand flies back over my shoulder and I bring it down in a hard, tight fist on the rough boards. I pound my knuckles against the wood. Joey might easily have guessed. He asked me last night if I was here. Exhausted, I drag myself down the steps and across the clearing to the Mustang.

I toss my duffel into the back seat and fumble in my pocket. My fingers have long since gone numb, and as I pull out my tangle of keys a small object falls from my pocket into the snow. It's Mark's spare key. Luxury, I used to think, finding this welcome sign under the terracotta flowerpot, the possibility of bartering a life of running for one of roots and claims. Now I know there can be no exchange, only an illusion of calm and the long wait for the unknown car engine, the gloved hand in the darkness, the glint of the knife or the metallic odor of the gun.

Cupping the key in my hand, I raise myself up and start back across the clearing toward the steps of the cabin. I bend down over the flowerpot and brush loose snow from its rim, rolling the base of the pot back to reveal the dry boards underneath. Something inside me wants to imagine the key always here, a porch light left on, a welcome to impossible return. I slip the key safely back in its place and turn to leave.

As I clamp my foot down on the accelerator of the Mustang and take the wide arching curve upward onto the interstate, I try not to think about Mark. I wonder if he knew they were coming, if a hum in their engine gave them away, the buzz approaching up the canyon without the familiar power of my car. Or did he look out the window of the cabin, expecting me or one of his cousins, and see instead the pale shapes of strange men.

I enter the gaping mouth of Hellgate Canyon and ease the car past sixty-five. Up ahead, the paper mill at Bonner coughs waves of smoke and steam up over the peaks of the Garnet Range. SEE A LIVE FIFTY-FOOT PYTHON! a billboard advertising the Snake Pit screams.

'Why don't you just take the disk to Langley?' Mark had said last night. But at the moment when he could have given the disk up, saved his own life or at least spared himself the pain, he had not done so.

We are not, I have come to believe, completely separate individuals. There is a part deep within ourselves that struggles to understand the nature of those who made us, to know the longings and fears of our mothers and fathers. We look up into the pained face of a parent and are bewildered that the end of a war, the fall of a city halfway across the earth, could cause tears. Somewhere on the mercurial face of that disk or in the grainy record of a base are traces of lives we will die without ever fully knowing.

One winter when we still lived in Brooklyn, I found an empty bird's nest on the sidewalk outside our apartment building. The nest was made of twigs and grass and thin, wiry bits of hair, with a few strands of pink knitting yarn twined in. The small things we lose in our lives, a forgotten sock, a comb, become the habitations of other animals, so that somewhere in Saigon or Hanoi a sparrow might be laying her eggs on a lock of my father's hair or the torn sleeve of his coat. In this same way my love for Mark has been transformed, taken on a new shape.

'I got it,' Mark had said to me as he steadied Keith on his good knee out of the Oxford. I try not to remember the slight dip in his walk, the delicate blue veins like small rivers in his hands and arms. Instead I take the dry seed of my pain and plant it deep in the earth of my body, hoping it will bloom someday, knowing I will meet Max again. Already I can feel the husk bursting, the germination of anger, the pale roots sprouting forth.

Eight

HARVEST DAWN, the package declares. A smiling, wholesome woman adorns the front of the box. I close the lid of the toilet and sit down, contemplating the model's perfect teeth, the lips curved up in a too-wide smile, the tip of the pink tongue showing seductively. Over the woman's shoulder a dewy field of wheat shimmers in soft morning light.

I know from experience that the foul chemicals I've just slathered on my wet head will not give me the same cute curls the package advertises. If I'm lucky the color will be closer to BRASSY TART. I was not born to be a blonde. The first time I had to do this was back when I was still working with the rentals. One of my connections got busted, and the DEA put such a fear of God in him that he rolled. For two months I went around looking like I belonged in a trailer court watching soap operas instead of out making runs.

Twenty minutes to go. I shake a cigarette from my pack on the rim of the tub. I've stripped down to my underwear, and the small bathroom holds the chill of the smooth porcelain fixtures. The floor is littered with clusters of brown curls. I've taken a pair of scissors to my hair, and even with the wet dye and the cap, my head feels lighter. A sign on the door reads THE BUTTE CHAMBER OF COMMERCE WELCOMES YOU! An image of tourists crowding into town to see the defunct copper mine springs into my head. I allow myself a silent chuckle. I see the camera-laden families staring down into the hideous pit which, over the years, has swallowed most of downtown Butte. 'Next stop is the Butte unemployment office,' a cheerful tour guide sings. The group turns and dutifully follows.

I'm laughing aloud now. The top of my head bobs in the mirror above the sink. My face looks comical under the flimsy shower cap. When I laugh my eyes squinch up above my round cheeks. I make a serious face and mouth the words 'Jeannette Decker' into the mirror. I look back at the woman on the Clairol package and wonder if the real Jeannette might look something like her.

Joey gave me the Jeannette Decker ID a couple of years ago, along with Rachel Park, Karen Clemson, and all the others. Rachel is a redhead from Michigan. I've never really used her much – red hair attracts too much attention. Karen is from California. She's another blonde. I pick up the blue plastic box I carried in from the car and rummage for Jeannette's Kansas driver's license, reading off the information in the small squares: weight, 135; height 5'8"; hair, blond; eyes, green. The picture on the license is of me with dyed hair and colored contacts.

I don't suppose there is a real Jeannette from Wichita. If she ever existed she is probably long since dead. I don't know where Joey got these licenses, but I have a friend who runs a bodega on Eighth Street in Miami's Little Havana who can make you into anyone you want to be. He reads obituaries and then sends away for the birth certificates of the deceased.

Identity is one thing about being a woman that I've always appreciated. We are not bound, like most men are, to being one person all our lives. We dye our hair, change our clothes, and suddenly Eva Duarte becomes Evita Peron or Norma Jean Baker becomes Marilyn Monroe. When changing myself like this first became a part of my routine, people close to me were surprised. I'd go home to the Keys with a short red bob or blond curls teased up around my face and no one would recognize me. Now my singularity has become so linked to these transformations that everyone expects them. I can see it in people's eyes, the strange identification of the parts of me that never change, the recollection of my lips, my chin, the way I walk. What's mutable about me is no longer important to the people who know who I am.

I lift the lid of the toilet and throw my finished cigarette butt into the bowl. There's a short hiss as the water consumes the tiny coal of fire. A contact case sits on the cheap plastic counter next to the Clairol box. I dip the tip of my index finger into the cold saline and carefully bring one of the green contacts up toward my face, pulling my right eyelid down with my left hand, pointing my eyes up to the ceiling. The cool imprint touches the slick orb of my eye. I nudge the contact up over my iris, stand back from the mirror, blinking, and then slip the other contact in.

My hair should be just about ready by now. I make my way back into the main room and over to the door, checking the lock for what must be the third time, peering out through the dusty drapes at the parking lot. The Sacajawea Motor Inn is a small one-story complex. It's one of those motels where you imagine the builder must have wanted to create an illusion of home. The units are all linked in one long row, and each doorway has its own miniature peaked roof. A sultry Indian woman with two long braids and a tight buckskin dress adorns the sign above the office. VACANCY blinks in pink neon below her bare feet.

I chose this place because there were no cars in the parking lot and because the complex is set in a small hollow far enough from the highway so that no one passing might pick out the Mustang. The police will be looking for me soon as well. Plenty of people in Missoula saw me with Mark. If I'm lucky, Keith is still sleeping off his drunk and I'll be across the state line before he goes in search of the GMC. Even if they don't think I had anything to do with what happened to Mark, they will want to talk to me.

A green Chevy Malibu pulls up in front of the office and a man in a cheap business suit gets out. I take a step back from the window and eye the Walther where I left it on the neatly made bed.

The man walks into the office and quickly returns. He gets back in the car and spins the tires around and parks in front of one of the units several doors down from mine. I can see now that there is a woman in the car with him. Cutting the engine, the man gets out and strides purposefully into the room, leaving the door under the little peaked roof open behind him. The woman puts her hand up to her forehead and leans back in the seat. Her hair is made up in one of those seventies Miss America do's with big bouncy curls teased up around her face and shoulders.

She sits for a minute, and then her white pumps come out first, landing delicately in the swirling river of blown snow. Office shoes, I think. The muscles in the woman's calves are strong beneath her pale hose. She looks to be in her late thirties, probably someone's idea of pretty once. She turns her back to me and closes the car door. Under her thin, tight blouse the outline of her bra presses into the skin of her back.

The door to their unit closes, and I move away from the window. The smell of peroxide from the hair dye has mixed with the stale, smoky odor of the room. Unhooking my bra, I throw it on the bed and slide my underwear down over my heels, then grab the Walther and head back into the bathroom.

I put the gun down on the back of the toilet, take the shower cap off my head, and stuff it in a plastic bag along with the empty Clairol box. Turning the shower on as hot as it will get, I step into the tub and scrub my head twice, watching the pale gold color run down the drain and grow fainter with each rinse.

When all the dye is rinsed out I turn off the taps and towel my hair, padding to the window again and checking the lot. The Malibu is still the only other car besides mine. I turn back into the bathroom to survey the damage.

The result is slightly trashy, somewhere on a scale between aging stripper and bad drag queen. My hair is uneven and sticks out at ragged angles. My eyes are unnaturally green against the vibrant yellow that frames my face. Perfect.

'Al, honey, you know Joey Perez, don't you?' When my father was drinking he had a habit of screwing his eyes shut until his pupils were only tiny slits, as if a smaller range of vision made it easier to focus. He raised his head, looked up in my general direction, and waved a limp hand toward Joey.

'I don't think so,' I said, glancing over my shoulder.

I slammed a mixing bowl full of fried chicken down on the table.

We were up on Big Pine Key, at a bar one of my father's friends owned. It was his last night in business, and we had been invited over to help finish off the remaining inventory. It was four in the morning and we were the last of a party that had started drinking at five o'clock that afternoon. The chicken was a desperate attempt on my part to sober everyone up.

'We met in New York last winter. Down at the bar near Tompkins Square Park,' Joey said. 'You were with that girl – Cathy, Christa? I don't remember her name.'

'Christine,' I said absently.

Richard, the owner of the place, was tilted all the way back in his chair. His head bobbed precariously on his neck, and he looked as if he was laboring to keep himself off the floor.

My father and Cyrus and their friends pawed sloppily at the chicken. I looked out across the dark restaurant toward the bar. The shelves were empty except for a bottle of sambuca and another of cinnamon schnapps.

Joey watched as I sat down and lit a cigarette. He and another man had just arrived. Joey's friend looked pretty small-time and I guessed he was probably hoping for some late-night business, looking to sell an eight-ball or two to the remaining drunks. The friend had obviously been drinking, but Joey was cold sober. My father slumped down over the table, his chin resting on a greasy drumstick.

'Wake up, Dad,' I said loudly, as if I were talking to a deaf person. I gave his shoulder a nudge, and he sat up and looked around. Oil from the chicken leg glistened on his skin. 'You've got to eat something.' I picked a napkin up off the table and wiped his chin.

Joey's friend finished a wing and threw the gnawed bones on the floor.

'Fucking animal,' Joey said. He scooped the bones up and put them on a paper plate. 'Where do you think you are?'

'Sorry.' The man shrugged.

It was August, and although the bar was open to whatever air was coming off the water, I was sweating in my cutoff jeans and tank top. Joey was wearing a pair of dark blue raw silk pants and a white linen shirt. His sleeves were rolled up neatly above his forearms, and every pleat and crease in the fabric of his clothes was perfect. He picked up a napkin and carefully wiped his fingers. His hands were beautiful and tan. A gold coin salvaged from the wreck of the Spanish galleon *Atocha* hung around his neck.

'You always take care of them like this?' Joey looked at me with interest.

'He's my father,' I said, as if this explained everything.

'Is there anything left to drink? Can I bring you something?' He put an emphasis on the word 'you.'

'I think there's some champagne left in the bar coolers. Why don't you bring us a bottle?'

Joey smoothed his pants with his palms. He came over to me and put his hand very lightly on my wrist. Even in the dense August humidity his touch held the cool dryness of wealth or power. He was out of place in the midst of such drunken carnage, seductive in his sobriety.

The ceiling fans clicked and whirred overhead. I reached up to my forehead and wiped a thin film of sweat from my skin. Beyond Joey the bar opened out onto a patio, and beyond the patio was a dirty courtyard with an ancient banyan tree at its center. A slight breeze had picked up, and the waxy leaves of the banyan shimmered as they turned in the wind.

The trunk of the tree was massive and its branches put down vines that, over the years, had rooted and grown into smaller trunks. Some time ago an avocado had attached itself to the banyan and begun to flourish. I peered through the darkness, trying to follow the twists of the scaly avocado wood over the smooth trunk of its host, but I could not see where the body of the one tree ended and the other began.

Joey came back to the table with the champagne. He set two plastic cups out and eased the cork from the bottle.

'Would it be okay if I called you sometime?' he asked. The champagne bubbled into the cups.

'Sure,' I said, watching the muscle in his jaw flex. I wanted him to touch me again.

Joey pulled a small book from his back pocket. 'What's your number?'

I gave him the number at my father's house, adding, 'Allie,' not wanting him to have to ask my name if he had forgotten it.

'I remembered.' He opened the book and showed me the page where my number was written. 'See? You're right here under A.'

Later, after the champagne was finished, Joey stood up to leave. I watched his brown forearms tense as he pressed himself up from the table. Halfway to the door he stopped and turned back to look at me. 'What's my name?' he asked.

I could see the first light of dawn in the doorway behind him. I hesitated a moment before answering, letting the force of the word gather on my tongue. 'Joey,' I said.

*

The sounds of a car engine carry from the lot outside. I walk from the bathroom to the window and see the woman leaning down to get into the Malibu. Her hair is still in place and she tucks a few locks back behind her right ear. I imagine the couple making love, the careful positioning of the two bodies so nothing is left in disarray, so no one will know.

Turning from the window, I begin to dress myself. I take my driver's license from my wallet, put it into the blue plastic box, and slide Jeannette's into the empty space. I tuck the Walther back in my jeans, sweep the hair up off the floor into a dirty towel, and put it into the bag with the shower cap and the Clairol box. Later, I'll stop at a rest area or a gas station and throw all these things away.

I paid for the room when I checked in, giving the grizzled old man in the office my best college-girl smile and someone else's name. I leave the key on the bedside table, switch out the lights, and close the door behind me.

I toss my bags into the front of the Mustang, open the trunk, and pull up one corner of the carpet. Sticking the flat end of a screwdriver into a small seam in the floor, I pop the metal open, revealing a thick stack of license plates. The plates click against each other as I flip through them, looking for the Kansas number registered to Jeannette. I scan the lot, reassuring myself that I'm alone, and trade the Florida plate on the Mustang for Jeannette's.

I replace the stack of license plates, smooth the carpet back into place, and climb into the Mustang, stuffing the bag with the hair and the Clairol box under the front seat. If they come here looking for me, they will find nothing but a slight rumple in the yellow bedspread where I sat to lace up my shoes.

The Malibu has left a set of pale tracks in the parking lot, and I turn the ignition key and follow them out to the road. It is so easy, I think, to find oneself in the life and skin of another. I see the careful folding of the woman's skirt over the back of a chair, the silent and calculated consent as she followed her lover in through the door.

Last time I was back home in the Keys I went with Cyrus and my father to Richard's old bar. An actress from New York had bought it and turned it into an upscale club. We sat out on the patio and had stone crab claws and overpriced Red Stripes. The old banyan was still there in the courtyard, but the avocado had grown through the crook in the branches and straight down into the heart of the massive trunk, leaving a dark gash in the gray bark.

Nine

The first rest area on I-90 outside of Billings is completely deserted. Whatever front scudded in over Missoula and Butte has snowed itself out over the mountains. East of Bozeman the vast white blanket slowly gave way to dry prairie grasses and relentless wind.

I pull the Mustang into a slot in front of the bathrooms. It's after dark and the clean silence of miles of empty land buzzes in my ears.

Behind me the junction of I-90 and 94 rises over the plains. When I'm driving the other direction, north from I-25, I love coming upon the tangled intersection from the flat Wyoming desert. The highways' mammoth concrete ramps and pillars leap up out of the scrub and sage like the buttresses and clerestories of a Gothic cathedral. Less than fifty miles to the southeast lies Crow Agency and, beyond that, the Little Bighorn battlefield where the Sioux defeated Custer.

I reach under the seat of the Mustang, pull out the plastic bag of garbage I've carried from Butte, and grab my cell phone. I walk over to the nearest trash can and throw the bundle in, smashing the phone against the concrete housing for the garbage. There should be no way for them to track me.

The flip-up mouthpiece dislodges and clatters on the cold ground. Gathering the broken bits of the phone, I walk down the length of the parking lot, depositing one piece into each trash can.

When I'm done I make my way back toward the main structure of the rest area. A sign on the highway advertised free coffee here, but I see no evidence to suggest that I will find any. I step onto the concrete slab surrounding the building and into the circle of harsh lights, fishing in my pocket for change. On the flat wall between the men's and women's rest rooms are two pay phones.

The phone rings twice on the other end and a woman answers. 'Blue Ibis,' she says cheerfully.

'Let me talk to Cyrus,' I say.

'May I ask who's calling, please.'

'No.' There's an exasperated sigh as the woman puts the phone down. The words to the Neville Brothers' 'Yellow Moon' are blaring in the background.

I pull a cigarette from my coat pocket and tuck the phone into the crook of my neck, cupping my hands around my lighter, shielding it from the stiff prairie wind.

There's scratching and bumping on the other end of the line as someone picks up the phone. I take a long draw on the cigarette and snap the lighter shut.

'Hello?' Cyrus's voice booms against my ear like warm silk.

'Has anyone been there asking about me?' I say. I don't want to stay on the line any longer than I need to. My supply of coins is short and I'm struck by the sudden irrational fear that someone could be listening.

'Allie!' Cyrus says. He sounds relieved. 'I got your message. Where are you?'

'Montana. Listen, I need to know. It's important. Did you tell anyone I was at Mark's?'

'No, Al,' he answers quickly. 'What's wrong?'

I take another drag on the cigarette and shift my feet from side to side, trying to warm myself. We are both silent. Part of me was hoping Cyrus had talked to someone he shouldn't have. The thought that they could find me there without asking him is suddenly more frightening.

'Are you out at the front bar?' I ask.

'Yeah.'

'Why don't you transfer this call back to the office. I'll wait for you to pick up again.'

The line goes dead for a moment. A car passes on the highway, throwing bright beams of light out onto the sage. I finish my cigarette and snub the butt out under my boot. I hear a click and then Cyrus's voice again.

'Are you okay, Al?'

'Someone killed Mark.'

'Shit, Al. Oh, shit. Oh, Jesus. Al, I'm sorry. I'm so sorry.'

'Listen,' I say, steadying my voice. 'I don't have a lot of time, but I need to ask you a couple of things. Have you been getting the news about David Callum, the old spook they think drowned while he was out boating?'

'They don't just think he drowned, Al, they know it. They found his body today, dredged it out of the little bay in front of his house. The story's all over the news. I heard about it on the five-thirty report this afternoon from Miami.'

'Did they say anything about him being killed?' I ask.

'No, just something about heavy tides at the full moon and his scull capsizing accidentally. Shit, Al, I've rowed those things a few times. They're pretty unstable.'

I take a deep breath and look out across the parking lot. The lights of the rest area magnify the arc of darkness beyond the little compound. The universe of stars outside the cloak of fluorescent light is invisible.

'Cyrus, I think I have something that belonged to Callum.'

On the other end Cyrus says nothing. The faint wheeze of his breathing rasps over the line.

'I got this disk outside of Seattle; it was a run Joey set up. He called me after I talked to you the other night, started talking money, said I could carry this package on my way down to the Keys since I'd be headed that way. Anyway, my pickup turned bad.'

'But you're okay. . . .' Cyrus fades off the line. The operator's mechanical voice breaks in, demanding more money. I pump more coins into the slot and wait to be reconnected.

'Allie, are you still there?'

'Yeah, I'm here.'

'Whoever killed Mark, you think they were looking for this disk?'

'Yes, and now they're looking for me. Cyrus, how did Darwin end up in Colorado?'

'What has that got to do with all this?'

'I need to know.'

'I'm not sure. I guess she needed a quiet place after prison.'

The wind has picked up even more, and I lean into the phone enclosure, sheltering my face. 'What do you know about Chau Doc?'

'Vietnam?'

'Yeah.'

'Little border town. The Bassac River runs right through it. Listen, Al, we're running out of time here. Why don't you call back collect?'

'No,' I say. I want more than anything to stay on the line with Cyrus, to keep hearing the familiar voice, but I'm afraid to say too much over the phone. 'Were you or my father ever there?'

'No.'

'What about Darwin?'

'Darwin?'

'Was she ever in Chau Doc?'

Cyrus hesitates. 'Yeah, Al,' he says finally. 'Darwin was in Chau Doc.'

'I'm going down to see her,' I say. 'I'll be there by morning.'

'This call will be terminated in thirty seconds.' The mechanical voice breaks in. 'For more calling time deposit one dollar.'

'I love you,' Cyrus says softly.

'Cyrus?' I'm about to hang up, but I bring the phone back to my mouth. 'Will you wait for me? I want to be there to scatter the ashes.'

'Of course, Al.' The line clicks dead, and I hear the dull sound of a long, flat tone.

Putting the phone back in its cradle, I look up toward the sky, to the flat wall of blackness that stretches out over the craned necks of the lamps that dot the parking lot. Short hard bursts of wind roll against my body as I walk back to the Mustang.

I remember the first time Cyrus took me out in the boat for a night dive. I was fourteen and it was late July. When we anchored, the top curve of the full moon had just begun to roll up over the black line of waves on the eastern horizon.

My tank and buoyancy compensator were sitting on

the deck of the boat, and as I bent down to put them on I caught a glimpse of the orange glow from the chain of electricity that ran down the Keys. It was commonplace on the islands on summer nights for the power to go out temporarily. Too many air conditioners and televisions being turned on at one time would flip a switch somewhere up near Homestead, and suddenly all one hundred miles of precarious land would be plunged into quiet darkness. As I straightened myself up under the weight of the tank I saw the colorful band of dim light flicker and disappear.

'You ready?' Cyrus asked.

He was sweating, and the light reflecting off the water gave his dark face a deep blue sheen. I shuffled closer to the stern and gripped the handle of my flashlight. I flicked the lamp on, watching the narrow beam play out over the water.

As the spot of light jumped from wave to wave I saw parts of things leap and move beneath the surface, the striped fin of a parrotfish, a swatch of the long muscular body of a barracuda, a single gray eye. Cyrus took a giant step off the end of the boat and crashed into the water. I trained the light on him and watched the top of his head sink down toward the reef.

I slid my flippered feet the last few inches to the edge of the stern, steadying myself against the bobbing of the hull, catching the thrust of each wave in my knees. Clamping my teeth around the mouthpiece of the regulator, I let myself fall forward into the water, closed my eyes, and let out a long breath through the bottom of my mask. Cyrus's hands were on my calves, his fingers guiding me down. The soles of my feet bounced off the rough coral of the reef. I opened my eyes.

The flashlight's thin beam lit up a wide tunnel of the water around us about fifteen feet long, revealing the brilliant colors of the anemones attached to the reef. The last few inches of the flickering tail of an eel swerved off, out of the range of the light. The bulging eyes of a grouper loomed into view and disappeared. Cyrus's left hand reached out and grabbed my wrist and slid up over my fist to the handle of the flashlight. He turned his face toward mine and held the fingers of his right hand up in the sign for 'okay.'

For a moment everything went black. I felt Cyrus move the flashlight into his hand. The line from his spare regulator brushed across my arm. I reached my empty hand out to him, grabbing for his mask, curling my fingers around the fabric of his buoyancy compensator. The pale green phosphorus of bioluminescence swarmed around us like sparks from a campfire. I caught the glint of Cyrus's eyes through the water. He placed two fingers on the front of his mask and motioned with them out into the darkness. His mouth formed the word *look* around his regulator.

I turned back to the reef. The ocean was lit up in the flood of light from the full moon. The long body of the eel coiled away from us and down into a crease in the coral. Twenty feet off, a small hammerhead circled through a school of tiny silver fish. I rolled over and looked up at the bottom of our boat. The curved hull cast a wavering shadow down through the clear water.

I step into the Mustang, switch the map light on, open the glove compartment, and reach inside, probing with my fingers for the small groove, prying the false back up against the roof of the compartment. I reach deeper and my fingers brush over the disk, over the slick face of the photograph of my father. In the very back of the compartment my hand finds the crumpled papers Mark left.

I pull the documents out and smooth them out on the passenger seat. My lips move as I read Callum's words: *any and all necessary force.* My eyes linger on the second signature, trying to unravel the scrawl of letters. J.R. I flip through the papers to the list of names: Jason, Henry, Darnell. . . . I imagine Callum's face, his wrinkles bloated away by seawater, his skin round and tight, the color in his eyes clouded with the milk of death.

Refolding the papers, I stuff them back into the recess in the glove compartment and slam the hatch shut. On the highway a semi rumbles by, its tailwind gusting across the parking lot and slamming into the side of the Mustang. I turn the key in the ignition and wheel out of the lot and onto the highway, following the red taillights of the truck across the rolling scrub and down toward Wyoming. The lights of the rest area recede in my rearview mirror. I look out across the shadowed surface of the desert and up toward the wide bowl of the sky.

December 18, 1969: four months before I was born, before the chilly April morning my mother felt the warm release of water from between her legs, the moist stain spreading across the black and yellow flowers of her bedspread in the small apartment in Brooklyn. Six months before my birth she had said goodbye to my father in San Diego and watched him climb through the doorway of a C-118. When I was born, my father was on his second tour of duty in Vietnam. He could have been outside of Chau Doc on December 18, might have seen Darnell Walker or any of the others. Or he could have been miles away, curled beneath waxy banana leaves in the forest near Da Nang or Hue, sleeping.

There should be a switch, I think, on the narrow beam of history, a way to turn off the one glaring thread of light and see the wide expanse clearly. There should be whole answers, not just slippery pieces of eyes or fins, a patch of black-eyed Susans stitched into a child's quilt.

And what about the Hmong from the Oxford, the red trail of the Chevy bouncing along through the valley?

Everyone who drives for a living, who's connected to this world I work in, has seen things they would like to forget. One night outside of Baton Rouge I got stopped for speeding. It was when I first started working for Joey, and I was still stupid enough to get caught on something small like that. The state trooper who pulled me over opened my trunk and found a pile of cocaine wrapped in kilo bags.

When he stuffed me into the patrol car I thought, This is it. I'm looking at ten years, easy. When I got to the Highway Patrol office I called my father and told him what had happened, asked him to call our lawyer for me. Then I sat in a back room for a good twelve hours, smoking cigarettes and sipping diet colas. Except for the officer who stopped me, I didn't talk to anyone, didn't even have my fingerprints taken.

In the morning the heavy door swung open and a man in a dark gray suit walked in. He handed me my car keys, told me I could leave, and walked me right out to the front door. I got back in the Mustang and drove straight to my arranged drop spot, a warehouse on the outskirts of St. Louis. I didn't even bother to look in the trunk, just assumed the merchandise would be gone, but when they opened the trunk in St. Louis I saw that not a single kilo was missing. I knew then what Joey meant when he said, 'No questions.'

There are always these incidents, a bust too well-timed, evidence miraculously lost. Usually you can trace the root of the deception to a few extra dollars slid across a table, a donation to a police retirement fund, a shiny new patrol boat. But sometimes, like that night in Baton Rouge, there seems to be a larger, slicker hand at play.

None of us ever speaks of these things to each other, but when we look up at the flickering images of covert wars and weapons deals on the nightly news we know we are somehow part of the whole scheme.

Maybe the Hmong were opium farmers? Maybe Air America was flying drugs off that base? But why all this interest in such old secrets? None of this explains the disk, the three men recently dead, the two dozen missing in the jungle, the obviously extraordinary value of the information I'm carrying.

In an hour or so I'll stop for coffee in Sheridan, then head down on Interstate 25 through Casper and Wheatland and Cheyenne toward Darwin's.

When Cyrus and I surfaced from our dive that night and clambered back onto the deck of the boat, I looked toward the Keys and saw that the power had come back on. The unmistakable orange glow reflected off the ragged surface of the waves, in much the same way a chain of artillery fire might reflect off a rice paddy or off the pools and eddies of the Bassac or Mekong.

Ten

It's nearly four in the morning by the time I pass Fort Collins, Colorado. Twenty minutes later, the Crossroads Truck Stop looms up out of the flat darkness by the side of the interstate. I shift the Mustang to the far right lane and pull off into the tight curve of the exit ramp. The plain to the east is dotted with the sparse lights of farmhouses and newer commuter subdivisions. I head under the interstate and onto the two-lane road running away from the mountains. A green and white highway sign flashes into view: PLATTEVILLE 9.

The narrow road rolls slightly over small hills and down across streambeds and irrigation ditches. There's a light fog, and my headlights flatten out against it. The dry corn rows fly past the windows and the land breaks open into intermittent flashes of beet and onion fields.

Occasionally a dirt road appears, the house it leads to just a few twinklings of light a mile or so off in the distance. Many of the names on the mailboxes sound foreign: Yamaguchi, Onaga, Mandelheim. I asked Darwin about this once and she told me they were all people left over from the war: Japanese Americans from nearby internment camps who decided to stay and farm here, German prisoners of war who fell in love and opened dairies instead of going home.

'Kind of like me,' Darwin said, 'survivors of wars.'

She opened her thick mouth in a wide grin. Her clean white teeth stood out sharply against her deep maroon lipstick and black skin.

The road dips down through a stand of cattails and comes up next to a field of dairy cows. The animals' heads turn toward the sound of the Mustang and their moist eyes glimmer through the fine mist. Across the field a yellow floodlight illuminates the weathered side of a barn, the blunt nose of a grain silo.

In the summer there is always lightning here. When I visit Darwin we sit in the metal glider on the back deck of her trailer and watch heat lightning or tornadoes or hailstorms raking across the plains. On this side of the mountains, weather is visible for hundreds of miles.

'Poor Fort Morgan,' she'll say, pointing out toward the rolling land on the southern side of the Platte River. 'Fort Morgan always takes a beating. It's a wonder there's still houses out there for people to live in.'

I crack the window of the Mustang. Odors of manure and fresh earth stream into the car. Several miles to the north the ringed lights of the reactors at the defunct St. Vrain nuclear power plant glow like docked spaceships. A low train whistle echoes from somewhere up ahead of me in the night. The road curves gently and, slowing, I head into a stand of cottonwoods. The fishy odor of the river rushes in through the window, the rotting logs and wet grass. The trees break open, the road narrows into a bridge, and the Platte stretches below me with its wide sandbars and oxbow bends.

WELCOME TO PLATTEVILLE, a sign says. I turn off the narrow bridge and cruise past the small school with its football field and jungle gyms. The cornfields form a high wall to my left. Plastic garden gnomes peer out from front yards. I skirt through the sleeping neighborhoods and over to the town's main street. Except for a few neons in the window of the town's one bar, everything is dark.

To the north the houses of the town thin out; the road slips away through more empty fields and turns to oiled dirt. My wheels spin against loose rocks as I take a sharp corner. In the distance, the windows of Darwin's trailer are ablaze with light. A figure moves inside, and a long shadow skates across a backlit curtain. I roll my window down as far as it will go. The rhythmic beat of disco music pumps out from the trailer over the fallow patchwork of land.

Easing the Mustang down the dirt road, I roll to a stop by the door. Darwin's pickup is parked on the frozen grass of the front yard, and behind it is a red Subaru that I don't recognize. I slide the Walther from where I've left it beneath the seat and reach into the back of the glove compartment for the disk and the papers, which I put in the inside pocket of my coat. Climbing the makeshift wooden stairs to the front door, I am fighting the fatigue of the drive, the stiffness in my neck and legs.

The trailer's door has been left slightly ajar. Through the crack I can see the back of Darwin's tall body and her hips, swaying and twisting to the music. She's wearing a tight purple miniskirt and shiny violet pumps with stiletto heels. Her legs are bare, and the strong muscles of her calves and thighs ripple with each movement she makes. Her wig is teased up over her head in a high bouffant style.

I clutch the doorknob, knock loudly, and call out over the music, 'Darwin, Miss Darwin!'

Darwin turns toward my voice and her face breaks out in a smile. She's not wearing a shirt, and as she saunters across the front room of the trailer to greet me, the black stubble of her shaved chest hairs sticks out above her delicate red lace bra. Her masculine shoulders are broad and defined.

'Al!' she says, pulling me deeper into the warmth of the trailer. She wraps her arms around me and steps back to survey my face in the lamplight.

'Babygirl, you look like hell.' Her voice wavers in the high register of false female speech. 'I like the hair, though.'

She leaves me and walks over to the stereo and turns the volume way down. I survey the worn but tidy furnishings: a sagging couch with huge purple flowers, two soft armchairs with lace doilies thrown over them to cover fraying upholstery, a console TV from the late seventies, a smoked-glass dinette set. A small kitchen juts off the living room.

I light a cigarette and slump down on the couch, glancing at the clock above the dining table, trying to count the hours it's been since I've slept.

'Where's Miss Kiki?' I ask.

Darwin navigates the marbled shag carpet in her stilettos. She nods her head toward the back bedroom. From the other side of the closed door come quiet rustlings and moans.

'She's got a visitor,' Darwin explains. She sits down beside me on the couch and gracefully crosses her legs.

I slip my shoes off. Darwin leans forward over the knotty-pine coffee table and opens the lid of a small mahogany box. 'So what you doin' out this way?' she asks.

Inside the box is a small mirror and several pieces of folded white paper. Darwin sets the mirror on the coffee table in front of her, opens one of the little envelopes, and sets the tip of a lavender fingernail against the paper, tapping out a mound of white powder. She pulls a short glass pipette out of the box and holds it toward me, motioning at the mirror. I shake my head, no.

'From the looks of your face I'd say you're in some kind of trouble, but then again you're always in some kind of trouble.'

I close my eyes and exhale smoke from my cigarette. There's a sharp sound of glass on glass, two loud sniffs of suction, and then I feel the weight of Darwin's body sinking back into the cushions beside me and open my eyes. Darwin reaches her hand out to the mirror, wipes away the cocaine residue, and runs the tips of her fingers over her pink gums. The undersides of her forearms are mottled with pink puncture scars.

'How's Cyrus doing?' Darwin stares up at the ceiling of the trailer and grins. 'Is he still with that Jamaican lady? What was her name?'

'Nicolette? No, not anymore. She moved up to Tampa, started a travel agency.'

Darwin seems satisfied by my answer. She flexes the muscle in her calf and props one of her sharp heels up against the edge of the coffee table.

'What about your daddy?'

'He died a few days ago, Darwin. I was up in Seattle when Cyrus called.'

'Shit,' Darwin says quietly. Her voice deepens into its natural tones. 'I'm sorry, babygirl.'

She props her elbow on the arm of the couch and leans her head on her fist. Her knuckles push against the hairline of her wig, tilting the mass of curls to the side.

I've known Miss Darwin since I was a little girl. She

was in Vietnam with Cyrus and my father and went through SEAL training with them out in San Diego. Back then she was just Darwin. The Miss part came later, when the war ended and she went back home to the Bronx. She started working drag shows down in Greenwich Village and turning tricks to pay for the heroin and opium habit she picked up in Southeast Asia.

I asked my father once why they called her Darwin. He said it was because during SEALs hell week she could stay longer in the frigid waters of the Pacific than anyone else, so they figured she was an evolutionary freak. When I was growing up I couldn't picture Darwin as a man so I always thought of her as the Mermaid Lady and imagined her sitting in the breakers with her green tail curled up under her and her thick hair studded with shells and seaweed.

When I was in eighth grade, Darwin got busted on a small-time heroin sale and spent a few years in the New York State prison system. The day after her parole ended, she and Miss Kiki stuffed their size thirteen platforms into the trunk of Kiki's rusty Pinto and evolved their way out into the heartland.

Darwin and Kiki work the Denver-Boulder-Fort Collins area now. They sell enough to keep themselves supplied and pay for rent and food. When I started driving I would drop in on the two of them whenever I was this far out. We worked out a nice barter system. Although Darwin will use whatever's close at hand, her preference is for drugs that lull and soothe and numb the brain. My needs and hers dovetailed perfectly. Darwin was always willing to trade coke for any spare package of heroin or opium I might have.

The muffled noises from the back bedroom have

stopped. There's a rattling against the doorknob and the door opens slowly. A man in a rumpled business suit emerges from the dark room.

'Hi, Frank,' Darwin drawls.

Frank grins sheepishly and navigates himself toward the front door of the trailer.

'You drive safe, you hear?' Darwin calls. Frank pushes the door open and steps outside. 'And say hello to your wife from me.'

The door swings closed and Frank's footsteps fade down the wooden stairs. The Subaru's engine coughs once and turns over.

'Thank God he's gone.' Darwin sighs. She reaches behind her back and unclasps the hooks of her bra. 'I've been wanting to get out of this contraption all night. Frank comes up from Denver about once a week. He likes to pretend Kiki and I are just two happy housewives.'

She takes the foam cones of her fake breasts out of the cups, folds the bra neatly in half, and lays it across the arm of the couch.

'Kiki, you all right in there?' she calls. She gets up and crosses into the kitchen, slipping the massive wig off her head, tossing it over the back of one of the dinette's chairs.

From Kiki's bedroom comes a snap of rubber against skin and then a muffled groan. I get up and push the door open wider.

'Miss Kiki, it's Allie,' I say, squinting into the dark bedroom.

Kiki's dull form is just visible in the swath of light from the living room. She's slumped on the floor next to the bed with her back pressed up against the wall of the trailer. Her knees are drawn up into her chest and her blond wig is wildly askew. Her thin arms hang at her sides; a thick band of surgical tubing is wrapped tightly around her left bicep. On the carpet next to her right hand is a hypodermic needle. She raises her right hand slowly and throws me a wide wave.

'Miss Alison,' she says, smiling absently. 'Help me up, baby.'

I untie the rubber tubing, move the needle off the floor and up to the nightstand, and hook my arms under her shoulders. The sour odor of sex fills Kiki's wig, a faint smell that reminds me of bleach and sweat. Her lipstick is smeared across her chin.

'You've got pretty hair,' Kiki whispers into my ear. She lifts her hand and runs her fingers over my head. 'Pretty, blond hair.'

I brace my legs and shift Kiki's weight onto my shoulders and pull her up off the floor and onto the bed. Then I walk back to the living room.

Darwin comes out of the kitchen with a stack of grilled cheese sandwiches. She sets the plate down on the coffee table.

'You get somethin' in you, and then I want you to tell me what this trouble you're in is,' she commands.

I pick up one of the warm triangles and take a bite. 'I need to know about Chau Doc. Cyrus says you were there during the war.'

Darwin lights a cigarette and sits down in one of the armchairs.

'Vietnam?'

'Yeah.'

'Sugar, I don't go there. I don't even want to start to remember that shithole. You don't need to know nothin' 'bout Chau Doc.'

'You know who David Callum is?'

'Sure. Guy used to run Phoenix. I heard he's dead. Drowned in his rowboat up near Seattle. It's all over the papers and the news.'

'Three nights ago I get this call from Joey, the same night Cyrus called about my father. Joey says he's got a package for me that's going south; the drop's basically on my way down to the Keys. He offers me a nice sum for this run. Anyway, to make a long story short, the pickup is bad. The guy who turns it over winds up dead, and whoever took him out is looking for me to give it up. Turns out it's a computer disk that's got Callum's name all over it – and Chau Doc too.'

Darwin flicks a long piece of ash from her cigarette and sinks back in the chair. 'You see these guys who are looking for the disk?'

'Yeah. They were slick. Pros. Darwin, I don't know what to do here.'

'You gonna finish those sandwiches?' Darwin raises one eyebrow and looks at me reproachfully. I pick another triangle from the pile.

'How long were you in Chau Doc?' I ask, sinking my teeth into the warm bread and cheese.

'Six months. I ran the PRU down there – Provincial Reconnaissance Unit. Six months was how long a special ops advisor could stay with one unit.'

'Why the limit?'

Darwin splays the fingers of her left hand wide and surveys her nails. 'Corruption, Al. That was the operative word over there. A man with his own little army can wreak havoc on the local population if he wants to. That was a joke, though. The whole Phoenix operation was so damn corrupt.'

'Were they Americans?' My lips are slick with butter and I run my hand across my mouth.

'Who?'

'The PRUs. Were they all American soldiers?'

'Shit, no. There were two words we heard over and over in Phoenix: pacification and Vietnamization. The idea of Vietnamization was to turn the war over to the South Vietnamese Army. Us special ops guys were just advisors. The PRUs were strictly Vietnamese soldiers.'

Darwin stubs her cigarette out and grabs a nail buffer off the coffee table.

'Can you imagine a more fucked-up system?' she says, running the buffer back and forth over her nails. 'There we were, "teaching" jungle warfare to people who'd grown up with it.'

'And the pacification part?'

'More like propaganda. Phoenix started with traveling medical clinics distributing medicine, immunizing villagers. Some white-collar spook in Saigon realized these clinics were a perfect chance to get people alone and talk to them.'

'And the South Vietnamese were willing?'

'Hell, yes. It was the same with the census takers later. If your neighbor's pig was shitting in your garden, all you had to do was hand his name over as a Commie sympathizer and he was as good as dead. Vietnam wasn't a regular war, Al. You couldn't just draw a line between North and South and know who was on your side and who wasn't. The South was crawling with Vietcong. We needed a way into the villages, and Phoenix was it.'

'And Callum started the whole thing, right?'

'I guess. It was the whole college-educated crowd in Saigon. That was the thing with the bird, a way of terrorizing the locals with their own mythology. From what I know, the CIA researched customs, religion. But terror's still terror. Sometimes if we had a special hit to do and we really wanted to make an impact, we'd go into a village the night before and paint a big eye on the hut of our target. Then it was almost magical when the guy got wasted, like God had been watchin'.' Darwin sets the buffer down. 'What's the biggest motivator, Al?'

I shrug.

'Think about it. What makes you talk?'

I reach for a cigarette and break a match out of its book. 'I don't know. Fear, I guess,' I say, running the sulfured tip over the grainy flint.

'Right on.' Darwin chuckles softly. 'Can I tell you a story?'

'Sure.'

'Maybe my second month in-country, we were loading a plane for air dropping. There was this whole pallet of crates marked CONDOMS. One of the guys from supply asked us if we wanted to see what was in the crates, said we'd get a good laugh out of it. Anyway, the boxes were full of rubbers, all right – elephant-size.'

Darwin laughs as if she's just told the punch line to a joke.

'Don't you get it?'

I shake my head.

'The idea was to let a few of these crates fall into enemy hands. In-tim-i-da-tion.' Darwin emphasizes each syllable of the word. 'Charlie was running around the jungle thinking we had superhuman dicks.'

I take a slow drag on my cigarette and look down the hall to see if there's any movement coming from Kiki. She's still.

I look Darwin straight in the eyes. 'When did you start with the smack?' I ask.

'My first tour we mostly just smoked a lot of dope to stay sane. But in Chau Doc, opium and heroin were easier to get than water.' Darwin motions toward the bedroom. 'That one, she's a different story, didn't get hooked over there. She wasn't even out of diapers when I was in Chau Doc.'

My coat is lying on the floor by the couch, and I reach into the inside pocket and pull out the sheaf of papers. I set the photo of the supply base down on the coffee table next to the stash box.

'I think this base is near Chau Doc. You recognize it?'

Darwin leans forward and picks up the paper.

'No.'

I reach over and put my finger on the bodies of the planes. 'What about these? They don't look like military.'

'Air America,' Darwin says instantly.

'In other words, CIA?'

Darwin nods.

'What would they have been doing there?' I ask.

'Anything, really. Could have been a way of getting operatives in and out. Could be they were transporting something they weren't s'posed to have. Dropping fliers, maybe. Hauling guns.'

'Narcotics.'

'That's one possibility. Al, you know the stories about body bags filled with dope. War costs money. The CIA is an expensive organization to have around. Running drugs out of Southeast Asia was just the Agency's way of having a bake sale.'

Darwin cranes her neck and looks at the remaining papers. 'What else you got there?'

I push the stack of copies across the table. Darwin fingers the papers gingerly with her long lavender nails, flipping through the maps until she comes to the copy of Callum's order. I watch her expression grow serious as she scans down through the body of the letter.

'You still got a drop arranged?' she asks. She knits her eyebrows together, forming a deep crease in the skin of her forehead.

'I called Joey from Montana. He told me the drop's still good. I'm supposed to drive to Houston and then call for details. Why?'

'You plannin' on goin'?'

I don't answer. I still don't know.

'You trust Joey?' Darwin asks.

'He's never screwed me on a delivery. I don't ask a lot of questions, but if Joey says he's gonna pay me, the money's always there. This drop is big money.'

'That's not what I asked you. I ask you, Do you trust him?'

I take another bite of sandwich and say nothing. Darwin scowls at me from her chair.

'I don't know. Someone found me in Montana,' I say. 'I've got a friend there, from the old days, guy doesn't drive anymore. He works with computers now, and I thought he could help me find out what was on the disk.'

'And?'

'And he's dead, Darwin. Whoever killed him was looking for me. I'm sure of it.'

Darwin leans back, letting a rush of air escape from between her lips. 'Girl, you're a fool if you go to Houston, you know that? Relative to your life, money don't mean nothing. Who knew to look for you in Montana?'

'That's just it, Darwin. Joey's the only person I can

think of who could have talked. But it's pointless. He knows I'll deliver. Why come and get me?'

'They payin' you good for this?'

'They were supposed to.'

'What does that mean?' Darwin asks.

'The money was supposed to come to me at the pickup, but it didn't.'

'Let me tell you something. This letter is some pretty serious shit. This base,' Darwin says, pointing at the grainy copy of the photograph, 'is American military. I can't understand why Callum would send Hmong on a foray out here.'

'What if they were just moving something? Picking up a load of drugs, say?'

'Could be.' Darwin wrenches her face up, thinking. 'But someone's trying to kill you, right?'

I nod.

'It's common knowledge we were into some dirty shit with narcotics over there. Plus we're talking about thirty years ago, Al. Thirty years is an awfully old secret to still be worrying. Shit. Me, I'm busy trying to forget, trying to put it out of my mind that I ever joined the SEALs.'

'Darwin?' I ask.

'Yeah.'

'Why did you become a SEAL?'

'Same reason your daddy and Cyrus did, I s'pose. We were poor kids, every one of us, never had much to be proud of. It's all about power, Al. Power and the high of believing you're something special. You remember that feeling you got when someone handed you your first gun? Suddenly you realize the Lord ain't the only one who giveth and taketh away. We used to leave these calling cards on bigwigs we killed back there. Nail the ace of spades into the guy's skull. Some units had their own little personal sign they'd draw on the card. It was like saying, "Look what I can do to you." We were eighteen or nineteen when we went in, most of us. They told us what we were doing was right, and we didn't ask a whole lot of questions.'

'Was my father ever in Chau Doc?'

'Not when I was there. I know he was up near Nha Trang for a while. He didn't get his six-month assignment until a few months after I got mine.'

The morning light shows through the opening in the curtains. I get up from the couch and walk over to one of the trailer's windows and pull back the thin fabric. A flock of crows is scattered across the empty field next to the trailer. The birds' wings are folded tightly down over their bodies. I put my mouth to the glass and let my breath form a foggy circle. The wind picks up momentarily, ruffling the birds' feathers, moving across the jagged silhouette of a neighboring cornfield.

One night during the summer after I graduated from high school, Cyrus and my father and I made a trip down to Cuba to pick up cargo. A tropical storm had moved through the Straits, and the open water was still churning from the storm's passage. We made it to the island with no problem, slipped into a small inlet on the northwest coast. It took us about an hour to load the boat in the darkness. When I think about it now, the trips we made to Cuba were just plain stupid. We got paid excellent money, but not enough to make the very real prospect of getting shot or rotting in a Cuban prison palatable.

The load on the boat was heavy. By the time we got everything on board, the hull was sitting low in the water.

When we reached international waters we turned our running lights back on and switched the radio onto a Coast Guard frequency. There was a small craft advisory out for the Straits of Florida. The waves around us were all cresting and white-capped, but none of us were particularly worried. We had run cargo through worse weather. My father disappeared below for a few seconds and came back with a bottle of Johnnie Walker Black Label. We were all happy because of our safe run out of Cuban waters, and we passed the bottle around the small cabin.

None of us saw the raft until we were almost upon it. Cyrus must have spotted it first because I remember he grabbed the throttle and slammed it down into reverse. The sudden slowing of the boat knocked me backward onto the deck. The engine labored to turn the propellers around. A few feet in front of us a tattered sail waved in the stiff wind.

In the waves below the boat was a battered raft made of inner tubes and sheets of plywood. The sail I had seen was a cotton work shirt tied around a rough mast. I counted eight people clinging to the raft. Thousands of Cubans make that trip across the Straits every year, but that night was the first time I had ever seen rafters. My father grabbed the bow line and flung it out to one of the men. I climbed back into the cabin and found a flashlight.

'How many are there?' Cyrus asked. He was working the throttle, trying to keep the boat steady.

'Eight, I think.'

I slipped back onto the bow and shone the flashlight down onto the silent brown faces. My father was guiding the raft back around to the stern, to the diving ladder. He turned toward me, and the beam of my flashlight caught him across the face.

'Al, I want you to open the hold and start tossing the cargo,' he said calmly, blinking his eyes against the bright light. 'We can't carry this extra weight without lightening up a little.'

I climbed around the cabin to the deck, popped the hold, grabbed one of the heavy bags of white powder, and flung it off into the waves. The package made a loud splash as it hit the water. I bent over again and looked up at Cyrus. He took his hand off the throttle, came out of the cabin, and bent down beside me. Together we emptied half the hold into the Straits of Florida, the weight of eight men in pure white powder.

In the field outside the trailer one of the crows opens his beak and lets out a sharp *caw*. The birds unfold their wings and spring into the sky, kicking up mounds of dirt as they lift their light bodies off the furrowed earth. I remember my father's face suddenly illuminated, his blue eyes blinking against the glare of the flashlight, his calm voice. I try to imagine him in Darwin's Vietnam, bending over a dead Vietcong, placing a card over the man's wide eyes, striking nail through bone. I try to reconcile this foreign father with the one I knew that night off Cuba. I try to see Darwin pressing the tip of a machine gun into the soft flesh at the side of another man's temple or lobbing a grenade deep into a dark hut, stepping back to watch the frail palm and bamboo structure explode. Or Cyrus putting a torch to the sail of a family's junk, motoring off into the night as the flames dance across Cung Hau Bay.

*

135

A thick line of russet clouds stretches across the eastern horizon. The crows spray upward and regroup far overhead. The flock circles and wheels.

'I'm tired,' I say, turning from the window. Darwin is hunched down over the coffee table. Her nose traces a straight path across her little mirror. There is more that I want to ask her, answers I know she will have, but they will have to wait until morning.

'If I crash in your bed will you promise to wake me up by ten? I can't stay here too long.'

'Sure, babygirl. You go get some sleep.'

I head for Darwin's room, then turn back and face her once more. 'Where you getting your supply from these days?' I ask.

'Here and there. You know.'

Darwin's room is small and neat. A lifesize picture of Marilyn Monroe is pinned to the closet door. On the bedside table is a small pipe and a long needle coated in thick opium, black tar. I have seen Darwin smoke before, have watched the delicate ritual she learned in some dim parlor in Saigon. Most addicts are hungry people; the faster they can bring the substance to the blood the better. But Darwin smokes with pure, deliberate style.

Never before have I thought about what brought Darwin here. I imagined a longing for silence, a desire for cleanliness and the neat midwestern order of the cornfields after a life of prison and war. I have begun to forget my own old cravings, the addict's panic, the desperate need to have the drug nearby. At the high point of my own long dance with cocaine I lived in a state of constant anxiety, desperate to maintain the umbilical attachment. 'Here and there' would not have been enough for me.

My eyes adjust to the pale light and scan the bedroom. A dressing table, cluttered with makeup brushes, false eyelashes, and eerie wig forms is pushed up against the far wall. The colorless features of the Styrofoam heads are dull and passive. Several pairs of falsies hang over the edge of the closet door. All the elements of self-deception are here.

'It was like you were someone else,' my father once said to me. It was after I had cleaned up, and I still don't know whether he was talking about the drugs or Joey. We never spoke about any of it again.

The days of exhaustion have made me strangely restless. I lie on my back in Darwin's bed and try to untangle the deepening puzzle of lies. Someone else. It is so easy to believe in the truth of this statement, in our own absolution from responsibility. What's difficult to swallow is that we live the lives we choose. Tomorrow I'll ask Darwin about the Hmong.

Eleven

'Oh, shit, Darwin. Shit, shit, shit.'

Kiki's muffled voice carries through the closed bedroom door. I roll over and look at the alarm clock. Nine-thirty. I've been asleep for a little over two and a half hours.

'Keep your voice down,' Darwin says. 'She hasn't slept for days.'

Throwing the covers back, I swing my legs off the bed, slide my jeans on, and instinctively grab the Walther from the pocket of my coat. I rub my eyes and open the door and step out into the living room.

Darwin is standing at the small stove in the kitchen. She's wearing green sweat pants and a black sweater. Her face is clean and masculine without her makeup, and her long lacquered nails are suddenly incongruous with the rest of her body. She eyes me as I come through the door and slices a thick slab of butter from a block on the counter.

'See what you've done.' Darwin glares at Kiki and scrapes the butter into the frying pan in front of her.

'What's wrong?' I ask.

'Well, good morning to you too.' Darwin reaches into the refrigerator for a carton of eggs.

'Shit, Allie,' Kiki says. She's sitting at the dinette table with the newspaper spread out in front of her. She looks up at me. 'You do this?'

'Of course she didn't do that,' Darwin snaps.

I set my Walther down on the smoked glass next to the paper. Kiki is wearing a fluffy pink robe and matching fuzzy slippers. She's sobered up some while I slept, but the smooth brown skin beneath her eyes is ringed by dark black hollows. An ashtray heaped with crushed cigarette butts sits next to her right hand. She folds the paper back to the front page and points at a headline in the lower right corner.

KILLING SPREE HEADED OUR WAY, the headline reads.

Darwin puts a mug of coffee down on the table. 'Drink this,' she orders.

Kiki snatches the paper and begins reading. ' "A killing spree that started in western Washington and moved through Montana may be headed our way, local authorities report. The suspected killer, Alison Kerry, is wanted by police for the murders of two still unidentified victims." Shit, Al, a spree?'

'What else does it say?'

'Just the same old bullshit. Drug-related crimes. You're armed and dangerous. Police suspect you've moved on into northern Colorado. A brief description of you and your car. You have a history of drug abuse. Blah, blah, blah.'

I take a long sip of coffee and reach across the table and pull a cigarette out of Kiki's pack.

'Shit, Al,' she says, 'someone set you up real good.'

Darwin sets a plate with two fried eggs, toast, and bacon in front of me. 'Why don't you just be quiet,' she snaps at Kiki.

I light the cigarette and pull the paper out of Kiki's hands. Underneath the headline is a poorly drawn pencil sketch of me.

'What was that guy's name?' Kiki asks Darwin absentmindedly. I half listen to them as I skim the article.

'What guy?'

'That guy a few years back. You know, the reporter down in Boulder. Old hippie guy. Crazy fucker.'

'Girl, I don't know what you're talking about.' Darwin stands back from the table with her hands on her cocked hips.

'What was his name? Wydel? Wykel? That's it, Wykel.' Kiki grabs my arm. 'They screwed him good.'

'That has nothing to do with any of this.' Darwin glares hard at Kiki. 'I tol' you to just shut up about that.'

'Oh, shit.' Kiki whistles, ignoring Darwin. 'Said he had some kind of underground marijuana farm.'

I put the paper down and shove it across the table. They've got the fisherman's death pinned on me, too. By now every cop and FBI agent west of the Mississippi is looking for me.

'So what happened to him?' I ask.

'He did some time, I guess. Lost everything.' Kiki stretches her arms over her head and yawns.

'Why'd they set him up?'

'I can't recall,' Darwin says, moving back to the stove.

'What's that supposed to mean?' Kiki snaps at Darwin. 'You gettin' senile in your old age?' She turns to me and continues. 'It was all that government conspiracy shit he was writing about in the Boulder paper, how the feds are still making money off Southeast Asia. How these refugees, right here in podunk Colorado, are helping the CIA store and distribute heroin and the like. Of course, everyone thought he was a nut.'

'Only you don't think he was growing?'

'Of course not. An operation like the kind they said he had? We would have known about that.'

I put my cigarette out and prod at the two eggs with the side of my fork. I have no appetite.

'Where've you been getting your supply? And don't give me that "here and there" bullshit.' I look Darwin straight in the eyes.

'Shit, not from the damn CIA.'

I grab the paper, crumpling it in my fist, and hold it in front of Darwin's face. 'Do you understand?' I say. 'They'll kill me. How long have the Hmong been doing business out here?'

Kiki and Darwin stare at me, silent.

'How long, Darwin?' I repeat. 'I know you wouldn't have come out here if you weren't sure there'd be a supply. And I know there's Hmong out in Morgan County. I know how it is. I've been there, remember?'

Darwin gets up from the table and takes my plate. She turns her back to me, and walks into the kitchen.

'Don't try to tell me this is some kind of coincidence.' My eyes follow Darwin.

'I worked with a couple of Hmong during the war. There was a team of them based in Chau Doc that used to help us with the PRUs sometimes: you know, lend a hand.'

'I thought you said the PRUs were South Vietnamese.'

'They were. The Hmong were additional, for special stuff. They were mercenaries.'

'We paid them?'

'Sure. We brought them in from Laos. They were

good fighters, but you sure didn't want to piss any of them off.'

'I thought they were farmers.'

'That too.'

'Who brought them over after the war?'

'I don't know. Mostly we just deserted them, left them to fend for themselves. There were a lot of refugees coming out of that part of Asia in the late seventies and early eighties.' Darwin takes the frying pan from the stove and puts it into the sink. She turns on the taps and squeezes soap onto a sponge.

'How did you know they were out here?' I raise my voice to be heard over the running water.

'Just before I got busted that last time I got a letter from one of them.' Darwin keeps her head down and scrubs at the pan. 'He said he was out here, said a spook he worked with had sponsored a whole group of them to come over here. When I got out of prison I couldn't go back to the city and that life, so I came here.'

'And this guy, Wykel,' I ask. 'Everything he was writing was true?'

Darwin turns and looks at me. 'After the war I was tired, Al. I haven't been out there asking around. Whatever's going on, I don't want to know. My friend comes by every once in a while with a package for me, enough to keep me going. You know how it is. You just want to forget what you've done, forget that person they turned you into. We killed little girls, old women. I don't want to know anymore.'

I stand up and reach for the Walther.

'I'm going out there. I need you to tell me the way.'

I throw on my coat and boots and pick the papers and the disk up off the coffee table.

'If anyone asks, you didn't see any of this shit,' I say.

Darwin gets up from the table and follows me to the door.

'You know where this Wykel guy is now?' I push the door open and step out onto the small porch.

Darwin shakes her head. 'He sure as hell ain't working for the paper anymore.'

Kiki is standing behind Darwin in the doorway. 'Where you goin', Miss Alison?' she asks.

'I don't know.'

I make my way down the steps and over to the Mustang. Darwin is right behind me. I get into the driver's side and slide my hand under the seat, feeling for the cold shapes of the Browning and the forty-five, making sure they're where I left them.

'Allie,' Darwin says, 'those MIA on that list?'

'Yeah?' Leaning across the passenger seat, I stuff the disk and the papers into the back of the glove compartment.

'The way I see it, MIA don't generally mean "missing." My experience is, it means "dead."'

I climb back out of the Mustang and throw my arms around Darwin, feeling the fragility of her lean frame, the small knots of muscles in her back.

'His name is Willie Phao,' Darwin tells me, taking a step backward. 'The place is easy to find. Head down to Fort Lupton and take Fifty-two east. About fifty miles out there's a marked turnoff to Hoyt. After Hoyt you hit a dirt road, and it's about two or three more miles. There's a big gate at the entrance to the Phao place.'

'I want you and Kiki to get some things together,' I tell her. 'Leave town for a while. Go up to the mountains.

144

Drive out to Vegas. Just promise me you're gonna get out of here when I leave.'

'Sure, babygirl.'

'I want you to swear.'

'Okay, I swear.'

The road out to Hoyt is flat and unpromising. Past Prospect Valley, all signs of farmland end and the only breaks in the dry monotony of the plains are the bobbing black figures of oil pumps. The metal structures are like strange waterbirds, tall and lanky and slightly menacing as they move their heavy beaks up and down along thin drilling lines.

As I turn off the small state road and head south to Hoyt, I pass an oil company service truck. Half a dozen men cling to the wooden walls that have been built up around the sides of the flatbed. The truck is the only vehicle I've seen for at least twenty miles.

The town of Hoyt consists of a few trailers, a tiny post office, and several low ranch houses spread out over the dry beargrass and scrub. After Hoyt, the pavement ends and the road turns to packed dirt and gravel.

About five minutes out of Hoyt I see the gate, the same inscription as the one in Montana. I pull off to the shoulder of the road and fish in my map box. I need to get my bearings, establish some kind of plan. According to Rand McNally, this road crosses I-70 about thirty miles on; then there's nothing but back roads until the Oklahoma border. Once I leave here I can head south toward Texas, keeping a good distance from civilization.

I rev the engine of the Mustang, spin the steering wheel, and head under the wooden gate and down the long gravel driveway to Willie Phao's house. The ceaseless wind of the flatlands is blowing hard, snapping a row of sheets and towels that hangs on a clothesline by the side of the two-story farmhouse. An old Ford pickup and a beat-up yellow Honda are parked on the cracked earth of the front yard. About fifty yards beyond the house is a long, squat cinderblock barn.

Some of the surrounding land has been tilled for planting, but the dirt is mounded in dry clods. Weeds and scrub poke up through the crusted ground. An irrigation system sits rusting along the fenceline, its giant wheels listing and broken. It's been a long time since anyone has farmed here.

I park the Mustang and step out, then climb the wooden steps and cross the porch. The radio is on somewhere inside the house, and the muffled twang of country music sifts through the walls. I stand staring at the weathered door for a moment, reasoning with myself. A town along the Bassac called Chau Doc. A thirty-year-old letter with the word HMONG typed in black ink. A truck with Colorado license plates. An old junkie ex-SEAL in a battered trailer. A farm without crops. Only the barest thread connects them, but it is all that I have. I knock on the front door and wait.

Since I quit doing coke I have become deeply fascinated with the machinations of that particular addiction. I suppose it is only normal to want to know my enemy, especially after defeat. Recovery is all about recognizing my lack of control in the face of such a powerful, almost divine, presence.

One particular article I read focused on rats who were given unlimited supplies of cocaine. The rats had two

146

buttons in their cages: one that fed them and one that released the drug into their bodies. Without exception, the rats pressed the cocaine button nonstop until they were dead. Food no longer mattered. Exercise no longer mattered. The animals just stayed with their tiny wet noses glued to the mechanism until they expired.

But the rats' deaths were not what interested me about the article. I had been at that particular stage of obsession in my own life and hardly needed research to highlight the deadly nature of my desires. What interested me was that the scientists had cut away the rats' skulls in an attempt to see the parts of the brain that were influenced by the drug. What they found was that cocaine sparked the most primal and persuasive area, the one associated with sexual pleasure.

I have had two relationships in my life that threatened to destroy me. The first was with cocaine, and my love for it grew out of an almost erotic desire. The first time I did the drug it coursed through my body with an electric thrill, imprinting itself indelibly in my memory. I knew it was bad but I wanted more. Even now, having been clean for some time, I can conjure up the physical details of my pleasure.

The second relationship was the one with Joey. Looking back, I realize I did not love him. I loved the perfection and power of him, the force of his body, the visceral way in which each cell of his physical being affected me. I liked the cleft in his shoulder where his muscles met, the way moisture collected on the tips of his fingers, the graceful knob of bone that protruded from his wrist. But what drew me was more than this physical desire or his power. There was something in him, some great unhappiness, that I wanted to cure.

They say the first high is the best, that, in an impossible quest, addicts are always searching to re-create that high. This was how I loved Joey, in a futile circle, wanting what I could never have.

There's no answer so I knock again, louder this time, pounding my knuckles into the wood. The music switches off and there's a thumping of feet on the floor. 'All right, I'm coming,' a voice calls from inside.

The door bangs open and a man appears. He looks at me briefly. 'Willie Junior's not here,' he says.

He's small and wiry, about the same size and build as the Hmong I saw in Montana, with a smooth face and patches of gray in his black hair. He's wearing a flannel shirt, jeans, and heavy workboots. 'He's got a game over in Brighton today.' The Hmong's voice is almost accentless, his words as flat and clear as the empty land around us. He places his hand on the door and moves to close it.

I take a step forward and put my foot over the threshold. 'I'm not here to see Willie Junior,' I tell him.

He stares hard at me, keeping his hand on the door.

'Are you Willie Senior?'

He doesn't answer.

'I'm a friend of Darwin's. She told me this is the Phao place.' I'm attempting to sound casual, trying to keep any hint of desperation out of my voice. I'm talking to a brick wall.

'How do you know Darwin?' the man asks, his eyes springing to life, narrowing. The door presses against my foot.

'She's an old friend of my father's. They knew each other during the war.'

The man looks past me, his gaze lingering on the Mustang. 'I'm Willie Phao,' he says finally, his grip still firm on the door. Smells of cooking waft from the house.

'Mr. Phao, Darwin tells me you were in Chau Doc during the war. I need some information, and I need to get in touch with John Wykel. It's important.'

Willie turns his eyes to me and blinks slowly. The only sounds are the whine of the wind and the violent clapping of the linens on the laundry line. 'I don't know about Chau Doc,' he says. His words are slow and deliberate and then he jams the door closed. I'm taken off guard by the force of it, and my foot slips backward. The lock clicks into place.

I can hear his feet shuffling away on the other side of the door and I raise my voice, trying to penetrate the wood. 'Doesn't look like you've got a real profitable farm here,' I say, trying desperately to hold his attention.

The feet stop moving but there's no response. I try another angle.

'My name's Allie Kerry. Maybe you've read about me. I don't care what you've got going on now. I just need to know about Chau Doc. I'm not here to bust you, Willie.'

The music has started up again, and I recognize the tune. It's an old Johnny Cash number, but I can't remember the words. Stupid. I cuff the side of my head with the base of my palm. It was stupid coming out here in the first place, a waste of time. Turning from the door, I take two steps across the porch.

'Alison Kerry.' The voice startles me and I snap around. The door is cracked ajar and the Hmong's face shows through the opening. 'Take this.' He holds his right hand out toward me. A folded square of paper flutters at the end of his fingers. 'Take it.'

I reach for the paper, crossing his fingers with mine. He loosens his grasp, and before I can say anything the door closes and I'm alone again.

One thing I've learned in my business is that most people are not willing suppliers of information. If they're smart they hold on to what they know, milking it for all it's worth. I knew this when I drove out here to the Hmong, understood the probable futility of my visit. I came because I was desperate.

When I slide into the driver's seat of the Mustang and unfold the slip of paper, I am profoundly baffled. Not by the penciled name and the phone number that follows, but by the reason behind my possession of them. Sometimes people surprise you, but they always have a motive. I scan the paper again before shoving it into my hip pocket: JOHN WYKEL. The letters, formed with soft lead, are dark and thick.

On the southern outskirts of Denver I pull into the parking lot of a Circle K store, go inside, and buy coffee and a pack of cigarettes. Neatly stacked newspapers in a rack next to the counter show the police sketch of me. The girl working the cash register is young and slightly pudgy. A small crucifix hangs from a thin chain around her neck.

'Could I get my change in quarters?' I ask.

The girl puts down the *Glamour* magazine she's reading and scowls up at me from beneath badly permed bangs.

'There's a five-dollar maximum. It's policy. I can't give you more than five dollars' worth.'

She rings me up, slams the quarters and the rest of the change down on the counter, and turns back to her magazine.

I push the door open and walk out to the pay phone in the parking lot. Through the front window of the Circle K, I can see the girl at the counter. She has put her magazine down and is staring out at me. Her eyes move from my face to the Mustang and back to my face. Smiling pleasantly, I shove a handful of coins into the slot and punch in the eleven digits of John Wykel's number.

A man's voice answers. 'Hello?'

'Mr. Wykel?'

'Yes.'

'Is this the John Wykel who used to write for the Boulder paper?' I say, trying not to sound threatening.

There's a long pause. 'How'd you get this number?' Wykel asks finally. His voice is wary, edged with manic energy.

'I was out to see Willie Phao this morn – '

'I already told you people everything I know.' Wykel breaks in, raising his voice so that I have to move the phone away from my ear. 'Who are you this time, DEA, Central Intelligence? Why don't you just leave me alone?'

'I'm not with the government, John. It's okay. My name's Alison Kerry. I'm –'

'Oh, my God. Alison. I should have known. He said you'd come. I should have known.'

'What?' I ask.

Wykel has gone from manic to irrational. 'I need to meet with you,' he says, ignoring my question.

The swiftness of the request catches me off guard. I press the phone against my ear and listen to the silence from the other end, unsure of what to say.

'Are you still there?' Wykel asks, desperate.

'Yeah,' I say, turning and looking in through the windows of the Circle K. The girl at the cash register smiles uncharacteristically. Something is definitely wrong. Her eyes are trained on my face, and she's cradling a black telephone receiver between her neck and her ear. On the counter next to the *Glamour* is a newspaper. Her mouth moves in monosyllables. She keeps her eyes on me, never losing her saccharine smile. I don't have much time.

'You're coming alone,' I tell him.

'Where are you?' Wykel asks.

'East of Denver.'

'Okay. You're sticking to the back roads?'

'Yeah.'

The girl puts the phone down and comes out from behind the counter and locks the front door. By now the cops are on their way.

'There's a place down by La Junta. You can make it there in maybe four hours if you hurry. There's a little town called Cheraw about ten miles north of La Junta. Pass through Cheraw and take the first dirt road heading east. About three miles out you'll see a sign for an old Koshare Indian kiva. It's a straight shot down there for me on the interstate. I'll be waiting for you at the kiva.'

'Alone.'

I slam the phone down and turn and walk calmly back to the Mustang. The tired wail of a siren drones in the distance. I wheel out of the parking lot and head east, away from the city and back out to the no-man's-land of the plains. Something tells me that the Kansas plate and Jeannette Decker's license won't be of much use to me now.

Twelve

The drive down to Cheraw is extremely slow going. Keeping my map open on the passenger seat, I stick to the roads that have no names or numbers, using the marked highways only when I have no other choice. I weave down through Kiowa and Elbert, slowing for intermittent breaks in the pavement and cattle guards. At Rush I take state highway 94 east and stop briefly in Punkin Center for gas. I'll be at the kiva before nightfall.

Two days after I saw Joey at the closing of Richard's bar, he phoned the house looking for me. I had placed him out of my league and hadn't expected him to call, so when he said his name I had to trace back through my memory to find him.

We went out that night. He took me to the restaurant at the top of the old La Concha Hotel on Duval Street. After we had finished our meal, we walked onto the rooftop terrace and looked out over the island.

'Do you know the story of Dr. Heinrich?' he asked.

It was one of my very favorite Key West stories, one of the island's more well-known myths. I leaned over the top of the terrace wall and peered down at the cars and tourists passing on the street below.

Dr. Heinrich was a German physician who had come to

Key West in the 1930s to work at the old Navy Hospital. He fell in love with one of his patients, a poverty-stricken young Bolivian woman named Laura, who was dying of tuberculosis.

After Laura's death it was discovered that Heinrich had robbed her grave at the old Key West cemetery and was keeping her body in the abandoned fuselage of a plane out on the base. When police stormed the plane they found the young woman's embalmed body laid out naked in the doctor's bed. Laura's deteriorating flesh had been carefully replaced with wax as it rotted. A sticky film of semen covered the corpse and a putrid stench rose from the half-flesh, half-wax body.

Laura was returned to her tomb, and the outraged citizens of the town banished the doctor from the island. At the moment the wheels of Heinrich's plane left the blazing hot tarmac of the Key West airport, Laura's grave exploded in a blinding flash.

'Sure, I've heard it.' We had finished a bottle of wine with dinner, and the drop to the street was giving me vertigo. I rested my cheek on top of the wall and smiled at Joey. 'What do you think?' I asked. 'Was she in the grave or did he manage to take her with him?'

'Most definitely she was in there.' Joey grinned back at me.

It was a stupid story, really, nothing more than a good way of spooking each other at slumber parties, but it had always fascinated me. Maybe because it catered to our adolescent fantasies of love and destruction. Joey's knowledge of it, the fact that we shared this childhood lore, was comforting.

The muscle in Joey's jaw flexed rhythmically against the tight skin of his cheek. He brought his face down close to mine and slid his hand under my hair and put his palm on my neck.

'You must look like your mother,' he said. 'Good thing, too.'

'I wouldn't know. She died a long time ago.'

Joey was quiet, his hand against my skin hot and moist.

'Cancer,' I explained.

'My mother died in prison,' Joey said. 'I was nine.'

'I'm sorry.'

'I'm not.' His voice was suddenly hard. He turned his head. His lips were right over mine, and I felt his breath in my mouth.

Just past Cheraw I see the hand-painted wooden sign that marks the turnoff to the kiva. It's late in the afternoon, and the low angle of the sun casts elongated shadows off the fence posts and surrounding brush. A thick bank of clouds approaches from the east. I take the narrow dirt track, searching for Wykel and the kiva.

About a mile or so off the main road, the track peters to a gradual end. I stop the Mustang and get out. The dry ground is crisscrossed by deep tire gouges, scars left behind by summer visitors turning around to head back to La Junta or Sugar City. A worn footpath leads off through the grass and over a small rise. There's no sign of anyone.

The wind has picked up and a gray swath of precipitation sweeps across the flatland, moving in my direction. Shivering, I flip the collar of my jacket up over my neck and follow the path down into the hollow on the other side. In the center of the hollow is a small opening in the earth, the entrance to the kiva. I check my watch, scan the prairie, and start moving back to the car. A loud clap of thunder rolls out of the storm.

When I climb to the top of the rise I can see a small blue pickup racing in from the west, kicking up a thick cloud of dust. I reach around my back for the Walther, clicking the safety off as the vehicle grows closer. The pickup pulls to a stop next to the Mustang and a middle-aged man with a thick full beard climbs out. I put the Walther up in front of me and sight down the nose of the gun at the man's chest.

The man cups his hands around his mouth and calls out over the wind, 'It's me, Wykel.' He makes his way toward me along the footpath. 'Jesus Christ!' he shouts. 'Put the gun down, Alison!'

'Where the hell've you been?' I demand, sticking the Walther in my jeans. My hands are shaking.

'I didn't mean to scare you. I watched you drive in. I had to make sure you were alone. C'mon. Let's get back to the cars. That storm is gonna be here any second.'

We're sitting in the Mustang, our breath glazing the windows with condensation. Wykel reaches into his coat pocket and pulls out a bag of loose tobacco. He slips a rolling paper between his thumb and index finger and stuffs shreds into the crease. Sleet pounds against the front windshield. I crank the heat up a notch.

'I knew you would find me.' Wykel says this matter-of-factly, as if he'd been expecting me to come. He runs his tongue across the gummed flap of the paper and seals the cigarette, then puts it to his lips and reaches out and wipes the front window clear with the sleeve of his coat. 'Can't sneak up on us out here.' He has a glazed, blissful smile, the kind I associate with poor mental health. 'We'd see them coming from miles away. You can't trust anyone, you know.'

Wykel's eyes are wide. He lights his cigarette and sits back. 'So what've you got for me?' He speaks in a nervous, disjointed staccato, with the same skittish energy I recognized on the phone.

'You said he told you I'd be coming,' I say, ignoring his question. 'Who's "he," John?'

Wykel's free hand drums on his pant leg. He motions with his cigarette out over the prairie. 'You know: him, the big honcho.' He raises his finger to his lips. 'Shush, they don't want us to know.'

I try to imagine what he sees out there. Little green men, possibly, or government thugs closing in on him. If I had known he was this far gone I never would have come.

'Who's that, John, the CIA? I heard they weren't happy with those articles you wrote a few years ago.'

'The CIA couldn't care less,' he says, cracking the window, exhaling a stream of smoke.

'Someone set you up.'

'Sure, sure. But it wasn't the CIA.'

'I don't understand.'

Wykel wipes the inside of the windshield again and peers out through the sleet. 'Didn't you read the articles?'

I shake my head.

'Just like in Vietnam,' Wykel says. He flattens his palm and slams it against the dashboard, exasperated. 'Special ops guys get fed up and go AWOL, hide out in Saigon, selling their services to the highest bidder. They've got their own little rogue operations.'

'You were in Vietnam?'

'Six years. I covered the war.'

'I still don't understand. If the CIA isn't working with the Hmong, who is?'

Wykel takes several quick drags on his cigarette. 'Them,' he says impatiently.

'Them who, John?'

'A few years ago I get a tip from this source who works Denver Vice,' Wykel explains, sighing and running his fingers through his hair. 'There's heroin everywhere. The stuff's flooding into the market, but no one knows where it's coming from and no one's talking. I mean nobody.

'So I start thinking about these Hmong out in Morgan County. They're not just selling corn and watermelons. And they didn't find their way out here themselves. You come into this country as a refugee, you need a sponsor.'

'So you started talking to Willie Phao?' I break in.

'Six years I watched them working with that shit over in Vietnam. American businessmen coming and going. Money, money, money. Opportunities aplenty. Those AWOL soldiers weren't the only ones making a little profit for themselves.'

Wykel picks a loose strand of tobacco from his lower lip and gives me a hard look, as if he'd just now heard my question. 'How do you know Willie?' he asks.

I shrug.

'I'm not stupid. I'm not crazy, either. They think I am, but I'm not. Willie's a nice guy, got a nice wife, a kid who plays football for Fort Morgan High.'

'A nice guy? The way I understand it, the Hmong were mercenaries.'

'Sure, sure. But you can't really blame them. Money makes the world go round, you know.'

Wykel stubs his cigarette out. He blinks his eyes and looks over at me. 'So what've you got for me?'

'What makes you think I have anything for you?' I can't

understand why he's told me all this. For a man who doesn't trust anyone, he sure talks a lot.

'You called me, didn't you?' He flashes me his crazy grin and starts to roll another cigarette.

'So what did Willie have to say?' I ask.

'Nothing I didn't already know. He said there were a group of American businessmen who used to come to his father's farm in Laos. He said they had passenger planes just across the Cambodian border in Vietnam where they took the product.'

'CIA?'

'Sure, sure. That's old news, though.'

'Did he tell you who sponsored them?'

Wykel clamps his lips together and nods.

'Who was it, John?' I feel like I'm talking to a child.

'Can't say. Not supposed to.' He presses his index finger to his mouth again. 'Shush. Quiet.'

'Where were you during the war?' I ask, trying to change the direction of the conversation, realizing I'm getting nowhere with questions about the Hmong.

'Everywhere.'

'How about the end of 'sixty-nine?'

Wykel stares at me in disbelief. 'Holy shit,' he says. He rests the unrolled cigarette on his knee and pounds the dashboard. 'That's what this is about?'

'What what's about?'

'Chau Doc.'

Wykel turns and grabs my arm, spilling loose tobacco onto the floor of the Mustang. I can feel the pressure of his fingers through the fabric of my coat, and my body stiffens instinctively.

'I knew you'd find me. What is it? What did you bring me? Callum said you'd come.'

The name hits me like a closed fist across the face. 'Get your hands off me,' I tell him. 'I don't know what you're talking about.'

Wykel sets his hands in his lap and looks down at them. 'Those men, those Americans. Gone. *Poof!* Disappeared. That's what I'm talking about,' he says frantically. Two white balls of spit have formed at the corners of his mouth.

'From Chau Doc?'

'The An Giang PIC, outside of Chau Doc, just north of Sam mountain.' Wykel grabs at his hair, pressing his palms against his temples. 'You know.'

I shake my head. 'PIC?'

'Provincial Interrogation Center. For "debriefing."'

'What happened?'

'Gone. *Poof!* Like I said. They didn't want me asking.'

'Who didn't want you asking? Callum?'

Wykel shakes his head. 'Them,' he whispers, reaching for his tobacco, starting a new cigarette. 'But he knows. That's why he sent you. They think I'm crazy. No more wife. No more job. I'm a janitor. But he knows.'

The bulk of the storm has passed over us, and the sleet has ebbed to a light rain. I've heard enough. Wykel is crazy, and I don't have time to waste with him. 'Get out of my car,' I say, flicking the wipers twice, clearing the glass. The water has darkened the colors of the earth around us to shades of chocolate and gold.

'You're out of your league here,' Wykel says.

'And I should trust you?'

Wykel doesn't move. The only sound in the car is the soft tick of rain on the windows. 'They'll kill you, and even if they don't they'll use everything you've ever done against you,' he says. 'I've read the papers. You're wanted for murder.'

'Thanks for the advice. Now get out of my car.'

Wykel opens the car door and swings one foot outside. He pauses for a moment. 'Who do you think hired you?'

I shrug. 'It's never really been my place to ask.'

'Maybe you'd better start.'

Wykel climbs out of the Mustang and walks around the front of the car to his pickup. My hands are shaking, and I close my eyes and take several deep breaths. Over the beat of the rain I hear Wykel's engine start up. The pickup idles for a few seconds and there's a sharp tapping on the glass by my ear. Opening my eyes, I see Wykel's face through the milky film of condensation. His hands are moving animatedly. I roll the window all the way down and peer out at him.

Wykel squats down so that his face is level with the window. 'Ten years ago, Alison,' he says. 'Take a look. CIA bigwig retires. He writes his memoir – only the original book never makes it to print. Reagan's in office, and the whole intelligence community is in an uproar. They're crying national security and all that. There are congressional hearings, and the media has a field day. And whatta you know? *Poof!* Gone! Just like those men.'

'I thought you said the CIA couldn't care less.'

'Sure, sure, about what's going on today.' Wykel leans his head back and laughs. The muscles in his throat tighten against his skin. His hands, curled around the window frame, are thick and powerful, and his beard is studded with fine drops of rainwater. A thin ribbon of fear courses along my spine.

'When you change your mind,' he says, suddenly serious, 'call me. If they don't disappear you first.' He straightens himself, turns and climbs into the pickup, guns the engine, and slips away into the rain.

It's well past dark when I pass out of Colorado and into the Oklahoma panhandle. I don't know why, but I keep thinking about Dr. Heinrich and Laura and about that first night I spent with Joey at La Concha.

When I was fifteen a man down the street from us kept the corpse of his elderly roommate in the kitchen for almost three months. The dead man was only discovered because neighbors complained of a terrible stench coming from the old house. The roommate told the local paper that he fed the man canned pork and beans and Schmidt beer. *I thought he was alive*, the paper quoted the roommate as saying. *He changed positions several times*. 'Of course,' the town's coroner explained, 'a body that is decomposing will seem to move and shift as the flesh decays.'

When I was growing up, a popular rumor was that the original builder of the Casa Marina Hotel had killed his lover and set her bones into the cement of the swimming pool. Before they ripped the pool out and replaced it with a new tile one, we used to hold our breath and run our hands along the cement bottom, feeling for a finger or a knee.

But there was something about Heinrich's story that resonated. Growing up, I was fascinated, not by the romance of the story but by the gruesome details. I watch the surface of the road disappear beneath the wheels of the Mustang and imagine the doctor in the cramped and humid fuselage. There is something powerful about such unwavering denial of death and time: how his singed fingers molded the wax to the shape of each rupture in the flesh; how he sprinkled her with drops of frangipani perfume to ward off the stench; how the buttons of his suit jacket brushed against her body when he rolled her back to change the sheets. It is these daily physical necessities that, even now, consume my imagination. Somewhere inside the labyrinth of Heinrich's brain was something that allowed him to forget the flies and the rampant decay and allowed him to wash away the tiny white eggs of the unhatched worms of death.

Shifting the Mustang into fifth gear, I head south in the direction of Abilene. Somewhere in Houston are the people who hired me, the same ones who sent the fisherman, the ones who'll know what to do with the disk. Before morning I'll have to find a place where I can catch an hour or so of sleep. Already the shapes of the road are wavering and shifting. I blink my eyes and light a cigarette, shaking off the ghosts of exhaustion.

I try to put everything together in my mind, but the details I have are like a cheap puzzle and the pieces don't fit. Nothing adds up, but one fact remains: Someone's trying to kill me. They knew about Mark and they guessed I'd head from his place down into Colorado. At least that's what someone told the papers and the police. And then there's Wykel. He knew I had something and he knew Callum was involved. I have every reason not to trust him, every reason to think he might be coming after me himself.

Some eight hundred miles stretch between me and Houston. I'll be there by noon tomorrow. No questions, I tell myself. Just keep driving. Easy money.

Thirteen

Houston has never been one of my favorite cities. It is where Texas meets the South.

A strange amalgam of oversized Baptist churches, all-you-can-eat steak houses, private men's clubs, and seedy strip joints, Houston has the hurricanes and humid summers of South Florida but very little of the charm. If I had chosen the location for this drop it would have been anywhere but Houston. Of course, mine is a rather dim view of the city. Most likely there are countless happy Houston dwellers who would be more than willing to point out just how wrong I am.

An hour outside the city I pull the Mustang into the parking lot of a Texaco station, use the filthy rest room, and fill my gas tank. I buy a can of Coke and a bag of Fritos and pay the old man at the counter. From the pay phone outside the station I call Joey.

'You know, Al, you're a big celebrity,' Joey says, when he hears my voice on the line. 'I've read all about you in the papers. Sorry about Mark.'

'I'll bet you are,' I say. 'Why'd you do it?'

'What, baby?'

'You think I'm an idiot? You're the only one who could have known I was at Mark's. How long did it take you to connect the dots? You set me up, Joey.'

'What are you talking about? Give me one good reason why I'd sell you out.'

'You're a greedy prick.'

'Listen, Al. Think for a minute here. You start shooting people, and the cops are gonna come looking for you. Besides, I know you'll deliver. Why would I send someone after you?'

'It's a lot of money, Joey. Maybe you figured you could save yourself my cut.'

'You're wrong about this,' Joey says. 'Whoever's out there looking for you, I'm not the one who sent them.'

'Don't worry, Joey. I'm still good for the drop,' I tell him. 'I want my money.'

'You in Houston?'

'Close enough.'

'Okay, you've used this spot before. Remember that drop you had under the Ship Channel Bridge last spring? You're going to the same place. How soon can you be there?'

'I'm not using your spot, Joey. I'll hand over the package, but I'm saying where and when.'

'Listen, you're the one workin' for me. Did you forget that?'

'You want the package or not?' My hands are shaking. I grip the metal cord of the telephone and feel it cutting into the flesh of my palm.

'Quit bluffing. We've still got your money. Ship Channel Bridge, one-thirty.'

'I won't be there. But there's a club out in Jacinto City called Jonah's. Too bad you're in Miami. It's the kind of place I think you might enjoy. You got a pencil?' I rattle off the address. 'I'll be there at two o'clock. And I want double my original price. With the shit I'm in here, I'm going to have to disappear for a while.'

'They're not gonna go for it, Al. You think it's easy to get that kind of money?'

'You've got that kind of money in your office safe. No money, no disk. I want to make this very clear. No more fucking around. I see the payoff straightaway or I'm outa there. We screwed up in Bremerton; it's not going to happen again. And tell them not to bring a crowd.' I set the phone into the cradle and loose my grip on the cord.

Skirting through the northern suburbs and around to the east of Houston, I hit the scan button on my radio and skim the AM band for news. A preacher on a Christian station belts out Bible quotes about the man being the lord of the household. On a sports talk show two men argue about the legislature's emergency decision to amend the Freedom of Information Act. It seems Texas A&M has used the act to claim their right to see the University of Texas's football playbook.

Finally, out of the static, comes the serious voice of a news announcer. I listen to the latest fund-raising scandal from the White House, the news of yet another broken cease-fire in the Middle East, the saga of the Russian soldiers still in Chechnya.

'In national news,' the announcer says, 'police are still searching for a Florida woman wanted in connection with two violent deaths. Police have still not released the names of Alison Kerry's two victims. Kerry is believed to be armed and dangerous. Police urge anyone with information regarding her whereabouts to contact local law enforcement. Officials suspect Kerry is on her way to Texas. Kerry is twenty-seven years old. She was last seen driving a pale-blue Ford Mustang. She has brown hair and eyes, is approximately five feet eight inches tall, and weighs one hundred and thirty-five pounds. . . .'

My watch reads 1:17 when I pull the Mustang into an alleyway a few blocks from Jonah's. The day has grown warm, even by Houston standards. I strip down to my T-shirt, get out of the car, walk around to the trunk, and rifle through the stack of license plates. It's more than likely the girl at the Circle K reported the Kansas number. I fish out the California plates and screw them into place, hoping the switch may at least buy me some time.

I find the boxes of clips and the spare guns beneath the driver's seat, roll up the leg of my jeans, strap a small holster around my ankle, and slide the Beretta inside. There are several Dumpsters in the alley, and the day's heat has magnified the stench of the rotting garbage. Brushing my damp hair back from my face, I roll the pant leg back into place over the top of my boot.

I slip out of my T-shirt, slinging the strap of my shoulder holster around my back and down between my shoulder blades, loosening the leather strap so that the holster rides just below my left breast, shoving Max's Heckler and Koch into place. The cups of my bra are wet with sweat.

As my head pops up through the neck of the shirt I see my face in the rearview mirror. The scab where the glass broke the skin of my cheek has grown smaller, but the bruises have deepened to a shade of ocher. Dodging my reflection, I bend down and rummage through the spare clips.

After loading the pockets of my jacket with ammunition, I find the disk in the glove compartment, thrust it into the back pocket of my jeans, and fit the Browning into the hollow at the base of my spine.

They'll kill you. Wykel's voice ricochets through my head. I'm not taking any chances. I grab a roll of duct tape from the back seat and fix the Walther up under the steering wheel.

It's 1:40 when I pull out of the alley onto a side street, find a parking spot, and cut the engine. Resting my hands on the wheel, I breathe slowly. I'll have to leave the car here. The lot at Jonah's sits just off a main street, and I can't risk anyone's recognizing the Mustang. I get out, slip into my coat, lock the doors, and walk the three blocks to the club. A handful of cars surround the windowless cinder-block building, and shimmering waves of heat rise off the asphalt. A marquee at the lot's main entrance reads ALL LIVE REVUE. HOUSTON'S HOTTEST LADIES. Before working for Joey I used to meet one of my regular buyers here. He had a partial interest in the business, and he told me that most of the money that goes in and out of these clubs doesn't come from the dancers, at least not from any legal activities they perform. Among other things, Jonah's is a cash-washing machine, and with the help of a few well-placed gifts to the police summer youth camp it prides itself on being cop-free. Even if someone at Jonah's recognizes me, they won't turn me in.

I cross the lot, replaying my earlier conversation with Joey. You're here for the money, Al, I tell myself; no money and you bolt. I check myself quickly in the two-way mirror of the front door, step into the dark air-conditioned entryway, and pull my wallet out of my coat. A wire cage runs the length of the narrow hallway. Heavy red-velvet drapes hide the walls. A grotesquely fat man stares out at me from a window in the mesh. Rolls of flesh spill out of the neck of his tentlike shirt.

'You here for an audition, sugar?' he asks. His eyes are set deep into his puffy face.

'No.'

The man raises a thick finger, points to a sign over the money window that reads FREE ADMISSION BEFORE 5PM, and waves me through.

I push my way through the curtains at the end of the entrance hall and into the main room. After the muggy heat of the air outside, the club seems unnaturally cold. The rings of sweat under my arms and breasts chill instantly in the cool air, and an involuntary shiver pulses down my spine. A long stage ringed by stools and a narrow plank bar juts out into the center of the room. Three poles are set at even intervals in the stage, and a bored-looking blond woman in a white teddy and black stilettos is wrapped around the centermost one. In the flaming-red glare of the stage lights, every crease and wrinkle in the woman's skin is visible. She arches her back and leans away from the pole, and I see the tiny dimples in the flesh of the backs of her thighs.

I cross in front of the stage and head for the bar. Strains of 'Desperado' blare from the sound system. A few customers sit at stools around the stage: a short Hispanic man in a dirty straw cowboy hat and jeans, a white businessman, and a group of three boys with military haircuts. A hefty bouncer leans up against the red curtains at the back of the room.

The dancer struts over to the group of boys and peels the lace cups of the teddy down off her small breasts. She turns her back to the group and leans forward, thrusting her thighs out behind her, running her fingers along the thin white line of the thong of the teddy, pushing the material to one side. One of the boys sticks a five-dollar bill into the crotch. His friends let out a few high whistles.

I turn my back to the stage and lean up against the bar. The bartender, a short, slightly plump brunette in a cropped T-shirt and cutoffs, looks up at me from filing her nails.

'A shot of Wild Turkey,' I say.

The woman eases herself off her stool and reaches for the whiskey. The mirrors that line the back of the bar reflect the image of the dancer. She has wriggled out of her teddy and is standing over the businessman with one foot propped up on the plank bar in front of him. She cups her breasts in her hands and bends her chest down close to the man's face.

The night Joey and I first went out, he took me downstairs to one of the rooms at La Concha after dinner. The room had a small balcony that overlooked Duval Street and the old Spanish church. I had worn a black silk dress with a thin mandarin collar and a long slit up my left thigh. It was an unbearably hot night, but instead of using the air conditioner, we left the doors to the balcony wide open. I was sweating, and the slick fabric of the dress clung to my stomach. A salsa band was playing in the hotel's downstairs lounge, and we could hear the sounds of the drums and horns.

Joey sat down at the room's small writing table and carefully laid out four delicate lines of cocaine. He took a twenty-dollar bill from his money clip and rolled it into a tight tube. Leaning over, he finished two of the lines and slipped the rolled twenty between my fingers.

As I bent over the table, he slid his left palm up along

my bare leg and across the inside of my thigh. Putting the twenty up to my nose, I traced the length of one of the lines. The fingers of Joey's right hand fumbled with the clasp on the back of my collar, and the long zipper opened smoothly across my skin and over each vertebra to the base of my spine. I finished the second line and straightened myself, letting the dress fall off my bare shoulders. Joey took his hand from between my legs and pushed the dress the rest of the way to the floor.

The bartender sets the Wild Turkey in front of me, and I tilt the small glass to my lips and down the shot. The businessman slides several bills into the fold between the dancer's breasts. The woman climbs up on the plank and crouches down over the man's face, putting her palm over her crotch, rubbing it against the thin line of her pubic hair.

'I'll have one more,' I say.

I watch the bartender pour the second drink and feel the warm buzz of the whiskey passing into my stomach. There was a four-poster bed in the room at La Concha and a ceiling fan with wicker blades. Joey pulled me up to him and took both my wrists in one hand and held them behind my back. He slid his other hand across my wet stomach and up over my chest.

There is a certain humiliation in desire, a kind of weakness in the acknowledgment that such longings exist within ourselves. I remember that Joey laid me down on the covers of the bed, and I could see raised patches of fading scars on his beautiful chest. They were the size and shape of silver dollars, stretched by growth. I reached out and covered them with my hand and I could feel their power, as if it were I who had been wounded.

'My mother,' Joey said. He lifted my fingers and pressed them to his mouth.

Taking the Wild Turkey, I sit down at a table a few feet back from the stage. I look at my watch: 2:10. The curtains over the entryway swing open and a tall man in a long leather coat steps into the club. He stands just inside the door and surveys the room, letting his eyes pass briefly over me. The music has stopped and the woman has come off the stage and is circulating among the customers, trying to sell lap dances.

The tall man moves from the curtains and starts across the room toward me, the shape of a gun bulging against the soft leather of his coat. His hands are empty and his palms are open and ready. I finish the second Wild Turkey and lean back in my chair, sliding my right hand slowly around my waist, easing the Browning out of my jeans and into my lap.

The music starts up again, a heavy disco beat this time, and a black woman in a sequined gold body suit twirls onto the stage. The tall man is about halfway across the room. He crosses in front of the stage, and the red lights flicker over his face. The blond dancer struts across the dirty carpet and approaches him. She tosses her hair back, puts her hand up to his face, and says something. The man shakes his head. His lips mouth the word 'sorry' as he steps around the dancer, moving in my direction.

'Where's the money?' I say. The man stops a few feet from where I'm sitting. He's just one step up from a cheap street hood, not much older than I am. He's wearing gray zoot pants and brown-and-white wing tips.

'Where's the money?' I ask again.

The man looks at me and shrugs. 'Outside,' he says, jerking his left thumb toward the door.

I click the Browning's safety off and bring my boot up hard and flip the table on its back. The empty shot glass shatters. A gray gleam of steel slides out from inside the tall man's coat and I slam the Browning up in front of me. The bouncer starts across the room in my direction.

'He's a fucking cop!' I lie, yelling the magic words over the music. Out of the corner of my eye I see the black dancer rush for the stage exit. The bouncer stops moving.

'Get your hand off the gun, cop,' I say, stressing the word *cop*, 'and put your arms up over your head. No money, no drop, that's the deal.'

I step around the overturned table and grab the arm of the blond dancer. 'How do I get to the back door of this shit hole?' I ask.

The woman nods at the stage. 'It's through the dressing room. I'll show you.'

I follow the woman across the room, keeping my left hand on her right elbow and the Browning trained on the tall man. We're about halfway to the stage when the curtains at the entrance shift again and two figures come rushing into the club. In the dim light I can just barely make out Max's compact shape. I loose my grip on the dancer.

'Get in the back,' I yell to the woman. 'Go!'

A flash of gunfire illuminates the deep red walls of the club. I point the Browning at the two figures and dive over the plank bar surrounding the stage, firing from midair. The mirrors behind the bar shatter. My shoulder comes down hard against one of the poles, and my face slams against the stage.

I bring my knees off the floor and crouch down, facing the club, blinking against the lights. The stage door is about ten feet away.

Pushing the fabric of my T-shirt up, I unholster the Heckler and Koch. Bullets whistle through the air around me. I wrap my finger around the trigger, brace my back against the pole, close my eyes, and squeeze two bullets from the barrel of the forty-five. Even if I don't hit anyone, the flash from the gun will partially blind every person in the dark club.

I rise up from my crouch and spring for the stage door, sliding the last few feet across the slick floor on my left hip. Keeping the Browning and the forty-five out in front of me, I fire through the haze of the stage lights.

Rolling up from my slide, I back the last few inches through the curtained stage door and into the dressing room. The blond dancer is rummaging through the drawers of one of the dressing tables. The room is sparsely furnished. Piles of rumpled clothes are heaped on chairs. An open closet holds racks of costumes: sequined halters, imitation buckskin, a neatly pleated schoolgirl's uniform. Through an open door on one side of the room comes the sound of a toilet flushing. The black woman in the gold suit comes rushing out.

'You find any more?' she asks the blonde.

The blond woman pulls a one-ounce bag of cocaine out of one of the drawers. 'I think this is it.' She tosses the bag to the black woman.

'What are you doing?' I ask.

The black woman looks at me incredulously. 'Shit, honey. You said they were cops.' She turns back to the bathroom, tearing at the bag with her long fingernails.

I slide a fresh thirteen-round clip into the Browning. My nose is bleeding from when I smacked into the floor, and I can feel the warm blood on my upper lip and chin.

Propping my hand on one of the dressing tables, I lean over and try to focus. The sounds of shooting coming from the club have stopped, and I hear the tick of hard-soled shoes on the stage.

Kiki was right: Someone sure set me up good. Someone who knew I'd be heading south from Seattle, who knew where to find me in Montana, knew exactly which friends I'd trust, someone who was sure I wouldn't ask questions. Someone who told the police I'd left Colorado for Texas. Joey.

The blond woman slams the door to the stage shut and pulls a bolt across the frame, locking the metal into place with her fist.

'You coming, Tasha?' she calls out over her shoulder, grabbing a robe off the back of a chair and slipping her arms into it. The black woman reemerges from the bathroom, tugging a pair of shorts up over her thighs.

'Jesus.' The black dancer, Tasha, tugs on her zipper and looks over at me. 'What the fuck you do, honey?'

I straighten up and run the back of my hand across my lips, wiping away a film of sweat and spit.

'How you gettin' out of here?' the blonde asks, not waiting for my answer to Tasha's question. 'You got a car?'

The knob on the stage door clicks back and forth, and then the entire frame shudders.

I nod. 'I'm parked a couple blocks away, down a side street.'

Tasha brushes past me and opens a door at the back of the dressing room. I can see a corridor and red EXIT sign. 'All right,' she says, 'let's get the fuck out of here.'

I push off the desk and move toward the corridor.

'Not that way,' the blonde tells me.

Tasha reaches out and puts her hand on my arm. Her brown eyes are wide, trained on my face. 'We're just gonna let them think we gone that way, sugar.' She grins. Both women are strangely calm, as if used to such intrusions.

The stage door shudders again, taking the impact of at least two bodies.

'This way,' the blonde says. She steps over to the open closet and disappears into the row of neatly hung costumes.

'Let's go!' Tasha's hand is on my back propelling me forward into the closet. Pushing aside the folds of fabric, I duck my head and dodge under the hanging rod. The costumes are musty with the lingering odor of old sweat. My fingers fumble across lace and wire and leather, the nubbed wool of the schoolgirl's plaid skirt.

'C'mon.' I hear the blonde's voice up ahead. A curtain at the back of the closet swings open. Tasha gives me one last shove, thrusting me forward, and we emerge into a small, dusty room.

'Follow me,' the blonde says. 'You're getting the VIP tour.' She turns and heads down a narrow corridor, the red hem of her robe flashing around her bare legs.

My nose is throbbing. I steady myself on the cool cinder block that lines the hallway and pitch myself forward. Tasha trails behind. My hands leave a faint red smear along the wall. The scent of my blood fills the passageway.

'We're almost home, sugar,' Tasha's voice echoes from behind me. 'Hang in there.'

The hallway makes a sharp corner. The blonde has stopped. She stands before us with one hand on the knob of a door. A bright slice of daylight shines in across the jamb.

'Dancers' side exit,' the blonde says, 'just in case.' She runs her fingers through her hair, brushing loose curls off her face. 'You can't see this door from the parking lot. We keep the Dumpsters right in front of it. My car's just outside.'

I rack the slide on the Browning and bring it up in front of my chest. 'Just in case,' I say, flashing a weak smile.

The blonde laughs. 'Here we go.' She flings the door open, flooding the hallway with heat and glaring sunlight. I hug the doorframe and creep down the back side of the Dumpster and check the parking lot.

'We're clear,' I say. I can see what must be the blonde's car, a yellow Camaro, in a slot a few feet away.

'Run!' Tasha calls from behind me. She and the blonde slip through the doorway and dash across the hot asphalt. Tasha flings the passenger door open, and I jump into the back seat. 'Get down,' she tells me. I put my head on the warm vinyl and listen to the slamming of doors, the sound of the engine purring to life. The Camaro jerks backward and wheels sharply around.

'Where's your car?' the blonde asks. I look up at the sound of her voice. She has the rearview mirror flicked down so she can see my face. Her eyes dart from the road to me and back. She guns the Camaro's engine and the car bumps as it leaps out of the lot and onto the street.

'Not far,' I tell her. 'I'll show you.' I roll over and train my eyes on the thin strip of her face in the mirror. Her heavy makeup is blurred. A swath of smeared eyeliner bleeds into the wrinkles in her white skin. In the daylight I can see that she is older than I thought, and harder. She looks over at Tasha and smiles and her cheeks lift upward elegantly, as if remembering some past grace.

I sit up and orient myself. 'Left here, then left again.' I

watch her hands on the wheel as she takes the corners, the red wings of her robe flapping against her wrists.

'It's the blue Mustang,' I say, when I can see the car. 'Pull up here.'

'Shit.' Tasha flips the back seat up for me and I crawl out. 'Honey, what'd you do?'

I pop the door of the Mustang and look back at her, not quite knowing what to say.

'Maybe you'd better not go there,' she says.

'Thanks,' I tell her. I hop into my car and watch them drive away.

When I was growing up, my father called hurricanes 'God's fingerprints.' In the early fall, when the storm season was at its peak, we would huddle around the television and watch the nightly reports from the National Hurricane Center on the late news from Miami. At times there would be five or six of the wild storms blooming in the Atlantic or the Gulf of Mexico. The multicolored whorls flickered across the screen like glorious, violent flowers. My father would hold his thumb up and I would trace the ridges in his skin and envision the stages of the storm: the green outer bands of rain, the orange and yellow inner circle of pounding wind, the black oval of the quiet center. The great eye was what fascinated me most, the promise of organized calm in the middle of such chaos.

As a child I always had a secret longing for a hurricane to strike the Keys. I would lie in my hammock on the upstairs balcony and look out over the dark island and imagine the sensual pounding of the rain, the wind forcing the royal palm in our front yard flat against the ground. We would lock the old shutters, I thought, and wait in the dark cave of the house and listen to the branches of the banyan and the poinciana scraping against the tin roof. There would be sound and wild power all around us and high waves washing up Duval Street and across the polished floors of the waterfront bars.

There would be fear, of course, but not terror. We would know the name of the storm before it reached us, the slow spin of its curved tentacles, its exact force and speed. Then, suddenly, the wind would stop and the booming of torn tree limbs flung against the side of the house would subside. I would step out into the clean garden and look up through the drenched forest of ficus and bougainvillea to the tunnel at the center of the hurricane. There would be absolute silence. The storm would hold us in its strong core like a woman's womb shelters a fetus.

I was in Homestead when Hurricane Andrew passed over South Florida several years ago, and my childhood wish came true. When the storm ebbed and the eye skated in off the water, I left my friend's house and wandered out into the stiff wind and the sputtering rain. I looked around at the sheared tops of the pine trees, the mailboxes blown off their posts, the streets flooded with garbage and debris, and didn't feel the long-awaited calm. There was a mahogany tree in a neighbor's yard that had held on through the first half of the storm. The tree's roots were loose in the ground and the trunk was tilted at a sharp angle, like evidence of some intimate betrayal.

I looked up at the clouds scudding across the sky and could sense the hum of destruction wrapped around us like an angry fist. It is better, I thought, not to know the heart of such a thing, better not to see the force with which it will return.

'Cops are like dogs,' my father used to say. 'If you don't run they won't chase you.'

Crawling through the back streets east of Houston, wending my way east toward the Louisiana border, I pray that he was right. I keep one eye on the speedometer and force myself to stick to the speed limit. My face is a mess and my shirt and hands are spattered with blood from my nose. Once I'm over the border and into Louisiana I'll stop and fix myself up.

I shift my thoughts from the pain to the tangled nest of lies that has followed me since Bremerton. Somehow everything goes back to Chau Doc. Whatever happened in that little town on the Bassac, twenty-four men went MIA because of it. But that was almost thirty years ago and people get on with their lives. I know, because I watched my father recover, and Cyrus with him. Willie Phao was in Chau Doc, and now he's moving heroin across the empty states of the great plains. I think back to the Nightshift, to the nervous fisherman. I thought he was a fed, DEA or FBI, but most likely he was someone Callum trusted, maybe someone from the Agency. In this business you never really know who you can trust.

I've seen this kind of thing happen before. Once, on a dirt landing strip in the Everglades, I saw a guy shoot his partner because the delivery we were waiting for came off the plane cut by a tenth. More potent than fear, money is the great motivator. When you're dealing with it in large quantities, you always have to watch your back.

I've always known Joey was connected high up. Maybe Callum hired me and someone in the Agency got wind of it. Maybe, with Callum and the fisherman out of the picture, they called Joey and set up this meet as a way of making me come to them. Joey wouldn't have snitched on me for the money. It wouldn't be good business. Once you start turning on people, the word gets out and suddenly no one wants to run for you. But then again, he might have snitched without knowing what he was doing.

Wykel was right. They would have killed me in Houston, like they killed Callum and the fisherman and Mark. And most likely those men on the list, dead in the jungle almost thirty years ago.

I hit Port Arthur and turn south, then cross the water at Sabine Pass and enter the bayou country of southern Louisiana. I keep close to the Gulf, pushing the Mustang, heading east to Chloe's, to the only place I know Joey won't look.

Fourteen

Just before dawn a sudden urgent stillness, a violent quiet, wrenches me from a skittish sleep. I sit up in bed. I'm in our house on Petronia Street, I think, in my father's room. Outside, the sky is marbled by black clouds against the deep shade of blue that comes in the hour or so before sunrise. The rain has gone. In the garden a cat lets out a lonely, tired wail. I swing my feet down onto the cool pine floor and make my way out into the hallway. Someone has left a light in the kitchen on. The stairs and the bottom hall are lit with a dim afterglow.

Rounding the curled base of the banister, I peer back into the kitchen, blinking my eyes against the harsh light in the doorway. To my right is the dark living room. 'Cyrus?' I call out, trying to shake the disorienting fog of sleep, but there's no answer.

I press one palm against the wall, steadying myself, letting the bare soles of my feet glide forward. My fingertips brush across fur. Thick velvet strokes the inside of my thumb, and I turn my head and see the shadowed profile of a moth, the outstretched wings glimmering in the slanted light, the two spectral eye spots glowing like tarnished coins, the silky feelers quivering against the back of my hand. The silent creature folds itself up at my touch. Its furry legs pulse twice and then it flutters its wings, stretches itself wide, and lifts off the wall. The silhouetted body disappears into the glare of the kitchen. In a split second it is gone from my view, and all I can hear is the panicked beating of its wings against the walls of the house, the heavy thumping of its body crashing against wood and glass.

I reach the doorway of the kitchen and stop, putting my hand across my forehead to shade my eyes from the light. In the center of the room is the kitchen table, its surface scarred from years of use. A half-empty bottle of Johnnie Walker sits in the middle of the table, and just in front of the bottle is a stack of playing cards. The moth flickers through the room like a phantom, darting aimlessly. It careens past my face, and the slight breeze from its wings brushes my lips and cheeks. Three of the kitchen chairs are tucked in neatly under the table, their rigid backs touching the thick wood, but the fourth chair, the one nearest me, has been pushed out.

Skirting the table, moving toward the door that opens onto the backyard, I cross the room. A distorted reflection of my face bobs in the blind window and I swing the door wide and hold it open, waiting for the moth to free itself into the darkness, inhaling the salty air, filling my lungs with the loamy scents of the moldering garden. It's no use. The moth moves closer to the globed overhead light in the kitchen, frantically battering the frosted glass, leaving dusty wing traces on the slick surface of the lamp.

I turn away from the creature and scan the yard. The rain has left a thick, wet haze. In the halcyon hush of the garden something moves. Letting the door fall closed behind me, I move out across the carpet of decaying petals and leaves. My shirt and jeans are clammy against my skin. Feathered poinciana limbs brush my bare arms, grope my neck, fling captured droplets of rainwater across my face. The air is rank with the sweet smell of rot. My toes graze the split skin of a fallen orange, slip over the nubbed leather of an avocado. The knobby ficus bushes that line the back fence ripple against each other.

'Who's there?' I call out.

No one answers, and I step closer to the ruffled wall of ficus bushes. 'Who are you?' I plunge my hands into the darkness behind the leaves, blindly groping the tangled branches, pressing my body into the cloak of the stiff plants, soaking my chest, sliding my arms deeper into the thick foliage.

'It's Alison,' I whisper, growing frantic, hearing the startled pounding of blood against my temples. There's a sudden thrust of movement in the ficus, a shuddered pulse in the empty air around my hands. I feel the head first, the curls slick with sweat plastered across the forehead, the two round sockets of the eyes, the lids fluttering against my fingertips. I skim my palms down over the mouth, under the curve of the chin, across the fleshy neck, and let my fingers touch the shoulders, the hollow above the collarbone. Sliding my hands down across the arms, I rest my fists in the calloused palms.

My face is drenched, salty with sweat. Here is my father, I think, smoothing my thumb across the fine hair on his knuckles, pressing his hand open so our palms can touch. Here is his body, and I will deliver him. I will open the woody limbs that divide him from my sight. I will deliver my father into the haze-soaked garden, into the first rustlings, into the wild azure inception of the day.

I grab his wrists, pulling with all my strength, but his body flakes under my fingers. He is as fragile as time-bleached paper, as the gray chrysalis of a sleep-drugged moth. And then, as if slapped by a great hand, I am thrust through the membranous threshold of sleep, pitched forth from the garden into the shadows of Chloe's house.

I lie in the soft double bed and listen to the hum of the ferry engine outside and the quiet scratchings of geckos in the ceiling. A candle is smoking on the windowsill, giving off the acrid odor of citronella. Shifting the sweat-soaked sheet to one side, I let the moist bayou air graze my body.

Whatever pills Chloe gave me have worn off, and my face is throbbing. I make a vain attempt to move from the bed, but I'm still exhausted. Outside, the ferry is docking. The groan of the hull against the pylons, the rattle of chains, and the thump of heavy rope thrown against wood drift through the window. Several cars purr off through the thick forest of cypress trees. Footsteps rumble on the porch and the screen door creaks open. Sophie's sharp nails click across the wood floor. The dog's shiny black head appears in the doorway of my room.

'Sophie!' Chloe's quiet command comes from the hall-way. 'Get away from there.'

Sophie crosses over to the bed and puts her wet snout on the pillow next to my head. I put my fingers behind the dog's silky ears and scratch.

'It's okay, Chloe,' I call out. 'I'm awake.'

'Well, you shouldn't be.' Chloe comes in and sits down on the edge of the bed.

'What time is it?'

I think back to Jonah's and remember the drive from Port Arthur, flocks of pelicans rising off the Gulf, the blacktop of the road stretching across the marsh from Grand Cheniere to Pecan Island. Outside of Esther I waited for Chloe's ferry.

'Around eight,' Chloe answers.

'I have to get to Miami.'

'Maybe in the morning.' Chloe leans closer and examines my nose. 'It was broken,' she says, 'but it'll heal fine. You must've taken a rough fall.' She gets up from the bed and crosses the room. Sophie follows her out the door.

Rubbing my eyes, I try to shake off the fog of painkillers. Chloe left my life long before Joey entered it. Her house here was the only place I could think to come. I can hear her in the kitchen, the sound of rattling pans and running water, the shuffle of her bare feet on the floorboards.

She comes back into the bedroom with a tray and sets it on the bedside table. 'Drink this,' she says. She lifts a bowl of hot broth to my lips, passes the bowl into my hands, and gets up and goes to the window. In the years since she left us, Chloe's fluid walk has not changed. She glides across the room more like a creature of air and water than of flesh. She pushes the sleeves of her cotton work shirt up past her elbows and leans against the sill with her back to me.

'What's going on, Al?' she asks.

Finishing the broth, I put the empty bowl on the tray beside the bed. Chloe turns from the window and lights a cigarette. She pushes the brown folds of her hair over her right shoulder and perches on the windowsill.

'What kind of trouble are you in?'

'Big,' I say.

The oily flame of the citronella candle flickers in the breeze from the ceiling fan, showering Chloe's face with light. My father met Chloe when I was ten. She had a float plane and used to fly illegal goods out of the Keys and up to Louisiana and Mississippi. When she wasn't working she would tie the plane up to the dock behind the bar and stay with us at the house. She was beautiful and dark and she smoked Lucky Strikes and smelled faintly of airplane grease and fuel. We never knew when she would come. Sometimes she would be gone for weeks, and then she would suddenly show up at the bar or the house. Sometimes she would leave without telling us, and we would wake up to find her small bag gone and her cold cigarette butts crushed in the ashtray like tiny pale ghosts.

One summer Chloe stopped coming to the house. Months passed and we didn't see her. I asked my father where she had gone, and he said she was home in Louisiana, that her father was sick and she had to run his ferry for him. Every birthday until I left home I got a card and a present from Chloe, but she never came back to the Keys. So when I found myself bleeding and exhausted yesterday, I thought of Chloe's letters from Vermilion County and the toll ferry she used to write about.

Chloe comes over to the bed and slips her lit cigarette between my fingers. 'Do you want more painkillers?' she asks.

I shake my head.

'I have to wash this. It's going to hurt.'

'That's okay,' I say.

Chloe dips her hands into a basin on the nightstand and pulls out a wet cloth. The fine hairs on her forearms are covered with hundreds of tiny soap bubbles. She runs the cloth over my face. I watch her hands, the strong veins in the tan skin, the graceful knuckles. The translucent bubbles pop and settle as she works.

'I heard about your father.' Chloe looks up at me with her dark eyes. 'God, Al. I'm so sorry.'

'I know.'

She puts the cloth down. I pass her the nearly finished cigarette, and she takes a drag before stubbing it out. When she turns her face back to me her eyes are rimmed with water.

'I loved him, Al. There was just so much to save. Too many ghosts for one woman.'

'Chloe?'

'Yes.'

'How did it happen?'

Chloe touches her fingers to the corners of her eyes. 'How did what happen, baby?' she asks.

'How did he die?'

'Cyrus didn't tell you?'

I shake my head. 'I figure he was drunk. I gave up on worrying about the details a long time ago.'

'Oh, God, Al. Why didn't Cyrus tell you? He shot himself. Cyrus found him in the office of the Blue Ibis. Your father shot himself, Alison.'

I sit up and swing my legs off the side of the bed, letting my feet touch the wood floor. 'That's not true,' I say. 'He wouldn't have done that.' A wave of nausea sweeps over me, and my throat tightens. I walk to the open window, gulping fresh air. 'My father wouldn't have done that.' My voice wavers.

'You couldn't have known, Al. You couldn't have stopped him.'

I'm aware of Chloe's hand resting firmly on the back of my shoulder, and the dark swath of the river cutting through the tall grasses and mossy trees. I press the heels of my palms against my eyelids and try to block the warm rush of tears.

*

The last night Chloe ever stayed with us, the beating of rain on the tin roof of our house woke me and I climbed out of bed and crept down the stairs. As I started down the front hallway to the kitchen, I heard low voices. I stopped walking and peered through the darkness.

The door to the back veranda was open and silver light from a streetlamp bathed the kitchen. I saw the shape of Chloe's back, the taut muscles between her shoulder blades, the thick swath of dark hair that fell down her spine. A shadow of rain reflected off one of the kitchen windows and poured over the hollows in Chloe's luminous skin. She was crouched on the floor and her arms were looped around my father as if he were a child. His shoulders were heaving against her chest.

I stood there and watched them for a long time, watched Chloe's fingers in his hair, the tension in her bare calves as she twisted her body around and drew him closer to her. Over the roar of water cascading off the eaves of the house and down into the garden a deep animal sound was audible, the sound of my father sobbing. He put his head down in the shadowed space between her legs and wrapped his hands tightly around her waist.

The next day Chloe flew away and out of our lives for the last time. I stood on the dock and watched her plane nosing upward until it was just a flash of silver wings in the unbroken blue of the sky. She came into the wreckage of my father's life fearlessly and left with her soul still intact. It's hard for me to imagine her here, fixed beneath the Spanish moss and cypress trees.

Long after Chloe has gone off to bed I lie awake and try to picture the details of my father's death. He would have been drinking, I suppose. Johnnie Walker, since that's what he liked for special occasions. He would have taken his old Colt revolver out and checked the cylinder for bullets. It would have been late, 5 A.M., after the bar closed, and he would have counted the cash from the evening and dropped the money in the safe, leaving the accounts for Cyrus as he always did.

From the office he would have been able to hear the slow lapping of water on the dock, the buzz of an outboard as a dinghy crossed the channel. It would not be easy to kill oneself. He would have looked around the office, at the painting of Haitian cane cutters, at the Johnnie Walker bottle, at the pattern of water from the marina dappling the walls. He would have smelled the salty odor of the Gulf and the faint sweetness of hibiscus and night jasmine.

Maybe he was tired, or drunk. He drained his glass and set it gently on the desk. He closed his eyes to everything around him, picked the gun up, laid the cool metal of the barrel against his temple, and pulled the trigger.

I shift in bed and throw off the sheets. There is a difference between the slow self-poisoning of alcoholism and the calculated violence of a gunshot. My father never thought he would die from drinking. He had visited death once and come out clean.

An accident would be easy to believe, a drunken fall in the shower, a slip off the end of the pier, a fire. But such a deliberate and cowardly act of self-destruction, I cannot begin to see. Heaving myself out of the bed, I slip into a cotton bathrobe Chloe has left for me and make my way through the dark house and out onto the front porch, stopping in the living room to grab Chloe's pack of Lucky Strikes.

I sit down on her white wicker couch, light a cigarette, and look out across the flat surface of the river. There is quiet here, but not stillness. Unseen figures slither through the marshy undergrowth of the forest. The moss on one of the great cypresses stirs, though there is no wind. In the last few moments of my father's life he would have heard the click of the round chambering in the Colt. He would have felt the burnished wood of the handle against his palm. And there would have been those last few seconds while his finger worked against the stiff spring of the trigger. So much time in which he could have stopped and worked back through the stages of death, yet he didn't.

My neck and back are stiff and cramped when I wake up in the morning still on the porch. Through the brush at the edge of the yard I see Sophie's sleek face. She's quietly stalking a ruffled ibis through the cool morning shadows. The hulking shape of Chloe's ferry glides across the river.

Chloe has left a full pot of coffee warming on the counter in the kitchen. A plate of fresh biscuits sits on the table and next to it a note from Chloe telling me my breakfast's in the oven and that I'm to help myself to juice and jam from the refrigerator.

I pour myself some coffee and open the oven and pull out a plate of sausages and grits with gravy and scrambled eggs. Starving, I devour the plate of food and two of the biscuits before hearing Chloe's steps on the porch. She calls Sophie inside. The screen door bangs shut and the dog's hurried steps echo through the house. Sophie bursts into the kitchen and runs straight for me, her pink tongue hanging from her mouth. Slipping her a biscuit, I rub the soft fur under her snout.

Chloe comes into the kitchen and lays her leather work

gloves on the counter. She sits down with me and lights a cigarette. There's a black smudge of grease across her right cheek.

'You okay?' she asks. 'I heard you get up in the night, but I thought you probably needed some time alone.'

'Thanks.'

'It'll take awhile to sort it all out. You know you can stay here for as long as you need.'

I shake my head. 'I can't stay, Chloe.'

'I know the business, Al. I did it for a long time. There's nothing you've got that can't wait. You're just making a lot of people real rich and screwing yourself in the bargain.'

I think back to Mark's. 'There are people looking for me. They'll find me here eventually. I know they will.'

'Christ, Al. You sound like a character in a spy novel, like the goddamn KGB is looking for you. So you pissed off some smack dealer or maybe even some rich Colombian. Al, you're a courier, right? These people have better things to do with their time than hunt you to the ends of the earth. It's not good business. Give it a rest for a while.'

'It's deeper than that.'

Chloe finishes her cigarette in silence. She gets up from the table and pours herself a cup of coffee.

'You gonna tell me about it?' she asks.

'It's a long story.'

Chloe shrugs and looks at her watch. 'The ferry doesn't cross again for another two hours.'

I tell her everything, starting with the call from Joey and the botched pickup in Bremerton and Mark's death. I tell her about Darwin and the Hmong and John Wykel insisting the disk was for him, about the meeting at Jonah's. She drums her fingers on the table while she listens, and when I've finished she leans forward and props her chin on her hands.

'So what do you think your father has to do with this?'

'Who?' I turn to Chloe, wondering if I've heard her right.

'Your father.'

'What do you mean?'

'All this stuff about Chau Doc. It seems like an awful big coincidence.'

'I don't understand. My father was never in Chau Doc.'

Chloe looks up from the papers. A strand of hair is caught in her mouth and she brushes it back behind her ear, smearing the grease farther across her cheek.

'Sure he was,' she says, hesitating for a moment. 'He headed the Provincial Reconaissance Unit there.'

'That's impossible,' I tell her. 'I asked Cyrus. He said my father was never there.'

Chloe straightens herself and moves away from the table. She grabs her Lucky Strikes off the counter. 'Cyrus lied to you, Al.' She puts the filterless cigarette in the corner of her mouth and lights a match. 'Your father was there for six months.'

'Cyrus would have told me.'

Chloe shakes her head. She lets the match burn down until the flame is almost to her fingers, then touches it to the end of the Lucky Strike and inhales. 'He was there,' she says.

My legs have gone rubbery and I slump into a chair, grappling with the weight of what she's just told me, my mind trying and failing to connect the word *lie* with Cyrus. My faith in him, even more than my faith in my father, has always been absolute.

'Maybe Cyrus didn't know. Maybe he forgot.'

Chloe doesn't say anything. She shifts her feet and leans back against the counter.

'What are you going to do, Al?'

'I have to talk to Cyrus. I'm going down to the Keys.'

'I can fly you. I've still got my plane. It's docked down by Intracoastal City.'

'I need to stop in Miami first, to take care of some unfinished business. I'll be better off driving.'

'I'm worried about you.'

I look at my watch. 'When can you take me across?'

The ferry makes a low groan as it settles into its moorings on the other side of the river. The roof of Chloe's house is just visible through the trees on the opposite shore. The ferry is small, with maybe enough room for half a dozen cars. I'm the only person on this trip, and I help Chloe tie up to the dock. Several cars are waiting in the makeshift parking lot for the next crossing.

Chloe has been silent on the ride over. When the ferry is secured, she walks with me across the deck to the Mustang.

'I want you to hold on to this,' she says. She slips me a scrap of paper. 'It's my number here. If you need anything, I want you to call. Cyrus has it too. I can fly you out of here. I've got a friend down off Honduras. She runs a little hotel on Roatán Island for the tourists who come to dive. I can get you a place to stay and a job. I've got a kid over in Delcambre who runs the ferry for me sometimes. He can watch the place while I go.'

'And then what? I spend the next ten years looking over my shoulder, searching every face I see, wondering which tourist isn't really a tourist? Then one day I'm found floating in the surf with a broken neck or a hole in my head.'

'Staying doesn't sound like much of an alternative. Call me, Al.'

I open the door of the Mustang and climb in. Chloe leans down and props her arms on the window jamb.

'Your father, Al. . . .' She pauses for a moment and looks past me to the river. 'I could have lost myself there. It was a matter of self-preservation, my leaving.'

'I know, Chloe. I know.'

Fifteen

The time I spent using cocaine was like a deep, unexpected plunge down a narrow well. It was not a fall from grace but from memory, a dreamlike plummet, constant and without end. My mind remembers events from that time fleetingly, as a body tumbling through darkness might suddenly brush the curved surface of its enclosure.

When I first quit using and clambered up from the depths, I was blinded by the landscape of my own history and teetered for a long time on the lip of the hole, breathless, struggling to remap my life's occurrences. In the months following my return I had a constant fear of losing things. Walking down the street, I would suddenly feel something slip from my pocket and would stop and look around fruitlessly for the object. I have learned now to accept these losses, to accept the dark hours and days, the solid recollections in between.

My life has been divided into three parts: the time before, still viewed through the watery membrane of addiction and distance; the trip through the void, lit by infrequent flashes of clarity; and the return, with the glistening cord of self-creation stretching before me. Tonight I am drawn back into a place where the landscape is ghostily familiar. Outside Pensacola I close my atlas and put all my maps away.

The sun is just beginning to set as I skirt around Ocala and head down through the porous, lake-studded land of central Florida. I've made good time from the border, and I'll be in Miami long before sunrise. Everything is intimate now: the rolling, evergreen hills of the north fading from horse country to farmland; the first waxy leaves of the orange groves; the tacky roadside stands that serve chicken disguised as alligator meat. I've crossed this state so many times that the names of towns are familiar to me long before they spring out of the darkness.

Outside of Avon Park the relentless booming from the artillery range punctuates the muggy quiet of the night. I stop for gas, then follow highway 27 down around the southern tip of Lake Okeechobee and on to Miami. The lights from what little traffic there is reflect off the canal and spray out across the Everglades. By three o'clock I've crossed Biscayne Boulevard and headed out onto the Julia Tuttle Causeway to Miami Beach.

After we moved down to Florida, my father used to send me to New York each summer to visit my grandparents. I would spend two weeks with my mother's parents and two weeks with my father's. My mother's parents lived out on Coney Island, and the weeks I spent with them were sheer freedom. They used to take me to the board-walk to watch the freaks: the contortionists and sword swallowers and fire-eaters. My grandfather would buy me cotton candy and hot dogs until I was sick. My mother's parents had come from Prague before the war, and they talked to each other in their own language and ate potato pancakes and thick cakes filled with shiny black poppy seeds and drank martinis with big green olives. My grandfather was a musician, and every night after dinner he took his violin out and played gypsy songs while my grandmother and I danced on the living room carpet.

My father's mother lived in Bay Ridge, near where the Verrazano Bridge runs over to Staten Island. My paternal grandfather died before I was born. Until my father found out and got angry with her and made her promise to stop, my grandmother took me to mass every Sunday when I visited. She taught me how to say the Lord's Prayer and Hail Mary and how to cross myself. We would go to church early, and she would sit in one of the straight-backed pews while I went into the confessional. I liked church almost as much as the boardwalk at Coney Island. I liked to sit in the dark confessional and talk to the dim face behind the screen. I liked the wavering rows of red candles in the back, the sound of the organ, the smoky incense, the delicate way the soles of women's shoes fit together when they knelt to pray. There was a St. Mary Star of the Sea Catholic church down the street from our house in the Keys, but my father and I never went inside.

Following Collins Avenue south off the causeway, I skirt over to Ocean Drive, park the Mustang in front of the News Café, and try to collect my thoughts. I know Joey as well as he knows me. He won't be home yet; it's too early. The bars are beginning to close, and a mixture of tall models and fat German tourists straggle along the sand-covered sidewalk. Art Deco hotels and café terraces overflow with after-hour diners. Well-dressed couples spill out of the bars into the hot night. Across the beach the waves of the Atlantic curl and tumble as they hurl themselves onto the sand.

When my grandmother sat in the pew, her flowered housedress covered just the tops of her knees. My neck was always hot and itching under the freshly starched collar of my one good blouse. There was a heavy curtain with little gold crosses stitched into it over the door of the oak confessional. When I pulled it shut behind me, the odors of wood soap and the priest's aftershave overwhelmed me. My grandmother had a rosary with a small silver crucifix strung between the beads, and I ran my hands over the shape of Christ's body while I talked, pressing my fingers against the three sharp nubs of the nails in his palms and feet.

I cruise up Ocean Drive, find a small public parking lot by the beach, and stop the car. By now Joey will be finishing up his late-night business, maybe smoking a cigar by the back pool at the Mark or the Clevelander, trying to find a woman who's still standing at last call. I load the Beretta, fit the silencer over its barrel, slip the forty-five into my shoulder holster, and change into a fresh T-shirt and a pair of shorts. With the disk in my back pocket, I head out onto the beach. Across the sand, Joey's building rises, hulking, into the darkness. The lights of several large ships glimmer on the sea.

I pass the scraggly sea oats and the wooden boardwalk, stopping halfway to the surf. Turning my back to the ocean, I sit down in the sand, draw my knees in to my chest, and count up through the stories of Joey's building until I find the blind, dark windows of his condo.

What is it that I want from him? Money or some catharsis of unburdening, an acknowledgment of my anger? Information that will help me find out where to go from here? The familiar tropical air fills my lungs. Wind sweeps in off the Atlantic, pushing my hair across my face. Running my tongue over my lips, I lick away a thin film of salt and wait for Joey to come home.

'Illusion,' my mother's father used to say, wrapping his

tongue around the foreign word while flames disappeared down the man's throat. The fire-eater was my grandfather's favorite, but my grandmother and I liked the woman who came after him. The curtains on the stage would fall back and she would glide out in a glittering cape and body suit, her pale legs rippling with power, her dark braid swinging across her back. She had a stairway made of swords that she climbed. My grandmother and I would hold our breath in the close, smoky darkness of the tent while she gingerly placed the soles of her feet against the gleaming edges of sharpened steel.

Better even than the staircase was her finale. She had a black velvet box full of long nails and a little gold hammer, and she would tilt her head back and hammer the nails up into her nose. She would take a sword from the staircase and slide it down her throat until the steel disappeared and then she would bend her graceful body at the waist with the sword deep inside her.

The lights in Joey's condo blink on and the silhouetted shapes of two bodies move through the living room. A woman steps outside onto the balcony. Scrambling up out of the sand, I head back across the beach, skirting the high cement wall that encloses the building's pool area. My calves work against the deep sand.

Through the glass of the front door I see the night doorman, Manuel, sitting at the front desk. I pull my T-shirt down over the Beretta and knock on the glass. Manuel looks up and smiles. He ambles across the foyer and opens the door for me.

'Hey, Manny,' I say. Manuel has worked this shift ever since I've known Joey.

'Mr. Perez just came in. I can call upstairs for you, Ms. Kerry, if you'd like.'

'He's expecting me. I think I'll just go up.' I head for the elevators. 'How's Dolores doing?' I ask. Dolores is Manny's wife. I push the button on the wall and the UP arrow lights.

'Oh, she's very good. We have a new baby girl.'

'Congratulations,' I say. The elevator doors open, and I wave to Manny and step inside.

On the fourteenth floor I step out into the hallway and follow the corridor to Joey's condo. Outside his door I draw the Beretta out of my shorts and knock. The hallway is air-conditioned and goose bumps are rising on my arms. I hear faint music from inside the door and the sound of high heels on the parquet floor of the foyer.

'Who's there?' a woman's voice calls out.

'I'm here to see Joey,' I say.

The heels shuffle away from the door and for a few moments everything is quiet. A shadow crosses the peephole and there's the click of bolts unlocking, then the door swings open and Joey's face appears.

'Where the fuck've you been?' he says. I step into the foyer, and he reaches behind me and closes the door. He looks down at the Jetfire and smiles. 'You come here to kill me, Al?' He slips his hand around my back toward the Beretta and I jerk the gun away.

'Get her out of here.' I look past him to the living room. I'm shaking.

'Julia,' Joey calls out over his shoulder. The woman appears in the doorway. She has red hair and is wearing a short white dress with sheer panels sewn into the sides. 'I've got some business, baby. You disappear for a while, okay?'

'C'mon, Joey,' Julia whines.

I bring the gun out from behind my back and let the light catch it. 'Now,' I say. 'Get your purse and go.'

I follow Joey into the living room as Julia scuttles past us and out the door.

'Where'd you find her?' I ask. 'Pembroke Pines high school cheerleading squad, or did you just pick the drunkest girl in the bar?'

'Jealousy's an ugly thing, Al.' Joey walks across the room to the bar and pours himself a drink. 'Can I get you anything?' He motions to the array of bottles. 'I'm sorry. I'm fresh out of coke.'

'You set me up,' I say. 'I was stupid to trust you in Houston.'

Joey crosses in front of the open doors of the balcony and sits down on the leather sofa. His bare feet sink into the creamy plush of the carpet. He's wearing beige linen pants and no shirt. A gold Indian Head pendant hovers over the deep crease between his chest muscles, and his old scars are bright pink against his tan skin. He puts his finger in his glass and stirs his drink. The ice cubes clink against each other.

'I don't know what you're talking about. You know, the rumor is you're using again. You must admit, your behavior has been rather rash lately.'

A round glass vase full of birds-of-paradise sits on a high table behind the couch. I raise the Beretta, aim for the vase, and pull the trigger. The glass shatters behind Joey's right shoulder, spraying water and flowers across the carpet.

'You see what I mean.' Joey calmly takes a sip of his drink.

'How much did they pay you?' I aim the gun at Joey's chest.

'Why don't you put the gun down. We both know you won't kill me.'

'How much? Or were you just going to take my pay?'

'Look around you, Al.' Joey spreads his arms wide. 'What do you think this place costs me? The money you were supposed to get – that's chump change to me. Put the gun down and think for a minute. I'm a businessman. Why the fuck would I want to start pissing off my drivers?'

'I want my money. Now. I carried the disk to Houston and I want what I'm worth.'

'Give me the disk, you get the cash,' Joey says.

'I don't have it,' I lie.

'Fuck you, Al.'

I move around toward the couch, keeping the gun trained on Joey. 'Get up. I swear to God I'll kill you. Do you know what they did to Mark?'

Joey takes another sip of his drink. I'm standing right over him, and I bring the butt of the Beretta down hard across his cheek. The metal of the gun connects with his skin with a sick smack. The glass flies across the room and slams against the balcony door. Joey's head snaps back and the skin in his neck tightens over his esophagus and tendons. A bright trickle of blood pops from his lip. There's a red welt growing under his eye and he puts his hand up instinctively, shielding himself from another blow.

'God, Al,' he whispers, and I know I've hurt him. His eyes are wide with shock and fear.

I put the gun down and look away. 'Start at the beginning, Joey. No bullshit. Who hired me?'

'The day before I talked to you about the job, I get this call from some guy asking to hire you for a run.'

'He asked for me?'

'By name.' Joey puts the tip of his finger to the gash at the corner of his mouth and winces. 'Fuck,' he says. 'That hurt.'

'How did he know to call you?'

'He wouldn't say. I'm being honest, here. At first I told him to fuck off. I explained to him that I'm not stupid. I don't take people on without references. He keeps telling me how he can't say where he got my name but it's all on the up-and-up. How the product you'll be running is strictly legal. It's just information, he says, of no interest except to the parties involved.' Joey looks up at me. 'So anyway, I say, "Why don't you walk down to the nearest mailbox and drop whatever this is in the slot and be done with it?"'

'So why didn't he?' I balance on the arm of the couch, keeping the Beretta trained on Joey.

'Whatever this "information" is, it's the only copy. He explains how he can't take any chances. Then he starts talking money.'

'And, for the right price, you kindly offered me up.'

'No. I told him to tell me who referred him or to go elsewhere. So he says his name is David Callum. He says, "How's the CIA for a reference?"'

'I told you no bullshit. I don't have time for this, Joey.'

'I'm not lying. You asked me who hired you, and I'm telling you David Callum did.'

'How would Callum know me?'

Joey shrugs.

'What about Houston?' I ask. 'Callum wasn't even alive when you arranged that drop.'

'When I agreed to set this up for him he told me you'd be taking this to Colorado, somewhere near Denver. He said you'd get all the information at the pickup, that I didn't need to say anything until you –'

'Denver?'

'Shit, let me finish. The night of your pickup I get another call. This guy says he's a friend of Callum's. He says everything's fucked. He tells me the drop's still good, but you're going to Houston. He says the money'll be there if you deliver.'

'But the original drop was for Denver?' Wykel, I think.

'Yeah. That's what I said the first time.'

'And who was this guy, this friend?' I ask.

'He didn't say.'

'And you didn't ask?' I can't believe Joey could be so stupid.

'You were out there, and I didn't know what to do. When you called from Mark's and said things went wrong, which is just what he told me, I relayed the message to go to Houston. How the fuck would he have known to contact me if he wasn't in with Callum?'

I stand up from the couch, move toward Joey, and press the silencer into the skin under his ear. 'So you told this "friend" of Callum's I was at Mark's.'

'No. I didn't tell anyone where you were. You've got to go with me on this, Al. I've told you everything I know,' he says, tilting his neck away from the gun. 'I swear.'

'How much money do you have in the safe?'

'I don't know. Fifty, sixty grand.'

'Go get it.'

Joey doesn't move. I bring the Beretta up and point it at the couch an inch above his left shoulder. 'They already think I've killed two people. You think a third really matters?' I pull the trigger, and the leather cushion explodes.

Joey gets up. I follow him out of the living room and down a hallway past two bedrooms to his office. He bends down behind his desk and turns the dial on his safe.

'I didn't think anything would go wrong,' he says. His hands are unsteady. 'I don't even know what's on this goddamn disk that's so important.' Joey puts his fingers on the handle of the safe.

'I'll open it.' I swing the safe door open, reach inside, pull out Joey's Sig-Sauer, and shove the gun in the front of my shorts. 'I suppose you weren't going to use this either. Take the money out,' I whisper, putting the tip of the silencer between Joey's shoulder blades. He pulls several stacks of bills from the safe and stands up.

'I need a bag,' I say.

'There's some grocery bags in the kitchen.'

We leave the office and head back down the hallway to the living room.

'Go sit on the couch,' I tell him, keeping the gun trained on Joey's chest, watching him from the open kitchen as I rummage through the drawers for a Winn Dixie bag.

'Can I have some ice for my face?' Joey asks from the living room. He has one hand over his cheek. More blood has leaked out of his mouth, and there's a thin line of red smeared across his chin. 'There's an icemaker on the door of the fridge.'

I open one of the cabinets and pull out a glass and fill it, then cross out of the kitchen to Joey. The money is lying on the couch, and I shove the stacks inside the bag. Through the open drapes to the balcony I catch a glimpse of the top arc of the sun breaking over the Atlantic. It's just a tiny red sliver of light crossed by the dark lip of the sea, like a new bruise forming in the sky.

'Why should I believe anything you've said?' I look

down at Joey. He's holding a crescent chip of ice to his skin. His fingers are delicate and strong at the same time, and the old pulse of longing wells up inside me.

He shrugs. 'Because it's the truth. Shit, Al. I need a drink.'

'I'll get it.' I put the money on the coffee table, walk to the bar, and pour a tumbler of scotch.

'I'm sorry.' Joey reaches for the glass.

'No, you're not.' I hand him the drink. 'Don't lie to me. I'm too tired.'

He brings the glass to his lips and takes a long drink. I put the Beretta back in my shorts and grab the money and start for the door.

'Someone else must have known you were at Mark's,' he says.

It's a simple statement, but it grabs hold of me and my stomach leaps up into my chest. I put my hand on the doorknob and look back at Joey. His eyes are closed and his head is thrown back over the couch. It is a moment of strange clarity for me, not unlike the moment when I knew I had to quit with the cocaine, when I realized it would destroy me. Desire has left me and pity has replaced it. I feel sorry for Joey and I know he's telling the truth. And I remember the message I left on Cyrus's answering machine, telling him I was at Mark's, and that Cyrus lied to me.

The little Cuban bakery next to the Bodega Melosa buzzes with morning activity. Men with hard hats and lunch coolers squeeze inside for *cafe con leche* and *boniato* rolls and hot egg sandwiches on *pan cubano*. I sit in the Mustang on Eighth Street, sip my frothy coffee, and wait. Melosa doesn't open until seven-thirty.

Callum knew who to call to hire me; he asked for me by name. He told Joey the documents on the disk, the orders, the picture of the base, were his only copy, all that remained of whatever happened in Chau Doc. But there were at least two Americans beside Callum who were involved. One was there that night, the one who led the Hmong team. The other person put his pen to the orders, scribbled his signature in the space below Callum's: J.R. And then there's my father.

At seven-twenty I see the bent shape of Luis Melosa round the corner, head down Eighth Street, and step into the bakery next to the bodega. Through the glass front windows I watch him order a coffee and joke with the girl inside. He has aged since I last saw him and fumbles with his keys as he works to open the security gate over the front of the little store. Putting his coffee on the sidewalk, he bends down and rolls the metal sheath up over the windows of the shop. He's wearing a short-sleeved tropical-weight cotton shirt, flat-front khaki pants, and red sneakers.

The fluorescent overhead lights flicker on and the ABIERTO sign appears in the window. I get out of the Mustang and head for the front door of the bodega. The morning sun casts long shadows across the cracked sidewalk. The day will be blistering hot.

I step inside the shop and walk toward the back through the rows of Goya canned goods and packets of dried yerba buena and achiote. Boxes of produce line the walls: green orbs of black sapote, bruised plantains, tuberous *boniatos*. The sound of Melosa singing to himself floats through the dusty little store.

'Luis,' I call out, moving in the direction of his voice.

He pops his graying head out from behind a tall shelf.

'Alison!' He scowls. 'Such a long time I haven't seen you.'

I smile. 'How's Maria?'

'Oh, we're both getting old, I'm afraid.'

'Nonsense.'

'It's true. We're grandparents now. Consuela had a little boy last year.'

'Is she still working at Mt. Sinai?'

Melosa nods, beaming. Then his face hardens and he loops his arm around my shoulder. 'I heard about your troubles,' he says, lowering his voice. 'Of course I knew it was lies. That's why you're here?'

I nod. 'I need a favor, Luis.'

'Of course.'

'I need a passport, a good one, not American.' I take several thousand-dollar bills from the pocket of my shorts and hold them out to Melosa. 'As soon as possible.'

'Canadian, perhaps?' he says, taking the money. 'I have several that would work for you.'

'That would be fine, Luis.'

Melosa shuffles to the front of the shop, flips the lock on the door, and removes the ABIERTO sign from the window.

'I'm sorry to disrupt your business,' I say.

Luis walks slowly back through the shelves and takes my hands in his, gripping them tightly. 'This is my business, Alison.'

The back room of the bodega smells faintly of photography chemicals and dust. Melosa sits me down in front of a blue screen, finds a pink bottle of Revlon foundation, and rubs the makeup into my skin with a small sponge.

'The bruises are not good,' he says matter-of-factly.

'What about the hair?' I ask. 'I don't want to be a blonde for the rest of my life.'

'The hair's okay. Even Canadian women make horrible hair choices. The passport will say you are a brunette. It is obvious this color is not real.'

When he's satisfied with the makeup he steps back to his boxy camera and takes a picture.

'It will be a couple of hours before I'm done. You can wait in the shop if you'd like. There are some magazines.'

'Thanks, Luis, but I've got some business to take care of. I'll be back in two hours.'

'What name do you prefer? I have Miranda and Helen and Sarah.'

'Why don't you choose for me?' I tell him.

'Oh, no. You must decide for yourself. This will be your identity. You must have a hand in it.'

'Helen's fine.'

Melosa presses his palm against a panel in the wall and a shelf stocked with canned goods swings open.

'Just like Batman,' he says, grinning. He steps through the opening and pulls the shelf closed behind him.

The periodical room at the Miami Public Library is empty except for a few homeless men reading the morning paper. The only sounds are the quiet shifting of newsprint and the buzz of the fluorescent lights. A librarian at the information desk looks up from her filing long enough to direct me to the library's computer system.

'I'm looking for an article from about ten years ago,' I tell her.

'Oh, yes,' she responds amiably, her voice barely above a whisper. 'Anything from the last fifteen years should be in there. Just search through, using your subject. The computer will give you an outline of each article. Print up the information on which ones you'd like to see, and I'll be happy to run back to the stacks for you.'

I take a seat as directed at one of the black and orange screens and scroll through questions, indicating a periodical search and typing the word CALLUM.

The computer labors for a few seconds, and a list of articles floods the screens. The first article on the list is from a 1987 issue of a quarterly business magazine. The article is titled COLD-WAR CASH. A brief synopsis reveals the article's content: The hoped-for success of a new computer game based on two archenemies of the Cold War, David Callum and Nikolai Gregorovich.

The rest of the articles are from the spring of 1986 and deal with the hearings concerning the publication of Callum's memoirs. I scan through the list, searching for anything that contains pictures, feeding the entries into the printer.

I rip the paper free of the printer and walk back toward the information desk. 'I'd like to see these, please,' I say, holding the slightly crumpled sheet in my fist, suspecting what the pictures will reveal but feeling the need to be certain.

The librarian looks up at me and smiles. 'Of course, dear.'

The magazines are dusty, their covers wrinkled by other fingers. I spread the slick pages out on a large table and begin thumbing through the articles chronologically. There are pictures of Callum, ten years younger than in the recent pictures the newspapers and networks have been using to cover his death. Callum in a dark suit and white shirt before the National Security Council. Callum with his lawyer. Callum in his office with a copy of his book. Callum with his wife at their home in Washington state, the two of them radiating unstoppable youth and vibrance.

One article is devoted to the issue of censorship. It's a spread of about ten pages in a popular news magazine with side comments written by well-known authors. There's an interview with Callum in which he seems somehow beaten down and reluctant to speak about the book. 'It's best for the nation. I can see that now,' he comments.

And then, in an article dealing specifically with the hearings, I hit paydirt. I recognize the fisherman first. He's seated with his hands resting on the table in front of him, bent forward slightly so that his mouth is almost touching a microphone. The mental picture I've held of him was of his posture in death, so it's strangely disconcerting to see him so alive, his lips captured in mid-speech, his eyes alert. *Robert Ghilchrist*, the caption below the picture reads, *Callum's security advisor in Vietnam, testifying before the council.*

I keep turning pages, and at the very end of the article I find what I'm looking for: a full-page photo of Callum emerging from the hearings into a bright crisp spring day. His wife is at his right side, her red dress dazzling against the drab coats and scarves of the media and onlookers. At Callum's left elbow is a short man in a blue suit. The man's fingers are just barely grazing Callum's arm. Callum's elbow is raised unnaturally, giving the impression that he's trying to avoid the contact between flesh and wool, between this small man and himself.

In the space below the picture, in black print on the slick white page, the caption reads, *Pictured from left to right: Jude Randall; David Callum; Callum's wife, Patricia.*

I trace the line from the man's fingers up his arm past his shoulder to his face. J for Jude Randall, Max, a man who likes his work. *J.R.*, the two letters penned into the ragged fibers, the ink still bound to the paper after all this time.

I flip backward, skimming the text as I go, until my eyes light on his name. 'Jude Randall testified on behalf of the government's effort to suppress publication of Callum's book. Randall, who is a former member of the Central Intelligence Agency, was in charge of American advisors in Southeast Asia. Mr. Randall cited "grave concern for national security," among other reasons. . . .'

I don't need to read further. I close the magazine and take the stack back to the desk.

'You find what you were looking for?' the librarian asks.

I nod.

The woman takes the pile from my hands, her eyes lingering on my face. 'You know,' she says, 'it's not really any of my business, but my first husband, he used to hit me sometimes. If you know what's good for you, you'll just get the heck out of there.'

'It's not that simple,' I tell her.

She smiles and shifts the magazines in her arms. 'It never is, honey.'

I stand in the front window of the bodega and look out over Eighth Street. Melosa's still in the back room, putting the finishing touches on the new Canadian me. On the sidewalk opposite the shop, a young Cuban woman pushes a baby carriage. Farther down the street

216

a boy who appears to be in his early teens leans in the doorway of a pawnshop. A man approaches him nervously. Pockets flash open and money changes hands. The nervous man slips a Baggie down the front of his jeans and scuttles away.

I look away from the window. My mind keeps replaying the slap of gunmetal across Joey's face, the muscles in his neck tightening as his head reeled back, his hand flying to protect himself, as if his body had lived such a wounding many times.

In the tent on Coney Island my grandmother's hand grasped mine through the darkness when the woman on stage bent over and her face disappeared, replaced by the jeweled hilt of the sword. In the audience, no one moved. I imagined the honed steel deep inside her supple body, the edge of the sword hovering over the tissues of her throat, the tips of the nails brushing the damp hairs in her nose. I can see now that power becomes ugly when it passes out of your body and into that of another. The real trick is to take it into yourself, to learn to wrap your skin around the stiff shafts of death.

Crossing to the counter of the bodega, I pick up the telephone. I take the scrap of paper with Wykel's number on it from my pocket, punch in the digits, and wait for him to answer.

'Hello.'

'John?'

'Yeah.'

'It's Alison Kerry.'

'Alison?'

'Listen, John, I need to know about the Hmong. Who sponsored them?'

'I'm not crazy,' he insists.

'I know you're not. I believe you.'

'Have you looked at a newspaper today?'

'No,' I tell him. He may have been right about Callum sending him the disk, but I still don't have time for his craziness. 'Who sponsored the Hmong? It's important.'

'What?'

'What was his name, John? You said the Hmong had someone who brought them over here. Did you ever find out who it was?'

'Sure, sure. I really think you should look at a paper, though. I'll bet it made the front page there, too.'

'I'll do that. What was his name?'

'Randall,' Wykel stammers. 'His name was Randall.'

'Thanks.'

'The paper, Alison –'

I hang up and call Joey. It's still early morning by his standards, and I let the phone ring and ring until he wakes up.

'Wha' do you want now?' Joey's voice is groggy with sleep.

'It's Al.'

'Oh, shit. I thought you were him. He's called twice already this morning. He keeps asking if I've heard from you.'

'What did you tell him?'

'I told him you hadn't been by here. Whatever you've got, he wants it bad.'

'Did he leave you a number?' I ask.

'No. He said he'd keep trying back.'

'Good.'

'Not good. What the fuck am I s'posed to tell him?'

'Next time he calls, let him know I'll be down in the

Keys tonight, at my father's house. I want to hand over the disk and be done with this.'

'Are you sure, Al? He's not fucking around. He knows you know what's on that disk. He'll kill you.'

'Just do this for me, okay, Joey? Just this one favor. I can take care of myself.'

'I wasn't lying last night. I want you to know that.'

'I know, Joey. And tell him to come by himself. No more hoods. I deal with him or I don't deal with anybody.'

I have one more call to make. I hang up, keeping the receiver at my ear, and rummage in my pockets for Chloe's number.

Sixteen

It's raining outside of Florida City, not the violent kind of downpour that sweeps in quickly from the sea and moves on to the Everglades but a slow all-day drizzle. Exhaustion buzzing through my body, I wheel off Highway 1 into the parking lot of the Circle K and fill my gas tank.

Inside the store, a middle-aged woman leans over the counter talking to a man in dirty jeans and a work shirt. They look up when I come in.

'It's wet out there,' I say, attempting a weak smile, heading for the coffee machine. 'Do either of you know if it's raining all the way down the Keys?'

I help myself to some coffee, pull a crumpled twenty-dollar bill from the pocket of my shorts, and lay it on the counter. The neck of the woman's tank top hangs down low over her freckled chest, revealing the red petals of a tattoo. She stares at my face, her eyes lingering on the yellowing bruises.

'I couldn't tell you what it's like past Marathon,' the man says, 'but it was pissing down there when I left. Plus it's slow going. The goddamn cops are stopping every car going in and out of the Keys.'

'They say why?' I grab a package of pretzels from a rack by the counter. 'I'll take these, and I got gas, too. I'm at the second pump,' I tell the woman.

'Nope. They've got a roadblock set up just past

Islamorada. They waved me right through. I figure whatever they were looking for, I didn't seem likely to have. It took me three hours just to get up here from Marathon.'

'Shit. Looks like it's going to be a long wet trip.' I roll my eyes.

'You just visiting?' the woman asks. She hands me my change.

'I grew up down in Key West. I'm on my way home.' I turn from the counter and head for the door. 'Thanks for the info.'

'You bet, sugar,' the man calls after me. 'Drive safe.'

After the artificial coolness of the convenience store, the air outside is dank and steamy. There's a *Miami Herald* box on the cement walkway by the door. Remembering what Wykel said about the paper, I fish for some coins, shove them into the slot, and open the lid.

I roll the paper up and stick it under my arm and dodge through the rain to the Mustang. It's still early and I have plenty of time to make it down the Keys. Wedging my cup between the seats, I unfold the *Herald*. The front page is of little interest. Another prisoner on the state's death row has lost his final plea. More scandals in Washington.

But when I open the paper to page three, I realize what Wykel was in such a hurry for me to see. I'm certain the black-and-white photo doesn't do the scene justice. Several men, all Asian, all dressed in black cotton peasant garb, stand in a field. The land beyond them is out of focus, but neat markings of agricultural divisions are visible in the distance.

The men all have tools in their hands. One leans on the handle of a shovel. One holds his hoe squarely level with his jaw. It could be a picture of bounty. Proud farmers. A good year for crops. But it is not. The men are not looking at the camera. Their gazes are directed downward, to a muddy hole where the ground has been loosened and moved away.

The hole is deep, large enough to hold the bodies, the fragments of arms and legs and skulls whose shapes are clear against the dark earth that contained them.

BODIES OF AMERICAN MIA DISCOVERED IN VIET-NAM. My eyes skim the headline and move down through the article's lead.

> Farmers in Vietnam's An Giang province made a startling discovery last week when they unearthed the bodies of some two dozen American soldiers. . . . The An Giang find comes at a time when renewed economic and political ties between the American and Vietnamese governments have aided in foster-ing cooperation in the search for and identification of MIAs. . . . Asked to comment on the mass exhuma-tion, officials on both sides say they intend to work together and that a serious investigation is planned. . . .

Callum must have known. If the bodies were uncovered last week, someone must have tipped him, someone still in the loop. Robert Ghilchrist, maybe. And then, after thirty years, some form of responsibility for those men had compelled him to act. He sent the list of names, the only information he had, to a man he knew would use it: John Wykel. I put the paper down and gun the engine, moving out of the parking lot and into the stream of traffic.

A mile or so down the highway, the sign for Card

Sound Road looms out of the rain. Slowing the Mustang, I cross over into the turning lane and off the highway, following a narrow two-lane road east across the toll bridge that spans Barnes Sound and into the mangrove forests of upper Key Largo. The rain has flooded low stretches of the road and the wheels of the Mustang hydroplane around corners. The ravages of Hurricane Andrew are still visible here. New foliage grows up around the jagged skeletons of pine trees stripped bare by the storm.

Several miles past the toll bridge the road splits, curving south to rejoin Highway 1 on lower Key Largo or north along the Intracoastal Waterway. I wheel the Mustang north, heading deeper into the mangroves, rolling my window down and letting the warm rain soak my face. Close to the outer tip of Largo, I find the road I'm looking for: two muddy ruts that jut west toward Biscayne Bay. I ease the Mustang through the mangrove hammocks and pull to a stop in front of a sagging one-story shack.

Several half-restored Harley Davidsons sit on blocks in the muddy front yard. A hammock swings from the makeshift porch. I cut the engine and climb out of the car, stretching my arms and neck as I make my way past an array of dirty, broken toys and greasy boat parts. Swarms of mosquitoes dive at my bare legs. From in back of the shack comes the sound of hammering. The rain beats quietly against the canopy of leaves, and the brackish odor of salty marsh water fills the air. I breathe deeply and let the smells of home flood my lungs.

'Charles!' I call out, crossing the yard, following the rhythmic hammering. A large Doberman pokes his head from around the corner of the shack. His ears go up and he lets out a low growl.

'Percy!' I bend down and slap my hands on my thighs. 'Come 'ere, boy.' The dog stops growling and bounds toward me. He leaps up to my chest and runs his wet tongue over my cheek. 'Hi, Percival.' I pet his long muscular back. 'C'mon, let's go find Charles.'

Around the back of the shack the thick foliage gives way to the wide blue expanse of the bay. A wooden walkway runs through the mangroves to a long dock. Charles's mammoth form is barely visible through the gray haze of the rain. He's at the far end of the dock, hunched over a large outboard motor, hammering furiously. Percy streaks across the walkway ahead of me and across the dock.

'Charles!' I call out again.

Charles stops the hammer in mid-swing and turns to the sound of my voice. The thick muscles in his upper arms glisten with rainwater and sweat.

'You trying to kill that thing,' I yell, working my way toward him, 'or just disable it?'

'Al!' Charles puts the hammer down and gives the motor a cursory kick with the toe of his boot. 'Jesus, you scared the crap out of me.'

'Sorry. I didn't see anyone at the house so I thought I'd just come on back. Where's Angela?'

'She took the kids up to her mother's in Atlanta.'

'You two fighting again?'

'Just the usual. It don't mean anything. You know us, there's always something to argue about. Shrimpin's been for shit lately. I've been thinkin' 'bout going back to the other. Of course Angela don't want me to. I know Cyrus is gonna need some help now that your father's –' Charles stops and looks down at his boots. 'Shit, Al. Let's get inside and out of this rain.'

*

'You know, it's funny him killing himself. I never figured Joe to be that kind of man. You remember when that crazy Steve shot himself out on Stock Island in that tourist's fancy car?' Charles hands me a dry towel and sits down opposite me at the scarred kitchen table. 'We were all at the Blue Ibis havin' a drink one night and that cop, Jorge Cora, walks in and says they found Steve. I'll never forget it. Your father turns to me after Cora leaves and says, "That's a fucking cowardly thing to do."'

I look past Charles to the open door of the shack. The rain is coming down harder now, and the bay is almost completely obscured. The teapot on the stove has come to a boil and a shrill whistle sounds through the kitchen. Charles gets up, opens a cabinet above the sink, and pulls out a jar of instant coffee. He pours hot water into two mugs, spoons out the dark crystals, and hands me one of the mugs as he sits back down.

'Sounds like you got some mean trouble of your own.' Charles blows at his coffee, sending dark ripples lapping against the edge of the cup. 'You don't have to tell me about it if you don't want to, but you've been all over the news the last couple days. Seems like every time I turn on the radio I hear your name.'

I run my thumb along the warm lip of my mug. 'It's probably better if you don't know the whole story, but it's not like they're saying it is. I got set up hard.'

'You look like shit, Al,' Charles says.

'Gee, thanks.' I attempt a weak smile.

'So what're you doin' back down here? The Keys are a pretty stupid place to run to, you know that. One way in, one way out. That blond hair's not gonna hide you forever. There's an awful big rap pinned to you.'

'I've got some unfinished business to take care of. You

226

know, my father and all. I'm heading to Key West.' I take a sip of my coffee, let the bitterness of it linger on my tongue. 'I've got a way off the island. It's arranged.'

Charles nods. 'So what are you doing here?'

'I need a lift.'

'Sure. We can take the truck. I've been wanting to go down and see Cyrus, anyway.'

I pull a cigarette from my crumpled pack and light it. 'Not in the truck. I want you to take me in the boat. They've got a roadblock down by Islamorada. I've got money, Charles. I'll pay you good. You can have the Mustang too, if you want it. I won't be coming back this way.'

Beads of moisture shine on the rich brown skin of Charles's neck and face. 'I'll keep the car for you, but I'm not takin' your money. You're like family, Al.'

I look around the small kitchen. Percy is curled in front of the door, licking his front paw. A striped lizard streaks along the wall above the stove. A child's picture of a shrimp boat under a bright-yellow Crayola sun hangs on the refrigerator next to a photo of Charles's two little girls.

'Angela's right,' I say. 'Keep fishing. Don't go back to work with Cyrus.'

Charles gets up and puts his mug in the sink. 'We'll take the small boat. I've got her runnin' fast. She'll make good time down the Keys. Why don't you get whatever you need from the car.'

'Thank you, Charles.' I stand up and head through the front room of the shack and out the front door.

Popping the trunk of the Mustang, I take the Winn Dixie bag and the disk and papers from the compartment under the rug where I've stowed them. I grab my duffel bag from the back seat, stuff Joey's Sig-Sauer and the other guns into it, and shove the Walther in my shorts. In the glove compartment I find the fisherman's wallet and, in the very back, the picture of my father.

'I s'pose they'll be looking for the Mustang,' Charles says.

'Yeah. I suppose so.'

'Why don't we move it around back to the shed. I can't imagine anyone'll come this way looking for you, but you never know.'

I climb into the driver's seat and follow Charles and Percy back through the mangroves to a rough little building. Charles motions for me to stop. I wait while he swings the shed doors open and then drive inside.

'You ready?' he asks, as I switch the engine off and step out into the musty darkness with my bag.

'Let's go,' I reply. I leave the keys in the ignition and close the door.

The rain is with us all the way down the Keys, shrouding the thin chain of islands, sizzling and humming against the calm water of Florida Bay. I curl up in a corner of the cabin with Percy and drift into a fitful sleep, waking occasionally to a twitch or kick from the dog's dreaming muscles. I'm vaguely aware of Charles's soft and constant singing and of our slow passage past the flank of this land that is creased into my memory like a deep scar into broken skin.

Just past Marathon I open my eyes to the underside of the Seven-Mile Bridge. The rush of traffic on Highway 1 shudders above us. The arc of the steel and concrete causeway spans out for several miles in each direction.

Daylight has waned to the fluorescent blue of dusk, and a fork of lightning rips through the sky to the north. The lights on the channel-marking buoys glow bloodred through the veil of rain.

I rub my eyes and stand up, adjusting my legs to the bucking of the hull. Charles's face glows in the cabin's dim light. 'You must be tired,' I say. 'I can take the helm for a while if you'd like a break.'

'Let me just get us through the channel here. Once we're around on the Atlantic side you can take over. You have a nice sleep?'

'Yes.'

'There are sandwiches in the cooler and a six-pack of beer. Why don't you help yourself.'

'Thanks.' I open the hatch of the cooler and pull two beer cans from their plastic rings. 'You want one?'

'Sure.'

I pop both cans and hand one to Charles. 'How many times do you think you've made this trip?'

'Shit. Hundreds. You?'

'More than I can remember.' I take a swig of beer and light a cigarette.

'You know how these islands were made?' Charles asks. We've crossed out of the channel, and Charles swings the boat to the right. Someone has lit a campfire on the beach at Bahia Honda. The flames echo across the shallow coral-ledged water.

'No.'

'Mangroves blew down from the mainland and started growing in the shallow water here. Their roots trapped coral and sediment and whatever else happened to float by.' Charles steps away from the helm and smiles. 'She's all yours.'

I take the wheel and push the throttle up. The boat gathers speed and leaps across the small waves. Water buffets the hull.

Charles sits down on the lid of the cooler and tilts his beer to his lips. 'It seems fitting, the Keys being made in that kind of aimless way. Angela likes to say the Keys are like the bottom of a cereal box, the place where all the broken bits collect. Everyone I know is kind of broken, runnin' from somethin'. I remember when I first came down here, twenty years ago, I'd ask people where they were from, their history. I was tryin' to be polite more than anything. You know, small talk. But no one here talks about the past. It's like you cross over the bridge onto Largo and all the old ghosts dissolve.'

I look to my right, to the passing lights of Big Pine Key, the cars snaking over the causeway. 'Charles,' I ask, finishing off my beer, 'what makes someone do such a thing, take his own life?'

'I don't know, Al. I s'pose for me it would be guilt, maybe somethin' happening to the girls or Angela, maybe some kind of betrayal.'

We both fall silent. The wind whistles across the front glass of the cabin. How many years would it take to make one tiny chunk of land? Thousands, maybe millions. I can't even begin to grasp the slow, patient effort of creation, the crooked fingers of the mangroves gathering the tiny coral creatures, clutching the brittle shells of the dead. Everything in the Keys is formed by plunder – even the house I grew up in, built from the timbers of a wrecked ship, a schooner lured to the jagged reef by a phony beacon.

I try to imagine the first crude islands, the small ripples in the coral that time has magnified. A snail shell stuck in the silt would be a wide fist of land now. What was once a barely visible wrinkle would be a lagoon or a bay.

Charles is wrong. Ghosts don't dissolve. Layers of time and great effort bury them, but their original forms remain. They may be somewhat misshapen, weathered or scarred by currents or storms or human passage. But they remain and determine the nature and shape of everything that struggles to grow around them. They persist, like the hungry cells of cancer that sifted through my mother's body and, in some small way, into each of ours. Like a cold, shivering little man from the PIC. Or an entire village, dead. Some kind of betrayal.

The Keys fall back behind me for the last time: Ramrod, Big Torch, Sugarloaf. I hoard the familiarity of name and place. I won't be coming back here.

Seventeen

Charles has taken the helm again for the last few miles into Key West. I look out the starboard windows of the cabin at the orange lights of Truman Annex. Neatly ordered rows of navy housing drift by, streets aglimmer with bright rain. The road to the beach at Fort Zachary Taylor runs straight through the base. Fort Taylor was a favorite childhood destination, and it was always with a sense of intrigue that we pedaled our rusty bubble-tired bikes through the maze of guardhouses and razor wire on our Saturday-afternoon swimming forays. Of course I now know there were no national secrets we could have seen here. The real top-secret stuff is all out at the deepwater base on the north-eastern side of the island, where they house submarines and ships the size of toppled skyscrapers. The piece of land the deepwater base occupies is always conspicuously missing from tourist maps.

Charles noses the boat around the far western tip of the island, past the base and the beach and the fancy hotels by Mallory Square. In the early days of the island, when wreckers made their living from the spoils of ships dashed against the reef, auctions were held on the pier. Survivors watched, sobbing, as their plundered possessions were parceled off and sold to the highest bidder. Now the beaches of the resorts around the pier echo with calypso music and steel drums.

Charles nudges the engine down close to idle and we drift into the marina behind the Blue Ibis. The rain casts spreading circles across the still water, like thousands of fish surfacing to feed. As we maneuver into a slip close to the bar, the side of the boat creaks against the rubber bumpers. Charles cuts the engine and I leap onto the dock to tie the bow line.

Percy nervously paces the deck, his rigid nose sniffing foreign smells. Charles finds my bag and hands it over to me. 'Is this all you have?'

I nod.

He crosses back to the cabin and pulls two Milk-Bones out of a drawer. 'You stay here, Percy,' he says gently. He tosses the two biscuits to the dog and climbs over the side of the boat and onto the dock. 'Stay!' He points his finger down at the deck of the boat. Percy doesn't move.

'So, the name Percy,' I ask. 'Is that like Percival of the Holy Grail?' Our footsteps sound on the hollow dock as we head toward the bar.

'What?' Charles stares at me incredulously. 'It's like Percy. As in Sledge.'

The walls of the front of the Blue Ibis come only to waist level. Rough posts support the roof over the bar. Through the sheets of water that pour off the long eaves I can see the crowd of drinkers gathered inside. Hank Williams blares from the jukebox and out into the wet night. Cyrus's boat sits tight up against the dock, snuffling at the wet wood. Charles and I skirt around to the rear of the building, past the dark windows of the office and down the back alley.

A trail of light leaks from the kitchen, falling across the slumped shapes of garbage cans. Salvador, the dish-washer, squats on a milk carton in the doorway, smoking

234

a cigarette. He looks up through the rain at Charles and me, searching my face, finding the familiar lines and angles beneath the tangle of bleached hair.

'*Hola!* Allie!' he says finally, jumping from the milk carton.

'Hey.'

'*Mira!*' he calls out over his shoulder into the kitchen. 'José, look! It's Allie.'

'Do you know Charles?' I ask.

'No.' Salvador shakes his head.

'He's a friend of Cyrus and my father,' I say, motioning to Charles.

The screen door opens and José steps out into the alley. His right hand is wrapped around the handle of a long knife. 'Allie! Charles!' He holds the door and motions for us to step inside. Age has shrunk him. He shuffles in behind us like a hermit crab, his muscles wiry on his slight frame.

The floor of the kitchen is covered with blood. The limp body of a shark, eight feet long, lies on the terracotta tiles.

'I caught him just a few hours ago.' José grins triumphantly. 'You know you must clean them immediately or their flesh will be poisoned.'

The shark's belly is slit wide open and its mammoth head has been severed from its body. Its black eyes are fixed on a plastic bucket heaped with glistening entrails.

'José, is Cyrus here?' I ask. The heat in the small kitchen is smothering, and the rich odor of blood is beginning to make me sick.

'No,' Salvador says. 'He left this afternoon. He was very upset.'

'Any idea where he went?'

235

'He didn't say.'

'He's not at home. I called him just now to tell him about the shark. I thought we would make a feast. See?' José gestures to a large saucepan of garlicky citrus sauce that's cooling on the stove. 'I made a fresh batch of *mojo*. But he wasn't there.'

Salvador cracks the screen door and flicks the butt of his cigarette into the alley.

'Allie, we are all so sad about your father,' José says quietly.

'Were you here the night it happened?' I ask.

'I was here earlier. But we had gone home. He must have stayed very late. I'm sorry.'

'I have to go find Cyrus,' I say. My eyes are fixed on the scarlet stomach cavity of the shark and José's blood-spattered tennis shoes beside it. I don't want to talk about my father.

'Try the Schooner Wharf,' Salvador suggests. 'He's been going there lately to drink.'

'And the three of you will come back later for shark,' José insists.

I turn my face from the corpse to José and Salvador. 'It's very important that you don't tell anyone you saw me.'

'Sure, Allie. Anything you say.' Salvador nods.

José squats down over the body of the dead shark. He sinks the sharp blade of the knife into the rough gray skin, cleaving the red flesh. 'Of course. I never saw you,' he says.

'Let's go this way,' I say to Charles, motioning to the front of the kitchen.

We skirt past the fryers and stoves to the office. The round windows in the swinging doors that lead into the bar show several couples scattered across the dance floor. I open the office door and step inside. Light from the marina streams in the window and falls on the desk, illuminating unruly piles of papers and the square body of the computer that Cyrus uses to do the books. I make my way through the semidarkness to the desk and set my bag down. Charles flicks the overhead lamp on and yellow light fills the room.

'This is where Cyrus found him,' I say, running my hand along the high back of the caned chair behind the desk. There would, I suppose, have been blood. Maybe even pink bits of brain or portions of ear or skull. Someone would have come, Cyrus or José, with a wet cloth and a bucket to clean it all away. Long after he was dead they would have erased these last intimate fragments of him. They would have cleaned his lip prints from the glass he was drinking out of. They would have rubbed the rustlike stains from the floor and the walls. Still, there would be strands of graying hair in the seams of the floor, sloughings of skin in the dust that now coats the window-sill.

'Al.' Charles comes toward me. The neck of his T-shirt is split open, and I put my forehead on the warm skin at the base of his neck. 'There's nothing any of us could have done.' Charles's voice reverberates through the hollows of his lungs and chest. 'You know that, right?'

'Yeah.' I whisper the words against the dark ridge of his collarbone, but I'm not convinced.

I step away, lean down, and open my bag, finding my ankle holster and the Beretta, strapping the gun to my leg. I change into a clean pair of jeans, pull my T-shirt up around my neck, fit my shoulder holster on, and shove the nose of the forty-five down into it.

'I want you to have this now. No arguments.' Pulling the Winn Dixie bag from the duffel, I count out five thousand dollars and hold the money out to Charles.

'I told you no money.' He thrusts his hands into the pockets of his jeans.

'I have plenty of money here. If you don't take it now I'll leave it with Cyrus and he'll make you take it. You helped me out, Charles.' I force the bills into Charles's hands, then shove the disk, the papers, and the rest of the money in the bar safe. The fisherman's wallet tumbles out of the duffel and I stick it in my back pocket. 'Now, let's go find Cyrus,' I say, pulling the Browning from the duffel, handing it to Charles.

Though the rain is still falling steadily, the Schooner Wharf is packed. Plastic skirts have been rolled down over the open walls to keep the water out. Charles and I push through the steamy crowd to the bar. A reggae band is playing in the back room, and the heavy bass beat of 'No Woman No Cry' filters out to us over the buzz of conversation. Cyrus is nowhere to be found but I recognize Douglas, a short, speedy little Englishman who cleans the Blue Ibis, teetering on a bar stool. Charles and I nudge up beside him.

'Douglas.' I put my hand on his shoulder, and he turns his bleary face to me.

'Allie?' he asks, squinting through the filter of inebriation.

'Yeah. How you doing, Douglas?'

'Not good, Al.' Douglas fiddles with a matchbook, ripping the thin cardboard sticks away from the cover. Even when he's stone drunk, Douglas is still nervous. 'You got anything on you? Just one bump. I ran out an hour ago. Just a little something to keep me going. Speed, even.'

'Sorry, man. I've got nothing. You know I don't touch the shit anymore.' My gums tense at the thought of cocaine. 'We're looking for Cyrus. You seen him?'

Douglas shakes his head and lifts his finger, signaling the bartender for another drink.

'Hey, Charles. Hey, Al. Sorry about your old man.' The bartender, Ken, comes over. He ignores Douglas and offers me his hand across the counter.

'Thanks,' I say.

'I guess you're in some pretty deep shit. You're a real local celebrity on the Miami news. I didn't expect to see you down here. The island's crawling with cops.' Ken nods at Charles. 'Long time no see, man.'

Ken has worked here since I was a little girl, and he knows everyone in the islands. He's wearing his customary Hawaiian shirt. 'What can I do for you, Al?' he asks. The hula girls on his lapels dance when he speaks.

'We're looking for Cyrus,' Charles tells him.

'He was in here a couple of hours ago.' Ken reaches into the cooler behind the bar, pulls out a bottle of Budweiser, and puts it down on the counter in front of Douglas.

Douglas takes a swig and slams the bottle back down. He grabs the sleeve of my T-shirt, steadying himself. 'I'm sorry about your dad. I would've stayed, you know. I was in to pick up my check and I could see there was cleaning to do.' I wrench Douglas's fingers from the fabric of my shirt.

Ken shoots a look of disgust across the bar. Douglas mutters something under his breath. He stands up from the stool and puts his mouth right up near my face, wheezing the stench of old liquor and tobacco.

239

'I would've stayed,' he whispers urgently, as if he's looking for forgiveness.

'So why didn't you?' I ask. I'm tired and, more than anything, just want Douglas to go away.

'Cyrus, he told me to take the night off.' Douglas grips the bar for balance. 'I don't feel good,' he murmurs. And before I've had a chance to absorb what he's said he shoves off into the crowd and weaves toward the men's room.

'Heads up, Al.' Ken taps my arm and nods toward the front entrance. Three bicycle cops have just pulled up outside and are moving through the crowd toward us.

'Motherfucker.' Charles grabs my sleeve and pushes me in front of him toward the back door, letting the crowd swallow us. I reach up inside my T-shirt and rest my fingers on the handle of the forty-five. The door looms before us and I put my hand on the wooden handle and pull. Through the rain I see the marina and the tall masts of the old pirate ship that belongs to the bar.

'Which way?' Charles asks.

'Number One Saloon.' The door closes behind us and we start down the side of the bar. I have to find Cyrus.

'Allie, stop!' A voice calls from the darkness behind us. I grab the Walther and turn. Charles freezes. The figure of one of the bike cops emerges from the wet shadows.

'Jesus. Put the gun down. It's me, Al. It's Pete.'

'Pete McCarthy?' I lower the Walther. Pete took me to the senior prom. He comes from a family of old bootleggers and his father still runs dope up to the mainland. His career choice made him the shame of the family, until they figured out what a help having a relative in law enforcement can be.

'Yeah. Hi, Charles.'

'Hi, Pete,' Charles says.

'Look, Al. I don't see you here, okay? But you need to get off the island. Everyone's looking for you.'

'I didn't kill those people, Pete. It was a setup.'

'I don't really care, Al. Just get out of here.' The rain is streaming off Pete's helmet and down onto his jacket. 'I'm sorry about your dad. The whole island is.' He turns and disappears back into the bar.

'Maybe it's better if you don't come with me,' I say to Charles.

'Probably. But I'm coming anyway.'

I put the Walther in my jeans and we start down the back streets that conceal the Schooner Wharf from the tourists.

A festive wedding party has just arrived at the front door of the Number One Saloon as Charles and I round the corner from Duval Street and step into the alley that houses the bar. Tall men in gaudy pink bridesmaid's dresses dash from a white limousine, holding the ruffled hems of their skirts off the wet cobblestones. A short man in a black tuxedo greets each bridesmaid at the door with coos of, 'Don't you look lo-o-ovely, dahling!' or 'Fabulous wig!' The Number One Saloon has always been the official drag queen bar of Key West, host to the truly happening all-male weddings on the island. The bar is also a haven for locals looking to get away from the ever-pervasive tourist crowd. Cyrus and my father and I came here often.

Somewhat underdressed, Charles and I follow the group inside. The doorman raises his eyebrows as we pass. A large portion of the saloon has been taken over by the wedding. A lanky black drag queen in tall white heels and a hoop-skirted satin wedding gown lounges on a banquette in one corner, surrounded by admirers. Spanish dance music blares over the dance floor. I spot Cyrus at the bar, engulfed in a sea of pink taffeta.

'Isn't it just wonderful?' A large black man in a flowing baby-blue chiffon gown approaches us. He has a full beard, and a spray of miniature blue roses has been pinned in his hair. 'Do have some champagne,' he says, offering us two glasses. 'I'm the mother of the bride.'

'Congratulations,' Charles says, taking a glass. The man whirls off into the crowd. We elbow our way to the bar and squeeze in next to Cyrus.

'Al! Thank God you're okay. How'd you get down here?'

'He brought me down in the boat,' I explain, nodding toward Charles. 'They've got Highway One blocked off up by Islamorada.'

Cyrus slides off his bar stool and moves toward me with his arms spread open.

'Don't touch me,' I say.

'What's wrong?'

'How was your fishing trip to the Tortugas?' I ask. 'You never told me. Did you get a good haul?'

Cyrus turns away from me and back to the bar. 'Shit, Al,' he says. 'What kind of a question is that? You think I don't feel guilty enough about being gone that night?' He taps on the counter, signaling the bartender. 'Three Johnnie Walkers, please.'

'Why'd you lie to me?'

Cyrus passes a shot glass to Charles and then hands one to me.

'Drink up,' he says.

I down the shot and turn to Charles. 'I think you'd

242

'better head back up the Keys,' I tell him, 'put a little distance between you and me.'

'I'm not leaving till I know you have a way off the island,' Charles insists. 'I can get you out of the country, Al. The boat won't make it too far, but we can at least get you to the Bahamas.'

'I'll be fine,' I say. 'Everything's arranged.'

'If you need anything –'

'I know. Thank you.'

'I'll be in touch.' Charles rests his hand on Cyrus's shoulder, then turns and lumbers off through the crowd.

'After you left SEALs training in San Diego, where did you all go?' I slam the empty shot glass down on the bar in front of Cyrus.

'I went with Victor Platoon to Soc Trang. Just opposite Dung Island on the Bassac. Darwin was there too, but just for a while. Then she went to Chau Doc. We left your father in Saigon. I didn't hear any news of him till seven or eight months after we were in-country. He was working with a PRU out of Khanh Hoa province.'

'And before Khanh Hoa?'

Cyrus doesn't reply. He waves to the bartender. 'Two more when you get a sec'.'

I shake my head. 'Not for me. Where was he before Khanh Hoa?' I ask again.

The bartender sets Cyrus's whiskey down. 'Where are you going from here?' Cyrus asks. 'You can't stay in the Keys.'

'He was in Chau Doc. Chloe told me.'

Cyrus doesn't say anything. He takes a sip of the whiskey and sets the glass down slowly. A coating of alcohol lingers on the beveled surface.

'You lied to me.' My face is flushed with anger, and my

243

voice rises to compete with the music. 'You told Randall how to find me at Mark's. You were the only one who knew I was there. And you told Douglas not to come in to work the night my father died.' I grab Cyrus's collar and pull his face close to mine. 'Don't give me this "I feel bad enough" bullshit,' I say. 'Did you kill him yourself or did you just clear out so Randall could have some space?'

I let go of his shirt and Cyrus reels backward, catching himself on the bar.

'Let me explain, Al.'

'I trusted you. My father trusted you.' I push off through the crowd and out the door, knocking people aside as I go.

When I hit the alley I break into a run, but Cyrus is right behind me, and he grabs my wrist and won't let go.

'Get your hands off me!' I yell.

'There were things in your father's life, Al.' Cyrus's grip is strong, his face contorted. He shakes his head. 'You have to understand. He never wanted you to know about Chau Doc. He made me promise.'

'Bullshit.' Swinging my free hand up under my shirt, I unholster the forty-five. 'Tell me what happened.' I click the safety off and bring the gun up level with Cyrus's face.

'I didn't kill him. I never would have left if I had known what would happen. I loved him, Al.'

'What happened at the An Giang PIC? They dug up the bodies. How'd those men go MIA?'

Cyrus stares at me, his face streaming with rainwater. 'It was right after the killings at My Lai,' he begins. 'The PIC was way out there. The end of the line. But rumors started filtering back to Saigon that the guys on the base were losing it.'

'What do you mean?'

'Like they haul these villagers in 'cause their files got red-flagged as sympathetic to the Vietcong. They're supposed to question these guys, make them a little uncomfortable, maybe persuade them to talk or even switch sides.'

'And?'

'And they were a little too zealous. Word gets out the soldiers who man the PIC are doing things like dropping cargo nets of Vietnamese villagers off helicopters, seeing how far up you have to take them before they talk. It was gruesome, Al. It was worse than gruesome.'

'I don't understand,' I say.

'After the hearings at My Lai, the American government was in a real bad position. Now they've got some soldiers on a backwater jungle base who are terrorizing the locals. The last thing the war effort needed was another hearing, so they just went out there real quietly and shut the whole thing down.'

Cyrus looses his grasp on my wrist.

'Two dozen of our own men, Al. We killed them.'

'And my father?'

'He was there.'

'You're lying,' I say, but even as the words slip across my tongue, I know Cyrus is telling the truth. Lowering the forty-five, I slip it back into my holster and turn to head out of the alley. I've heard enough.

'Please, Al. Let me explain.' Cyrus's voice is weak over the drumming of the rain.

'Too late,' I say, looking back over my shoulder. 'Goodbye, Cyrus.'

The windows of our house on Petronia Street are dark. I step onto the front porch and sit down and light a cigarette. The iron bench in the front garden where my father sat all those years ago is still in its place. I tilt my head to the second-story balcony. I'm no good at judging distance. High overhead, the leaves of the royal palm nuzzle each other.

How many feet was he from me? Twenty, maybe. I count the seconds it would have required to cross through my bedroom and down the dark hallway. Ten, fifteen. Twenty-five would have seen me down the stairs, and thirty would have put me in the garden with him, my small arms wrapped around his neck. Yet I stayed up there.

I stand up, flick my cigarette into the rain, and slip my key into the lock on the front door. The bolt clicks and I push the door open and step into the foyer. Rain spatters against the tin roof. I walk down the hallway to the kitchen, find a flashlight in the drawer next to the sink, cross back through the hallway, and climb the stairs.

Rain reflects from the windows onto the walls, onto the timber that once crossed the sea. At the top of the stairs I flick the flashlight on and let the beam play out across the wood floor, searching instinctively for the flickering tail of a scorpion. Termites swarm into a crack in the baseboard. I pass the door to my father's bedroom, the upstairs bathroom, my old room.

At the end of the hallway, opposite the spare bedroom, a narrow door leads up to the cramped attic. Squeezing into the passage, I work my way upward. I'm slick with rain and sweat, and damp strands of hair cling to my face. The light from my hand catches the rough roof beams, and the rain is deafening as I emerge from the passageway and scan the attic. A small window under the back peak looks out over the yard. Ducking to avoid the slope of the roof, I head to the very far corner. December 1969, while webs of tissue disappeared miraculously into my fingers, while I lay curled listening to the watery heartbeat of a woman I'll never know, my father was in Chau Doc.

I find the box I'm looking for and open the lid. From amid the stacks of papers and photographs, my father's dog tags gleam. I loop my fingers through the chain, testing the weight of the metal. Beneath the tags is a stack of letters. Training the beam of light on the creased papers, I flip through the pages of my mother's handwriting until the date April 23, 1970, jumps out at me.

'Today we had a daughter,' the letter begins. It must have been raining when he read this. Some of the ink letters are smeared: the *L* in Love, the *A* in Alison. It was raining, like it's raining tonight. He sat in a tent or under a tree somewhere in the jungle and read that he was a father.

I dig farther into the box, flipping through a jumble of photographs, turning each picture over to read the inscription. *Cyrus and Darwin in Soc Trang. With Cyrus on leave in Hawaii. The PRU in Khanh Hoa.* Everyone is smiling absurdly, their cheeks shining with camouflage paint. The very last picture is of my father and an Asian man. The man comes only to my father's neck, and my father has his arm hooked over the man's shoulder. They are dirty and tired. Both are wearing sandals and what look like black pajamas. The flashlight is dimming, and I slap my palm against it. The beam springs back to life. I turn the picture over and read the faded scrawl. *With Willie Phao, point man, Chau Doc PRU.*

So Willie had been there too. And that day at his house, on the dust-webbed porch, it wasn't fear, or anything I said, but my last name that had caused him to open the door to me.

Setting the photograph aside, I run the beam along the bottom of the box. Colors leap out, the body of a bird, curling feathers, small eyes etched onto the back of a playing card. I put my fingernail under one edge of the card, flip it over, and hold it up into the light. The inverted black heart of the ace of spades. In the white border, blurred by sweat and humidity, is a hand-penned picture of an arm, and in the curled fist an arching sword.

I reach into my pocket for the fisherman's wallet and slip the creased card from the leather, laying the two cards together, matching the arms, the blades of the swords, the smudged black ink. Some kind of betrayal.

I start at the bottom of my father's house and work my way up through the stations of his daily life, putting the flashlight back in the kitchen drawer, navigating by touch, and by shadow and crest of light. Slipping my tennis shoes off, I press the soles of my feet into the nubbed linoleum in the kitchen, let my toes find the paths worn across the floor, the trails from sink to cupboard, from doorway to refrigerator. I run my fingers along the patterns of frequently touched surfaces, the ribbed grains in the table, the grooves dug in the counters from slicing bread or onions.

In the living room I page through magazines, old newspapers, aware of the oil from his hands that still coats the tables. I open and close the curtains, press my palms against the swollen rings in the coffee table where condensation from cold drinks leaked into the wood, trace the threadbare arms of the couch, its crooked back, the angular tips of leaves and swirls of flowers etched into

248

the upholstery. On the hall table are cold mounds of spare keys, fallen stacks of unopened mail.

This, I think, is the mystery and the miracle of war. It has little to do with physical survival, with the luck and timing that lets a foot miss a trip wire on the path, lets a body move back two inches from the line of a bullet. Such fabulously close proximity to death may keep one awake some nights, may leave one sweating in wonderment, but it is not important. The mystery has everything to do with the return. The miracle is that we learn again to live among others, to live with ourselves.

And so my father and Cyrus came home to live in their wide silences. They celebrated birthdays. They made love to women. They lost people in the way that all of us lose people: sickness, old age. My father sat on the edge of my bed each night and brushed my hair out in a dark fan on the pillow. He smoothed the flowered sheets and tucked them under my chin. Cyrus sewed patches on the ragged hands and feet of my stuffed bears and lions. On Sunday mornings he came over early and made French toast and fluffy mountains of grits and fried eggs that were crisp around the edges.

And I never even imagined what things they might have done. I remember reading a few years ago a story in the newspaper about a man in South Africa who had tortured people during apartheid. He covered the heads of his victims with a burlap sack and poured cold salt water over them until they choked and gagged and eventually threw up on themselves or suffocated. He worked standard office hours, nine to five, and at the end of the day he would scrub clean his hands and roll the sleeves of his starched work shirt back down around his wrists and go home to his wife and two children.

Did they marvel at me? Did my father not stand before me, my scrawny child body emerging flushed from the shower, my wet hair dripping onto the bathroom tiles, and wonder at the clean charm of it all? And was it not constantly somehow there between us, in nightmares, in the unspoken spaces? It seems to me now that I always knew, that knowing tainted us all.

I work through the events of the last week, worrying them like an open sore. It began simply, when a farmer thrust his spade into the mud of the delta and felt the metal tool strike against bone. Who would have been notified? A handful of people in both governments: those involved in the search for missing Americans; someone in the CIA, Robert Ghilchrist, the fisherman, David Callum's security chief in Vietnam. Perhaps loyalty compelled him to tell Callum, perhaps fear, perhaps something I will never understand.

I find my father's bed by touch, easing my hands up the banister that lines the stairwell, along the cracked walls of the hallway, down the doorframe, through the vacant darkness of his room. He has left the bed unmade. It's a tangle of twisted sheets and pillows still concave from the weight of his head. I lie down and curl my knees up into my chest.

'We killed our own men,' Cyrus had said. I clear my brain and let the questions and answers sort themselves out into two neat piles. Jude Randall's signature was on the order, but the killings in Chau Doc are too far in the past to matter much today. The government protects itself and its own; Randall would know that. No, something greater is at stake here.

Randall had met Willie Phao in Chau Doc, had cut himself in on the merchandise coming off Willie's father's farm. Then when the war ended he brought Willie and the others over and started his own business in the States. But what about Cyrus? Randall ran the PRU advisors in Vietnam. They would have known each other from the war. But why betray my father now?

Easy money. It all goes back to that.

The butt of the forty-five cuts into the skin below my breast, and the holster chafes at my back. Tomorrow there will be rawness there, pink indentations in the flesh, a crease at the base of my spine from the Walther, a red welt around my ankle where I've lashed the long silenced body of the Beretta. My father had left the window open and rain splashes over the sill, loosening the white paint, warping the wood. I press my face into the cotton covers and breathe the sweaty odor of his last sleep.

It doesn't matter who pulled the trigger: Cyrus, Jude Randall, or someone he sent; some part of my father the war created. Whoever it was, my father knew him well.

I listen to the steady pulse of the rain, to the blood battering my veins. He knows where I am. All I can do now is wait.

Eighteen

Sometime in the early hours of the morning the rain stops. I lie face up in the bed, my body rigid, my ears alert to anything foreign. Just about the time I've resigned myself to the possibility that he won't come, I hear him. Snapping my eyes open, I scramble up from the tangled covers. The house creaks around me. Final heavy pearls of rain roll off green fronds, shudder against the pressed tin roof. Somewhere in the house below a screen door sighs open. Feet stutter across floorboards, searching. I kneel in the knot of sheets and slide the Walther from the back of my jeans.

It was the deep of night when they left Chau Doc. They followed a small river north across the border. How many were they? A dozen, at least. One of them for each two men to be killed. The foreign voice of the jungle chattered around them, the screeching of monkeys, the singing of insects. The Hmong rarely spoke, and when they did it was in a language my father couldn't understand, their words clipped and nasal.

Sweat rolls off my forehead and I release one hand from the Walther and wipe my eyes. The feet probe the house with practiced quiet. A heel scuds across the rug in the living room. I click the safety off.

Willie Phao, the point man, took the lead. He combed the air for invisible wires. He stepped carefully over each root and fallen branch, listening for anomalous snaps, feeling the slightest pressure on his calves or the balls of his feet. They slid from a dike into the muck of a rice paddy. Mud sucked at their ankles.

The loose board on the third step of the stairway squeaks. Fabric rustles against the wall. I slow my breathing and try to block out the rush of blood against my skull.

Total pacification, my father thought, remembering Callum's orders. Razor wire hung like delicate lace between the towers of the base. Searchlights played out, glimmered across the marsh. They sank deeper into the reeds, let their bodies float down through the darkness, let the weight of their heads roll up, let their lips hover just above the surface.

Tensing my thighs, I dig my knees into the mattress, lock my elbows up in front of my chest.

They came around through the airstrips, skirting the mined fields, the memorized placements of each explosive charge. They took the towers first. They crept up the rough rungs and slid knives across the throats of the guards inside, one hand clamped over each mouth, death cries muffled against palms.

A body stirs the air in the hallway, whispers closer. I unfold my knees from under me, slip off the side of the bed, ease my bare feet across the floor, and lean my shoulder against the wall next to the door. Holding my breath, I let the pads of my fingers tug at the trigger. A dim shape materializes in the doorway, the outline of a gun, a curled hand, the length of an arm. I sight down my arms, raise the Walther slightly, wait for the shadowed head to appear.

My father stayed below in the deserted yard. He

watched the searchlights go blank, the figures creep downward. He took his knife from its sheath, heard the steel whistling against the leather housing. He crept into the barracks, moved down through the rows of canvas cots, dealing a card at each bunk. Bodies stirred in sleep. A snorer stuttered, breathed, snored again. Green faces turned below mosquito netting.

Waves of anger and fear roll through my body, and I lock my thumbs tightly over each other. From the doorway comes the whine of slow exhalation. The man blinks once, slowly, and turns toward me, the white crescents of his eyes disappearing until he is almost invisible. His gun is level with my face, and the dim smear of his mouth curves up into a tight smile.

'Alison.' He says my name carefully, slowly laying out the three clear syllables into the half darkness between us. 'Did you really think I'd come alone?'

There's a dull pop of silenced gunfire from the hallway. The wall next to my shoulder explodes and the heavy shipbuilding timber splinters into jagged shards. I squeeze the trigger once and the Walther jumps and snaps. A sudden flash illuminates the room around me, the unmade bed, the open window, the empty doorway. I'm too late. Already Max – Randall – has slipped back into the murky maze of the house.

I grip the Walther, holding it out in front of my chest, and skirt around the doorframe, scanning the empty hallway, letting my eyes readjust to the darkness. A half-moon skimmed across the rice paddies, crept, broken, through the palm trees. Or maybe there was no moon, no soldier snoring, nothing growing in the marsh. The only sound in the camp was the clap of rain, the gush of water through the gutters. There was the dull thwack of knife into flesh, the snapping of neck bones, the eyes rolling inward. Some things I will never know for certain. I will always guess at the permutations of heat and light, the angle of precipitation, the path through the jungle.

But my father was there. Willie Phao was there. And David Callum was there, if not in Chau Doc then in a dusty little room in Saigon, watching the hands on his watch tick past 0300 hours and on toward morning.

How many tonight, I wonder? There could be a dozen of them waiting in the garden, crouching like specters in the smooth brown folds of the giant banyan tree, faces pressed behind the rippled fans of banana leaves. Sliding the Walther into the cradle of the small of my back, I ease my pant leg up over the silenced Beretta. I've fired one loud shot already. If I fire again I don't want to give myself away.

I push off the doorframe and head down the hallway toward the back of the house, toward the two other rooms on the second floor. My eyes are stinging and I blink back a salty trickle of sweat, trying to keep my vision clear. I stop at the door to my bedroom and scan the far walls with the Beretta. Nothing. My bare toes curl against the thin pine slats of the floor.

I move on to the spare room, sweeping my body in slow, full pirouettes, trying to cover myself from all directions. They could come from anywhere, the stairs to the attic, the guest-room door, the stairs from the first floor. Motherfuckers. I move my lips inaudibly, cursing to myself. And then I hear it. Just a muted shudder of movement above me, not much noisier than a tree rat or a cat leaping across the roof might be, but distinctly, haltingly human. I turn toward the attic stairs, forgetting the blank door to the spare room just a few steps away.

Two hands grip my chest from behind and I feel the rush of my breath leaving my lungs as my face careens toward the floor. I can sense the weight and build of the body above me. It's not Randall but someone taller and leaner. The man's grasp loosens for a split second as our bodies take the jar of the impact, and I jerk my right elbow forward and bring it up hard into the sharp ridge of the man's collarbone. He heaves upward and I roll over onto my back, fumbling with my right hand, trying to hook my finger around the trigger of the Beretta.

'You bitch,' the man's voice rasps out of the darkness. He slams his fist down across the left side of my face, whipping my head to the side, disorienting me. There's a sharp click above me and I recognize the slick, mechanical sound of a safety uncatching. I find the cool crescent of the Beretta's trigger with the tip of my index finger and squeeze. The man reels backward, his weight lifting from my legs. His left hand flies to his right shoulder. His gun skims across the floor, hits the baseboard with a metallic smack. 'Fucking bitch,' he says again. I push myself up off the floor and sight into the shadows, searching for a target. He's crawling for the open door of my bedroom and I scan the length of his body, aiming for the top of his shoulder.

'How many?' I whisper, taking two steps toward him, clamping the heel of my foot down on his good hand. I press the barrel of the Beretta against the cotton fabric of his shirt. 'The way it is now, you'll live. Don't make me shoot you a second time,' I tell him. 'How many are you?'

He wiggles his hand under my foot and I slam the Beretta down across his wounded shoulder. His body shudders with pain. I put my face down close to his face.

'I'm listening,' I say.

'Two more outside.' He chokes the words out. His breathing is labored.

'Where's Randall?' I murmur.

He tilts his head up to the ceiling, to the floor of the attic.

'Thank you.' I release his hand and smack him hard with the gun one more time, aiming for the base of his skull. His knees buckle and his weight collapses forward.

Leaning my back against the wall, I catch my breath and try to assemble some kind of plan. Two outside and Randall somewhere above. There's no point in even trying to take the attic stairs. I'd be trapped in the narrow passage like a rat in a maze, dead before I made it halfway. I close my eyes and make a mental map of the house and yard. Two men outside probably means one in the front and one by the back door. I could easily get out one of the downstairs windows, but it probably wouldn't do me much good. The back garden is surrounded by a high whitewashed fence that runs the length of the house. If I did get out a window, I'd be corralled in the yard, with my only ways out through the front and back gates. The fence is taller than I am by several feet, and my body would be an easy target against the white wood if I tried to scale it.

Opening my eyes, I blink away a fresh trickle of sweat. Through the door to my old room I can see the window that looks out over the garden. The sky has lightened a shade as sunrise nears. I creep back down the hall and into my father's bedroom, heading straight for the open window, slipping the Beretta into my jeans, pressing my hands against the wet wood of the sill, ducking my head into my chest as I crawl outside. My toes grip the pressed tin and curl over the pattern of ridges stamped into the metal.

Steadying myself on the window's dormer, I look up. I'm on the lower tier of the roof and the slope is gentle here. About ten feet above me is the roof's gable, splitting sharply upward. I start climbing, groping my way with my hands and feet. The tin is slick from the rain and humidity, and I have to move carefully to keep myself from sliding. When I feel the tin seam and the abrupt shift in the grade, I stop. There are two windows in the attic, one on each end of the sharp peak. I rise up, lean my back against the gable, and shimmy toward the back of the house, away from the street.

This far up I can look across the tin sea of conch-house roofs all the way to the inky Gulf. A lumbering cruise ship is docked at Mallory Pier. A festive strand of white lights twinkles across its deck. Below me, to the north, is the treeless rectangle of the old cemetery. The La Concha hotel and the twin towers of the Spanish-style cathedral loom behind me on Duval Street.

I reach the end of the gable, redraw the Beretta, and kneel down, easing carefully onto my stomach, crawling on my elbows toward the attic window. At first I don't see him. The attic is dark through the watery glass. Then slowly the figure of the man resolves itself. He's crouched low and unmoving with his back to me. He brings his right hand up to his head, brushing loose hair back from his face, and I see the outline of a gun, the sleek barrel, the blunt handle nestled in his fingers.

My plan, which has come to seem more insane up here on the roof than it did in the adrenaline-driven panic of the house, is to slide the attic window open and surprise Randall, getting off a few rounds, I hope, before he has time to collect himself. I put the Beretta down next to my stomach, wedging the handle against a ridge in the sloping tin, balancing the weight of my body on my toes. I raise my hands, press my fingers against the weathered sash, and start gently pushing the window open.

All I need is a few inches through which I can sight a clean shot. I work slowly, keeping my eye on Randall, knowing the slightest squeal of wood, the barest creak, will give me away. The window moves about half an inch and sticks. Lowering my hands, I rest them on the peeling trim around the window and press my lips into the sloping tin, easing the burden of my weight from my toes. Somewhere across the island a siren shrieks. A car passes on the street in front of the house, its tires sizzling on the wet pavement. The island has moved closer to daylight. Out of the corner of my eye I can just make out the first ocher welts of dawn. I take two deep breaths and raise my hands again to the sash.

Then, suddenly, there's a heavy thump and a loud scrambling on the gable above me. Just a rat, I think, but through the rippled panes I see Randall rise from his crouch and move toward the center of the attic. He stretches his arms out and scans the ceiling with his gun, angling sideways, keeping his legs tensed, his knees soft. I duck my head back down and shift sideways. My hip brushes the Beretta and the gun clatters dangerously down across the ridged tin.

I snap my hand out and pin the handle of the Beretta. A deaf man would have heard the clamor a mile away. Grabbing the gun, I roll onto my back and away from the window. In a second I'm on my feet, scrambling around the side of the gable, propping myself against the steeper slope of the roof with my free hand.

Wood rasps against wood as the window slides open; then everything is dead quiet. I shift the weight in my thighs and try to steady my breathing. The muscles in my legs are burning. One one-thousand, two one-thousand, three. . . . Counting off the seconds to myself, I survey the drop to the garden. I'd survive the fall but certainly not without injury. If I hit the ground lame I'd be an easy target for the two down below.

There's a dull pop from around the corner of the gable as the tin compresses under new weight. I unlock my knees and begin working backward across the roofline. A second pop echoes through the darkness, the soft sole of a shoe bracing itself against the slope. I tense my arms and hold the Beretta straight in front of my face, sighting down the barrel to the edge of the gable.

Randall's hands appear first, the tip of his gun in stark silhouette against the orange-streaked sky. I exhale and give the trigger of the Beretta a smooth tug, aiming for the butt of Randall's gun. There's a sharp howl from around the corner of the gable and the gun flies through the air, skimming down the length of the roof and dropping into the darkness below.

Randall staggers forward, his compact frame struggling to hold its balance. He drops to his knees and rolls once, catching himself with one foot on the lip of the eaves. His left hand has taken the shot. Randall curls his knees into his chest and groans, cradling the smashed and ragged fist.

I sidle along the roof, balancing with my left hand, keeping my right hand and the Beretta rigid before me. They will have heard us by now, no doubt, the two below. Or seen Randall's gun in its arching free fall. I don't have much time. They'll be in the house soon, searching for a way up here. Randall looks up at me like a wounded animal, his face passive, his mouth set in a grim line. I step closer to him. I could reach out with the flat of my foot and, with one swift push, send him tumbling through the perilous expanse of air to the ground below.

Randall reaches out with his good hand and grabs my ankle, pulling my foot out from under me. My knee hits the cool tin and my body reels, listing toward the edge of the roof. His grip is strong; I can feel each finger through the fabric of my jeans. I twist my torso around, trying to keep my balance, and fire the Beretta blindly. The shot ricochets, pinging off the tin. I fire again, trying to aim for the figure struggling below me, counting how many shots are left in the clip. If I'm right, there should be two more. The grip on my ankle loosens and I fall back, my shoulder jarring against the steep pitch of the roof.

My eyes snap shut at the force of the impact. When I open them I see him beside me, his sightless face turned up to the rouged and glowing sky, a dark stain pooling like a halo around his head. Sitting up, I lean over the still figure, lift his head, and run my hands through his matted hair. I slide the tip of my finger into the hole at the front of his skull, feeling the layers of tissue and bone. Blood leaks down my arms. He would have killed me, I think. He wouldn't have stopped until I was dead. I turn and grope my way to the gaping attic window above me, trailing smeared prints on the pressed tin.

Two more, I say to myself, trying to keep focused. The one I met earlier should still be out cold. Stopping outside the window, I trade the nearly empty Beretta for the Walther and make a quick check of the attic from outside, assuring myself that it's empty before ducking across the sill and into the house.

The first one is easy. I can hear them below me, two distinct sets of feet crisscrossing the landing, checking doorways, searching in the semidarkness for the attic stairs. Then one set falls momentarily silent and there's a hesitant shuffling and breathing at the open door. I cross through the attic, making just enough noise to give myself away, and kneel in the far corner, leaving myself a clear view of the hole in the floor where the stairs break through.

He comes up slowly, pivoting from side to side, covering himself from all directions. He is breathing hard, and even from this far away I can smell the rancid odor of sweat and fear. He balances one foot on the landing, pulls the second foot after him. I sight down the barrel of the Walther and wait for his whole body to appear, pinning my eyes to the flesh just above his knee, pulling the trigger. The man cries out and teeters precariously over the stairs, then pitches forward, his arms waving frantically, his legs gone slack.

I cross toward him and bend down and pull the gun from his hand. His eyes are squeezed tight against the pain, and he's gripping his leg with his free hand.

'Randall's dead,' I tell him, flinging his gun into the shadows of the attic. 'You're lucky. You'll live.' I loop my arms under his shoulders. 'Now stand up. You're going to help me get out of here.'

'Fuck you,' the man wheezes. His mouth is dry and his breath smells of sickness and decay.

'Now!' I tug at the man's shoulders and he struggles up onto his healthy leg, muttering curses. I press his back into my stomach and aim him toward the bottom of the stairs, bringing the Walther up to the base of his head. 'We're going down,' I whisper into his ear. 'One word and you're dead. Got it?'

The man nods. He braces his body against mine and takes the first step. I strain my ears against the silence of the house below, trying to pick up the faintest sound, anything that might give the second man away. Nothing.

'Keep going,' I tell the man in my arms, nudging the nape of his neck with the barrel of the Walther. He takes another step, keeping all his weight on the good leg, wincing at the pain. 'Where the fuck is he?' I whisper, thinking out loud.

And then I hear it.

A floorboard in the attic behind us lets out a sharp creak and I snap my head around, wrenching the injured man with me. I glimpse a figure emerging from the roof through the open window. There's a flash of gunfire.

'The bitch has me,' the man in my arms yells, his voice high and panicked. 'Don't shoot!'

I duck down into the passageway and lean against the wall of the stairwell, keeping the first man pinned to my chest, firing back, trying to track the figure as he disappears into the shadows. The second man. He must have slipped out through a downstairs window and come up the roof the same way I did. He holds his fire, but I hear his feet shuffling above me.

I shift my body under the injured man, keeping his chest in front of mine, jabbing the Walther back into the flesh of his neck. 'C'mon, asshole, let's go,' I say. 'Haven't they told you how dangerous I am?'

I keep my back to the wall and we take the stairs together.

'Oh, please,' the wounded man groans as we near the landing. 'I'm gonna be sick. I'm gonna be sick.'

When we're both free of the doorway I loose my grip and shove him aside. He slams against the floor, his stomach heaving visibly. Heavy footsteps resound on the ceiling, racing from the perimeter of the attic to the top of the stairs. The air is sour with the stench of bile and blood.

Switching the Walther to my left hand, I fire up the passageway. My right hand fumbles with my drenched T-shirt, sliding the damp fabric up over my stomach, unholstering the forty-five with one easy movement. I pepper the stairs, hammering at the wood with both guns. Leaning my hip against the banister, I descend backward toward the first floor, keeping up a steady stream of gunfire.

When I reach the bottom landing I grab my father's keys from the hall table and turn for the door, flinging it wide. My feet hit the peeling boards of the porch, and I race down the steps and out across the damp lawn, keeping my eyes on the path, not daring to look back. I hit the street and break into a dead run, aiming my body toward the Gulf, mapping the twisting network of alleys and back-garden shortcuts that lead to my father's bar.

My ears are still ringing from the gunfire, and I look up at the quiet conch houses that line the street. There should be sirens by now, the wheels of cop cars rushing over the slick blacktop. Someone must have heard us. My bare soles smack the pavement as I veer left and take the weed-choked lane that runs behind the cemetery, then turn down William Street and head west. Someone must have called the police. I inhale deeply, gulping the briny air, wondering at the early morning silence, and skirt behind the library and out onto Margaret Street. My breathing finds a rhythm and my legs hit their stride and then, in an instant of wild clarity, I realize where I am. There will be no cops, no wailing sirens. I am in a town of criminals, where juries can't be sat for drug cases because no one is impartial, where neighbors politely pull their shades at the sound of shots, where the cop that comes to arrest you was your high school prom date. No one will call. No one will have heard anything. I am home.

Nineteen

When I hit the crushed oyster shells that line the parking lot of the Blue Ibis I stop running and slow to a walk. Silver ripples undulate across the surface of the marina. The lone figure of a pelican waddles past slips filled with yachts and fishing boats, its webbed feet slapping against the planks. I scan the lot and find my father's red Toyota pickup where I'd seen it last night, parked in a slot close to the docks, then skirt around the side of the bar, past Cyrus's boat, and let myself into the little utility shed that juts off the side of the building. The shed is a mess and I have to rummage through tangles of anchor ropes, musty floats, boxes of spare flares, and cans of paint and fiberglass filler to find my diving gear. I make one trip to the truck with my buoyancy compensator, fins, mask, and snorkel. On my second trip I grab two spare tanks and my regulators.

My father's spare bar key is on the jumbled ring I took from the house. I slide it into the front lock and dodge through the empty bar, past overturned chairs stacked neatly on table tops. In the office safe I find the money, the disk, and Helen's passport. The first lashings of sunlight on the bight are visible through the window. The pelican stops at the end of the dock, thrashes its wings, erupts into the air.

I work back through the bar and out to the truck. I take

the Palm Avenue Bridge and then follow North Roosevelt Boulevard along Garrison Bight and onto the causeway to Stock Island and Cyrus's house. The wheels of the truck hum beneath me. My diving gear rattles in the bed.

A high-combed rooster is scratching in the moist dirt of Cyrus's front yard, spraying small stones from his lizard-like feet when I wheel into the driveway and cut the engine. Hazy morning sunlight filters through the canopy of leaves still wet from last night's rain.

'Cyrus!' I yell, climbing the steps to the front porch, past the money tree and the rigid red bodies of mating palmettos. I knock once on the screen door and slip inside, not waiting for an answer.

The slow blades of a fan creak overhead. A speckled gecko scrambles across the canyons of a jalousied window, his tiny feet rustling against the glass slats. I edge down the hallway and into the kitchen.

The back door is open and Cyrus is sitting at a glass and iron table on the porch with a cup of coffee in front of him. Mangroves and buttonwood trees line the far end of the yard, and beyond them the sea spreads to the horizon. I draw the two playing cards from my pocket, step outside, and slap them down on the table.

'I want you to start from the beginning. How long have you been working for Randall?' I demand.

Cyrus says nothing. His eyes are trained on the black spades. I sit down opposite him. Crescents of dried blood ring the tips of my fingernails. I light a cigarette and pull the Walther from my jeans and cradle it in my lap. Under the dimpled surface of the table, the porch is littered with damp leaves.

'Did it start over there, Cyrus?'

He shakes his head. 'I knew him in Vietnam. All of us

who worked as advisors did. He got in touch with me after the war. I was staying up at my mother's in Jacksonville, working as a bouncer in a bar there. He called and said he had a business proposition for me. You have to understand what it was like for those of us who came back, Al. I couldn't have stuck it out in the Navy; I just didn't believe anymore.'

'So you started working for Randall?'

'Not really working for him. He fixed me up down here.'

'What do you mean?'

'He bought me the bar, Al, the Blue Ibis. He gave me a chunk of cash to start the business.'

'And in return?'

'In return he had a funnel for his earnings.'

'You were laundering money for him?'

Cyrus nods and gets up from the table. He disappears inside and returns with two fresh cups of coffee.

'How long's it been since you slept, Alison?' he asks, handing me one of the mugs and sitting down again.

'Did my father know?'

'He'd told me what happened at the PIC. The whole thing had been Randall's idea, and your father hated him because of it. When you two came down here I couldn't tell him.'

'And you did all the bookkeeping.'

Cyrus shrugs. 'He wasn't interested.'

'I guess it worked out well for you.' I flick my cigarette off the porch and take a sip of coffee.

'Your father and I were smugglers. It hardly seemed to matter that we were tucking away a few more illegal dollars. Without Randall we wouldn't have had the bar.'

From the front yard comes the sound of the rooster

crowing. I look across the grass toward the water. 'I killed him,' I say.

'Who?'

'Randall. He came to the house last night and I killed him. How did he find out about the disk?'

Cyrus drums his fingers on the glass of the table. 'Christ, Al,' he murmurs.

'Callum was looking for me when he called Joey. How did he know where to hire me?'

'The night before your father died he was on one of his benders. He came out here after the bar closed and got me out of bed. He wouldn't shut up. Kept on about Callum and some information and how Randall was really going to be pissed off. He said he'd got you all mixed up in it too, that he'd given Joey's number to Callum. He didn't say anything about Chau Doc or about the PIC. He wasn't making much sense. I kept asking him questions, but he was piss drunk. You know how he used to get.'

Cyrus looks up at me and I nod. 'I know,' I say. 'So you called Randall?'

'I had to. Your father didn't know it, but we were pulling in good money off the cleaning we did for Randall. I wanted us to retire, Al. We were lucky to survive as long as we did without getting caught or killed or whatever. I wanted us to have a better life. Can you understand that?'

I nod wearily. 'Sure, Cyrus. I can understand.'

Cyrus continues. 'So I called Randall just to let him know something was up.'

'And to let him know I was involved.'

'No, Al.'

'He knew to go to Mark's. He knew to call Joey when he wanted to find me. I'm not stupid, Cyrus. You told him.'

Cyrus leans forward and runs his fingers back and forth through his hair, sending motes of sweat into the sunlight.

'I didn't know they'd kill him,' he says. 'It was the same with your father. Randall told me to clear out, that he just needed time to talk to him. He asked me for Joey's number and where you'd be likely to stop. The last thing I wanted was for you to get hurt. I didn't know it would all go to shit.'

'So Randall didn't even know what was on the disk. He thought Callum was ratting on his business.'

Cyrus nods.

'You might as well have pulled the trigger yourself,' I say.

For a few moments neither of us speaks. Cyrus shifts in his chair. A power boat motors close to shore, sending its wake lapping against the concrete bulwark at the edge of the yard. It is so quiet I can hear bougainvillea flowers dropping softly around us.

'You hate me, Al,' Cyrus says, breaking the silence. 'You should.'

'What about Callum?' I ask. 'All these years go by, and then he just calls my father and knows I'm in the moving business?'

Cyrus reaches for his coffee cup and takes a sip. He works the tip of his finger across a small smudge on the glass surface of the table. The skin on his hands is dark and his knuckles are dry and weathered.

'You remember a few years back when you first started working for Joey? You got stopped in Louisiana on some stupid speeding charge.' Cyrus sets his cup down and looks at me. His right eyebrow arches sharply upward. 'You remember?'

I nod. 'I remember. I was outside of Baton Rouge.'

'What do you think happened up there?'

'I don't know.' I pick at a patch of dried blood on my forearm. 'I always figured I was carrying for someone important. I thought the interested parties intervened. It happens all the time.'

'Who'd you call when they hauled you in?'

'I called down here, you know that. I talked to my dad. I figured I needed a lawyer.'

'Didn't you ever think it was a little strange that these "interested parties," as you say, found out about it so quickly? You think your freedom mattered that much to them, mattered that much to Joey?'

'I don't know what I thought. I figured the drugs mattered. I figured I was carrying a load of valuable cocaine in the trunk of my car. Listen, Cyrus,' I say, my voice rising with irritation and anger, 'I don't want to talk about fucking Baton Rouge.'

'Don't you get it, Al? He's the one who got you out that night. Your father called him, asked him for a favor, asked him to pull a few strings for you. He didn't want to see you spend the next ten years in prison. Callum must have known the right people. A couple of hours after your father talked to him, Callum called back and said you'd be out by morning.'

'So when he needed a courier for the disk he thought of me?'

Cyrus's gaze is hard on my face. 'No one gives a favor without expecting one in return,' he says. He shakes his head and looks down at the pattern of dead leaves at his feet.

Turning my head toward the blue sprawl of the Atlantic, I light a fresh cigarette and lean back in my chair. 'I need the boat,' I tell him.

'It's back at the bar.'

'Not yours, my father's.' I tilt my head to the edge of the yard where my father's old boat lists on wooden blocks.

'You know that boat won't last more than a couple hours in the water. Your father never fixed the rip in the stern.'

'I know. The radio still works, right?'

Cyrus nods.

'Good, and I need to use the compressor. I brought my tanks and gear.'

Cyrus knits his eyebrows together. 'What's going on, Al?'

It's early afternoon by the time everything is ready. Cyrus starts the engine of his truck and slowly backs the trailer down the boat ramp and into the water. I wade down the slippery cement, holding the bow line. Water creeps up around my knees. Two horseshoe crabs glide along the sandy bottom. The hull settles into the water with a loud sigh and the boat floats free. Tugging on the line, I ease the boat up alongside the dock. Cyrus cuts the engine of the truck and climbs out.

'You gonna at least tell me where you're going?' he asks.

I don't answer. A shrimper skates across the horizon of the Atlantic, its nets tilting like the outstretched wings of a butterfly.

Cyrus shakes his head. 'I have something for you.'

He turns and walks back across the yard. I watch him climb the stairs to the porch and disappear inside. The oversized leaves of a banana plant ruffle across the side of the house. I sling my diving gear into the boat. After a few moments Cyrus emerges from the kitchen and crosses back toward me, his arms cupped around a box.

'I love you like you were my own daughter, Al.'

Cyrus puts the box in my hands and I open the lid. Inside is a plain clay urn.

'He never wanted you to know about Chau Doc, about any of the things that happened during the war,' Cyrus says. 'It was his greatest fear, that you'd find out and stop loving him. I want to tell you something.'

I shift the box in my arms and lean against the side of the truck.

'When Darwin and I were in Soc Trang, our team got sent to do this job for Phoenix in a little village just up the river. A gunboat dumped us on shore and we were on foot the rest of the way. It was night, and we had been told there was this bigshot VC staying in one of the hootches in the village. They even told us which bed was his, exactly which corner he slept in.

'It was severely dark in the hootch, and as soon as I got my hands on the VC I knew something was wrong. Darwin knew too. I put my hands over the VC's mouth and Greg, that's our buddy, slid the knife right up inside the chest.

'My hand slipped and the VC let out a little moan. Just real quiet. The whole thing was quiet. Then I heard Darwin's voice through the darkness, just a whisper. "Oh, fuck. Jesus," he said. "It's a girl. It's a motherfucking little girl."

'My hand slipped away from the VC's mouth and down across her chest and I knew Darwin was right. Darwin just kept whispering, "Jesus, Jesus, Jesus." See, Al, we didn't have the right information. We didn't kill some VC leader, we killed a fourteen-year-old girl.'

I shield my eyes from the sun and search the glaring ocean for the shrimp boat.

'It was so dark,' Cyrus whispers. 'Always. And we were always afraid. There's a way a young girl sleeps, like you used to sleep. I'd watch you in the boat sometimes. I'd watch your fingers curled against your cheek, the slope of your back in a protective curve, the quiet ease of your body breathing. There's an unmistakable way a girl feels in your hands, surprisingly alive, like the first fish you ever catch. You expect it to move like liquid against your fingers, but it fights you instead.'

My father was wrong. And Cyrus was wrong. I don't hate them. I hate their weakness, their deception. But I forgive them everything. Cyrus raises the toe of his boot and kicks at the grass. It is a familiar gesture, one my father used to make when he was frustrated or thinking.

'We were all guilty, Al,' he says. 'We all knew.'

I cross the flats and head out toward Woman Key, running the boat at full throttle, keeping the hull as far out of the water as I can. About an hour out of Cyrus's dock I find the two dredged hills, slow the boat, and nudge into the cove. The stern is already low in the water. I slip the disk out of my pocket and release it into the deep hole. The iridescent surface flickers like a silver-scaled fish as it spirals downward. Whoever wants to know these things will have to come to it themselves; I won't help them. How could I possibly explain the entirety of his life, the scope of my forgiveness?

Once, in a fit of greedy carnage, Joey and I stripped the blossoms from an orange tree and scattered them into the sheets of my bed. We put the white petals into our mouths and tongued soft pollen onto each other's lips.

Tearing the papers into small shreds, I sprinkle them onto the waves. Bits of planes, ripped words, and names float across the cove: force, pacification, MIA; Henry, Darnell, Jason. I lift the urn and crush it against the hull. Gray flakes stipple the water.

How to describe the smell of orange trees, the lush seduction, the great welling desire to take all of it into your body? I pressed my nose into the crease of Joey's spine, the rich valley of scents. I drew the citrus-infested air into my lungs and held it there.

The bow of the boat bucks upward and I start the engine again and head for one of the deep channels. The propeller scrapes against the fine sand of the flats. Rocks and seaweed brush the hull. I aim for where pale blue gives way to a stretch of dark sapphire, for deep water.

When I see the rippled brown crease in the Gulf that is Woman Key I stop the boat, take the radio from its hook, and scan the dial for the Coast Guard frequency. Muffled static blares from the speaker. I click onto the channel and make my distress call.

'This is Alison Kerry,' I say, stating my position, ticking off the registration number of the boat, waiting for the garbled acknowledgment.

Salt water is seeping over the stern. I wrap the belt of lead around my waist, slip into my BC and fins, and clip the waterproof bag that holds the passport and the money onto my vest. The boat lets out one last shudder as the bow juts straight up toward the sky. Pushing off the deck, I let myself fall free.

Just below the surface of the water, barracudas hover around the sinking boat, knife-thin witnesses. I reach for my compass string and find my bearings. It'll be a good hour swim to Woman Key. I kick myself forward. The muscles of my arms and legs work against the elastic resistance of the water. The great vertiginous chasm of the sea drops below me.

How to explain the bloom against the throat, the ragged scrim that separates violence from longing, longing from love? It would be necessary to go to the tree, to stand under the boughs and bend your neck to the creamy faces of the flowers, to the dense perfume. I look back at the boat, at the hull settling into the sand, the curtain of silt rising around the cabin.

All afternoon and into the night, Coast Guard rescue boats and helicopters crisscross the stretch of ocean where I went down. After sunset their search beams fan along the water, comb the wrinkled coral of nearby islands. I sit, half submerged, in the tangled camouflage of mangrove roots that line Woman Key and listen to the chopper blades cutting through the air above me. Spotlights dance across the gnarled branches. The bright sickle of the moon emerges from the sea and shrinks upward, throwing a long rippled wake over the Gulf. It is after three before they leave. Nothing more to be done until daylight.

I hear Chloe long before I see her. She comes in from the north, running with her lights off. The hum of her engines whines through the clean silence as she buzzes the island once and loops south. A sliver of starlight catches the rim of her pontoons. I flip my flashlight on and wave the beam through the sky. Chloe dives down and scuds into the sea.

They will come back tomorrow: more boats, more planes. By the next day, if I'm lucky, they'll give up on missing and presume me dead.

I haul my diving gear out of the brackish water and

stumble to the beach. Across the ledges and foamy crests of breaking waves, the door to Chloe's plane pops open. She waves to me. The curve of her arm is silhouetted by the green dash lights of the cabin.

Bad navigation, they'll say. They'll trace the long scar across the flats, the rocks dislodged, the choppy crease left by the propeller. They'll find the damaged hull, the small cleft in the stern, the rift my father never fixed.

I drag my gear behind me. The surf curls gently around my waist, up under my arms. Chloe reaches her hand out and I pass her the BC, push the tank up over the pontoons, swim around to the passenger side of the plane, and scramble inside.

'You all right?' Chloe asks. She hands me a dry towel.

I pull the door shut and nod.

The plane skims forward across the water and jerks upward. Pressing my forehead against the rattling window, I look out at the shrinking curve of lights that is the Keys. I close my eyes and envision the topography of the flats, the miles of channels branching to meet the hazy arterial rush of the Gulf Stream, the subtle divisions of shading that are depths. This subaqueous terrain is as familiar as the gestures of my first great love, familiar as the near-weightless pressure of my father's palm against the low curve of my back, his fingers riding the crest of my spine.

How to convey the complications, the mysterious, unexpected ways in which tides shape depths, shape strength of current? It is not easy knowledge. I have learned it all my life. And still there is that always receding curve of the ocean, the natural horizon of another's grief, beyond which we can never see. When I released the disk into the water it clung for a moment, buoyed by surface tension, the weight of its secrets suddenly defying gravity.

They will imagine some violent end to my life, the thick jaws of a shark slicing into my flesh, foam billowing in my lungs as I inhale seawater.

They will think I lost my way. I am certain this would never be possible.